"It's getting late," Mercy whispered, inching closer.

Leopold glanced at the window. Night was closing in. Since the new moon had just passed, he needed to leave now while he could easily see his way back to the Vulture and return early tomorrow, if she was sincere in her wish to allow him to continue. God alone knew if he would get a wink of sleep tonight after kissing her today. He had to get away.

The duchess' hands settled on his arms. "Will you dine with me?"

Heather Boyd

BESTSELLING AUTHOR

Engaging the Enemy

Wild Randalls

1

The characters and events portrayed in this book are fictitious. Any similarity to real persons, living or dead, is purely coincidental and not intended by the author.

ENGAGING THE ENEMY © 2012 by Heather Boyd
ISBN: 978-0-9872619-0-8
Editing by Kelli Collins

Dedication

For my two very different grandfathers' who showed me how to live my life and love my family. I miss your health food, your nighttime drinking and pipe smoking, your chiming clock, but not the cold seat on the outside dunny. Forgive me, Joe and Mack, for following pipe-smoking strangers down the street. The scent reminds me of everything I no longer have since I lost the two of you. You were the best!

Chapter One

No matter how much time had passed since his last visit to Hampshire, Leopold Randall, heir to the young Duke of Romsey's title, would rather return to exile in India than beg help from Romsey Abbey. If not for his quest to be reunited with his family, two brother's and sister, Leopold would never have desire to set foot on Romsey soil again.

He stared across the mist-shrouded valley to where Romsey Abbey, a sprawling mishmash of architectural foolishness, slowly revealed itself in the early morning light, and the place filled Leopold with a growing sense of foreboding. All his life, he had gazed at the place that had been the home of his ancestors and wished he might have been born into another family.

The stench of betrayal lie thick upon Romsey Abbey. Even when the duke in question was too young to understand the power he would one day wield, his existence was far from innocent, steeped in lies. Born and bound in deceit. The Romsey dukes crushed those who stood in their way without a passing thought for the pain they would inflict. Leopold's side of the family had suffered such a fate, scattered them to the four corners.

Leopold had been denied any return to England in the past five years. His existence considered both a threat and a commodity for the old duke's schemes. The last time he had been summoned into His Grace's presence, Leopold had made a bargain with the old devil to keep his brother's and sister safe. Even if he'd not had any choice in the matter, the memory of that night still haunted his dreams and robbed him of any peace.

Behind him, in humble whitewashed cottages, the sleepy village came to life. They were happy, secure in their lives, confident in the benevolence of the Duke of Romsey, and the continuation of years of endless tradition, pomp and ceremony. Going about their days with no idea of the ugly, calculating power of the family he was sadly a part of.

Leopold slipped a pistol into his hand, finding reassurance in the familiar weight, and then let it go in disgust. Three months ago he'd been sweltering in Surat on the banks of the Tapti River, unaware of the changes at Romsey, going about the old duke's business with no idea he was free. The news he had died a year and a half ago had pleased him. But it was only by chance that he'd heard the duke's only son, his cousin Edwin Randall, had also died six months after acceding to the title. To say he was shocked was an understatement.

Now, only a child stood between him and gaining the title of the Duke of Romsey.

Somewhere in the depths of hell, the old Duke of Romsey must be writhing in agony.

Many men might covet such a situation, but Leopold was free and, if he lived a quiet life, now he'd returned to England, he might never have to bow to the current duke's demands again. The idea had been gratifying—intensely so. He could go wherever he chose without having to account for his actions.

Freedom after a decade of servitude was sweet. It had taken him a very short amount of time to wrap up his affairs, set aside his mistress, and return home on the first available ship. Not even a run-in with a marauding American privateer had dimmed his enthusiasm.

His heady sense of excitement had lasted until his feet touched English cobblestones in Portsmouth. Hearing so many English voices at once had overwhelmed him momentarily, but a single voice—clear and insistent—had turned him about in his tracks. A girl, calling out to a young lad named Toby.

His missing brother's name was Tobias.

It hadn't been his brother; just a street scamp dodging his pursuers. But at that moment, he'd reaffirmed his purpose in coming home. Come hell or high water, he would put his missing family back together. He would search the globe if necessary to find out what the old Duke of Romsey had done with Oliver, Rosemary, and Tobias. His younger brothers and sister had been moved and hidden from him for years. Only Leopold had been granted a limited liberty, forced to dance to the old duke's tune in order to keep them safe.

Unfortunately, information was hard to uncover. He had spent weeks in London, engaging a private investigator to discreetly question staff at the ducal mansion and the duke's man of business with the hopes of hearing of their fate.

He was informed the London mansion had been closed since the old duke's death a year and a half ago. The current duchess, his cousin's wife, widowed a year ago, was mired in the country with her son and had no plans to come to Town that anyone knew of.

The man of business was new and clueless about the past, or Leopold's side of the Randall family. Aside from striking up a careful friendship with Viscount Carrington in London, a man an old friend had vouched for but with too many problems of his own to be of help, he'd had no choice but to grudgingly return home to Hampshire and beg for information himself.

Now, he had no idea what future lie before him, but his audience today would set the wheels in motion for the rest of his life. He would get his answers and be done with Romsey once and for all.

"Your breakfast is ready, Mr. Randall," the innkeeper called. "Same room as last night."

"Thank you, Brown." Leopold turned from the view and graced the innkeeper with a smile reminiscent one he'd worn in his former life before his exile. The man need not have any reason to question his motives for returning. He need not see how bitter Leopold had become. "How is your daughter faring these days?"

"Very well, sir. She's got three young ones now and another on the way. Her husband comes home irregular from sea and refills her belly at each visit."

Leopold smiled but made no further comment. He'd only asked to be polite. The former Fanny Brown had been the local tart. Tenderhearted, but a tart just the same.

"If you don't mind me saying so, sir, it sure is good to see another Randall in the district. The place has been far too quiet since your family left." Brown touched his cap and hurried away. "The Duchess of Romsey will be pleased to see you," he called.

Anger swirled through Leopold like a rising tide, and he hesitated to follow. He had to work hard to force his bitterness away.

Left? His family had not left of their own volition. His parents had likely been killed on the duke's order, his siblings abducted certainly. But until he had proof of their whereabouts, he'd keep his eyes open and his opinions to himself. Until he'd met the current Duchess of Romsey and determined how big a threat she was to his family's survival, he'd do well to distrust anything and anybody.

With one last glance at the distant abbey, he turned toward the inn and the warmth of his breakfast. The private dining chamber was so familiar, so unchanged during his absence, that he expected to hear his family laughing around the battered table over a meal. He shook off the memory—it did no good to dwell on happier times—and wearily sank into a chair.

Leopold spooned food into his mouth mechanically, offering a smile to the shy innkeeper's wife as she added fresh rolls to the table. But his mind was on the frustrating question of where his family had been taken and, more importantly, what kind of life they were living, now that the old duke was dead. Despite his promises, there was always the danger that Romsey had lied from the start and disposed of them ten years ago.

He shook his head. He could not think too much about that possibility. That way led to the same panic he'd experienced a decade ago when he'd discovered Oliver had disappeared overnight from his lodgings.

Would Oliver still be calculating the odds of every conceivable circumstance? Would Rosemary still be ordering everyone about as if she were a duchess and driving young men to distraction? No doubt Tobias would still be knee deep in trouble, hopefully nothing that Leopold couldn't get him out of.

Despite the old duke's tight noose around his life, Leopold had made his fortune in India and had the satisfaction of being able to buy almost anything he wanted now. But all he required was his family back where he could see them every day, where he could return to a life where he'd been a happy and content man.

Sadly, he could barely remember those days.

Wishing for a miracle hadn't helped him so far. Only time and determination would get him where he wanted to go. And that was as far away as possible from Romsey.

Leopold threw some coins onto the table and strode out to the stables, eager to get on with the hard day ahead. His valet, Miles Colby, awaited him, their two mounts saddled and ready in the yard.

The cheeky fellow bowed deferentially, as if he did so every day. "Are we still to look about this morning, sir?"

"Yes, it cannot hurt to refresh my memory of the land." Leopold ignored Colby's behavior—it really was better than asking him to stop yet again—and swung up into the saddle.

His valet had taken the news of him being connected with the Duke of Romsey, of being next in line for the title, far better than Leopold had done. Colby had tried, unsuccessfully, to have Leopold turned out in a style befitting a duke's heir while they had been in London. But Leopold had resisted. He was content enough as he was and had no need to gild the lily, since he very much doubted he would live to inherit anything. The current duke was young, but he might manage to live longer than his father and spare Leopold of the unwanted responsibility.

He urged his horse out into the lane at a trot. He'd not told Colby outright that he was refreshing his memory in case he was pursued. Colby would be all right, should the duchess prove to be dangerous. In Leopold's experience, the Dukes and Duchesses of Romsey considered outsiders, someone without Randall blood, useful indulgences—not potential threats. At least, not at first glance.

Familiar vistas greeted him as they made their way to the estate entrance, but from the outset it was apparent that all was not right with Romsey. The road was deeply rutted in places, and when he glanced into the empty fields, he could see that the lower lake's eastern shore had choked with withered reeds. The old duke would never have allowed lapses like that to occur, not in his lifetime anyway.

All about him, Romsey suffered from the lack of rain, as the rest of England seemed to do. The upper dams should have been breached earlier to feed the lower streams, to ensure the harvest was a good one this year. What he saw hinted that the estate did not prosper.

Leopold's chest tightened with a mix of gladness and regret at the other signs of decay. As much as he hated the dukes, Romsey was home. The memory of cool, lush green fields had sustained him in sticky, sweltering India. What lay about him soured his return.

Suddenly, a woman screamed, "Get your hands off him!"

Leopold twisted in the saddle, searching for the feminine voice raised so furiously in alarm.

In the distance, farther along the lane, stood a shabby thatched cottage where a tall man held a child captive in his arms. A woman beat ineffectually at the man's body, begging for the boy's release.

Leopold kicked his horse forward. "What the hell is going on here?"

Both man and woman turned. Beth Turner—garbed much more poorly than he remembered—gasped in surprise, and then ran toward Leopold. "Sir, he's trying to take my George away with him!"

Like hell he would! Leopold swung from the saddle and sidestepped the distraught mother. "Let George Turner go. Now."

The other man—a rough-looking brute—scowled at the interruption. "Stay out of my business and be on your way."

The Turners' welfare was very much his business. Leopold withdrew his weapon and pointed it at the man's head. "What happens here *is* my business. You are on Romsey land. We rule here."

"You ain't the duke. He's but a child. Besides, the woman can't pay her husband's debts. The son will work them off."

Behind Leopold, Colby was attempting to reassure the distraught mother, but Beth Turner had a full head of steam up and wasn't about to be silent. "You imbecile! Don't you know who stands before you?"

The man blinked. "He ain't anyone important. Just some gent come ta sniff 'round your skirts."

Beth gasped. "You're blind."

Leopold waited, patience wearing thin. "Let go of the child and be on your way before I put a ball in you."

"Listen. I got orders. She can't pay, so I'm to take the child in place of payment."

"How much?"

The debt collector licked his lips. "Ten pounds, it is."

Beth Turner shrieked at the sum named. Obviously, this debt collector attempted to line his own pockets and considered him a gullible cull.

Leopold debated his options. He could shoot the man, but he'd rather not risk hanging over ten pounds and have to flee the country. Besides, the man could probably use the money. Judging by his shabby attire, debt collecting didn't pay well. Or he just wasn't very good at it. "Colby. Ten pounds. Now."

Behind him, his valet rushed for the horses and Leopold could hear him digging around in his saddlebag. The debt collector's eyes widened, and the child slipped from his grip. Once released, the boy rushed for his mother.

Paper pressed into Leopold's palm and he lowered the weapon. He held out the notes. "I will expect no further demands to be made of the Turners. Come to *me* in future."

The brute lumbered forward to retrieve the money and tucked it into his pocket. "I would if I had your name, sir."

"Leopold Randall."

The debt collector paled and took two steps back.

"Begging your pardon, Mr. Randall. I didn't recognize you."

"Quite. Be on your way."

The other man turned, dragged himself into his rough cart, and set off down the lane at a fast clip. Once he had disappeared from view, Leopold turned to look at the cottage.

The Turners had been a moderately prosperous family, but it appeared they had fallen on hard times in his absence. They hadn't lived in this shabby place before. Their last place had a prettier outlook. William Turner, a man with a well-known temper and pride to match, would be furious when he found out what had just transpired between his wife and the debt collector.

He turned to Beth. The once pretty woman appeared neatly dressed, but closer inspection revealed careful darning on the sleeve and a tattered hem dragging on the dry road. Her expression was one of exhaustion and embarrassment as she clutched her son to her with every appearance of never letting go.

"William always said you would come back when the duke died, but I never believed him," she whispered.

He smiled. "Of course I returned. I have unfinished business at the abbey." Leopold glanced around. "When will William return?"

The boy started to speak, but his mother shushed him by pushing him toward the cottage. "William's gone, Mr. Randall. He died the spring before last."

Leopold rocked on his heels, shocked at the news. He glanced around the cottage again, noting the disrepair, the signs that the man of the house was long gone. A feeble curl of smoke drifted from the chimney in a roof that needed re-thatching. The gardens were wild with neglect, too. He couldn't believe William was gone, but the proof was before his eyes. "I'm so sorry, Beth. I hadn't heard of his passing."

"Why would you?"

An awkward silence stretched between them. Leopold had counted on William's presence to make his return bearable. Without him, there would be no reason to dwell in the memory of happier times. He'd get what he came for and leave as soon as he could. And if there was trouble, he'd battle his way out alone.

"Will you come in, sir?"

Beth Turner's formality grated on his nerves. Although William had been his friend since childhood, Beth had remained in awe of his familial connections since her marriage. She refused to behave any other way, even if his chance of acceding to the ducal title was slim.

Resigned that little had changed between them, Leopold allowed her to lead the way into the cottage. She hurried to bring order to the cramped space, hiding scuffed shoes and pails set at random about the bare floors.

Eventually, Beth dragged on a frayed shawl from the chair by the hearth and motioned for him to sit in William's former chair. Leopold took up his usual seat, on a three-legged stool, on the other side of the fire.

Gingerly, Beth sat in William's place. "If I may ask, what brings you back to us now after so long, Mr. Randall?"

"Family business, Beth. But I had intended to see William. How did he die?"

Beth tucked a lock of hair behind her ear and then rubbed her palms over her knees. "Poacher's shot caught him in the thigh when he was gathering wood. Sawbones couldn't save him."

Appalled by her toneless statement, Leopold sat forward. "I'm very sorry, Beth. He was the best of men. I had intended to offer him a position, now that I've returned to England for good. I wanted to bring you all with me to a better place."

Beth shrugged and glanced over at her boy. "All I've got is my George now. We do all right here."

"He looks to be a sturdy lad. Quite the image of his father at that age."

The boy, laboring at his chores on the other side of the room, straightened his shoulders. Leopold bit back a smile. A little encouragement was all it took to make a boy see his future as a man. William Turner's child would grow to be an honorable, proud man if given the chance. But not in this place as it was now.

Leopold looked around him again, noticing the absence of small things that had come into the family upon William's marriage to Beth. The delicate rosewood table and chairs he'd teased William about were gone. So too were the carpets. He worked to keep his face clear of emotion. They had fallen far in his absence, but getting distressed over the matter would solve nothing.

Leopold stood. "I must take my leave of you now. But I will want to hear if you have any more trouble. Be sure to send word to me."

Beth scrubbed her hands over her knees again, a sure sign his request troubled her. "Where exactly are you staying?"

"The Vulture." He'd not be welcome at the abbey beyond an hour, and most certainly never asked to stay so he might have the chance to decline graciously. The village inn was preferable to anywhere else.

Beth Turner's shoulders relaxed. "I'm glad, sir."

Leopold nodded then stepped out into the yard with Colby hurrying in his wake. At the horses, he set his foot into the stirrup with a heavy heart. "Make it right, Colby." He swung into the saddle. "Food on the table for tonight, speak to Brown about fixing the roof, and see to it that the boy and mother are properly prepared for the coming winter. Tell Brown I'll settle funds on him this evening to cover every expense required. Once I have matters settled at the abbey, I'll make arrangements for their future."

Colby's eyes widened with surprise, but he wisely nodded and directed his horse back toward the village. As much as Leopold didn't want the responsibility here at Romsey, he wouldn't turn his back on William's widow and son. He would see she had the protection of the Randall family, even if it was from the disreputable side.

Chapter Two

The trouble with Mercy Randall's friends—childless friends in particular—was that they did not understand the great responsibility placed upon her shoulders as the widowed Duchess of Romsey. She shook her head to deny the latest invitation to revisit London and take in the delights of the capital. She was the mother of a young duke, the last of his line, and thus her sole responsibility. She could not come and go from Romsey Abbey at will, even if she might *wish* to run away at times.

The responsibility was so great that Mercy often had nightmares in which she imagined all manner of duties she may have neglected that day. Romsey Abbey comprised eighty-nine chambers, four greenhouses, various outbuildings, and one hundred souls dependent on her largess. Fifteen hundred acres of fertile farmland—hers to care for until her son came of age.

What had she been thinking to accept a proposal of marriage from a seemingly healthy marquess seven years ago?

"You are kind to invite me again," Mercy said firmly. "But my life is here now."

Anna, Countess Barnet, gave her arm a squeeze. "Now, my dear, dear duchess, I shall hear no arguments this season. You are out of mourning and it is much too long since you've come up to London. I cannot allow you to wallow here forever. Your husband died over a year ago now. He would never want you to remain after he was gone."

Mercy glanced beyond the gardens to the dark woodlands and shuddered. "I could not leave Edwin here alone."

When Mercy had married Edwin Randall, the Marquess of Manderson, at eighteen, she wasn't told that he had a weak heart. If she had known from the start, she'd have at least considered the likelihood that she'd be left to manage everything, should he die before her. But she'd lived in ignorance until the day he'd collapsed while out walking the grounds a year into their marriage.

At the time, the doctors had said the exertion, coming so soon after a mild fever, had brought on the attack, and they had cautioned Mercy to limit her demands on his time. Not something a new wife particularly wants to hear when she was just coming to know the man she had married. Since her husband's sudden death, Mercy had decided that she would have to think of the future. Too many people depended upon her to think of old pleasures.

Anna waved her hand dismissively. "The child will go on well enough without you."

If Anna knew the truth, she wouldn't be so sure. There was danger circling her son. He was too young to face that alone, abandoned to the servants care.

Mercy forced a bright smile to her face. "I do wish it were that easy, Anna. But I would not rest without Edwin by my side."

Anna shuddered. "A child in London is quite out of the question. How could you consider it? What if he should stumble into your private chambers while you were entertaining a friend?" Anna smiled wickedly. "I can think of no faster way to cool a man's ardor than to have a child thrust into a room with him. I'm told it is quite draining."

Although Mercy was terribly lonely, what Anna suggested was impossible. As much as she might miss the intimacies of the bedchamber with her husband, she had no time to spend with a lover. All her energy was devoted to her son and his welfare and education.

Anna's earthy laugh filled Mercy's ears. "Speak of the devil. Look, here comes Shaw, now."

Lord Shaw, Anna's elder lecherous brother, strolled about on the far side of the garden with Mercy's sister, Blythe—Lady Venables—by his side. Blythe seemed content enough in Shaw's dubious company for now, but Mercy would have to rescue her soon. Shaw was not the sort of gentleman Blythe approved of. He was too bold, too forward and lusty for long conversation. According to Blythe, a gentleman should convey his heart's desires discreetly. Shaw made no bones that he was eager for bed play with any woman he met.

Mercy wished with all her heart that Shaw would have stayed in London and found another lady to call on. He came to visit with too much frequency for her peace of mind as it was. Despite all she had done to dissuade him, Lord Shaw was determined that he would be the first man to spend a night in her bed.

Mercy shook her head. "I care not if a man's ardor is drained or not by the appearance of my child. I have no intention of going anywhere without my son, and I have no intention of taking a lover. Why must you always be going on about that?"

Anna tipped her chin toward her brother. "You cannot deny Shaw hasn't expressed a particular interest in you, and it is to his credit that he seeks to entertain Lady Venables in such a way. She has a prickly demeanor that you know many find unsettling. However, he sacrifices his time so we may have an enjoyable visit. What more could you want in a man?"

Mercy bristled. Perhaps what she wanted was someone who did not fake pleasing manners around her family in the hopes of getting beneath her skirts. "He does not need to play my sister false on my account. I enjoy my sister's company tremendously."

Anna's brow rose as if she didn't believe her. "We shall never agree on her character, and I want no ill will between us. However, in order for my brother to court you, you must see that a trip to London will give you time to come to know him better. He cannot spoil you as he wishes if your sister is close by. Oh, when you come up to London, things will be easy. No more bothersome Blythe shooting daggers at our conversations. It is hard to imagine a woman of her reticence captured a husband at all, let alone Venables. They say he had an adventurous disposition while he lived."

Mercy smiled, but the conversation was growing tiresome. She liked Anna, when they discussed other matters besides Blythe and Lord Shaw. They had been close friends since her first season, but Anna's obsession with Mercy's love life, or lack of, was driving her to the brink of being rude. The snide comments against her sister were a problem, too. Blythe might be laced up tighter than necessary, but she had a good and generous heart under all her frowning.

As Blythe and Lord Shaw joined them, Mercy forced herself to smile.

"Ah, Your Grace, you do know how to please a man." He looked about the garden with a proprietary smile. "Nothing could give me more pleasure than to remain at Romsey Abbey for the rest of my life. The quiet, the solitude, the breathtaking vistas. I do not wonder that you prefer this locale to anywhere else. I know I would remain here for all my years if given a chance."

A scandalized expression crossed Blythe's face.

Mercy could feel a headache coming on. The very unsubtle suggestion that Shaw particularly liked Romsey Abbey would bring on yet another lecture from Blythe later. She would have to assure Blythe, again, that she wanted nothing from him. But first, she had to dismiss him, gently, for the sake of her friendship with Anna. Surely it was time for them to go. "You are kind, my lord. But obligations must be met, despite the disappointment of our feelings. Please give my regards to your mother. I look forward to seeing her again one day soon."

He took up Mercy's gloved hand and pressed a kiss to the back of it. "I look forward to that day as well. My mother is almost as fond of you as I am."

The look Shaw directed to her was hot and heavy with suggestion. Mercy ignored it, recovered her hand and led Anna toward the waiting carriage.

She gave her friend a quick hug. "I am so glad you could stay overnight, Anna. All going well, I'll see you again next week, as we arranged."

Anna lips turned up into a devious smile and Mercy's heart sank. "Sooner than that, I should imagine."

Anna kissed her cheeks and climbed into Lord Shaw's impressive new carriage.

One down. One to go.

Lord Shaw kissed the air above Blythe's hand, and then put his back to her as he captured Mercy's again in a firm grip. "Until we meet again, Your Grace." When he squeezed her fingers, head dipping to kiss them too, Mercy tugged them back. A predatory smile curled his lips.

Insufferable bounder. Could he not take a hint that she wanted none of him?

He swept inside the carriage and raised his hand in salute as they started off.

As soon as the carriage was at a greater distance, Mercy turned to her sister. "Oh, thank heavens they are gone."

"Lord Shaw visits you too frequently." Blythe scowled. "He is enamored of you."

Mercy caught her sister's arm and dragged her back toward the safety of the abbey. She did not like to be outside for long with so few people around her. The open spaces and dark woods beyond sent a chill racing up her spine. "I do not encourage that man. I enjoy Anna's visits, but I do wish Shaw would take himself back to Town. He is forever gossiping and causing trouble between us. I do not like him at all."

Blythe's frown grew. "He is on good terms with many people. He is wanted everywhere. I cannot understand it."

"Well, not by me." Mercy shut the terrace doors quickly. "Come, let us take breakfast together. Cook wanted to try out a new dish. Hopefully, it has not been ruined by Anna's tardy departure."

Although Blythe moved along with her through the abbey, there was a stiffness to her posture that Mercy did not like. No doubt her feelings were still prickling over Shaw's rather obvious intentions. She would be preparing yet more sternly worded lectures on the subject of a duchess' responsibility to observe the utmost propriety. Mercy was all too aware of her responsibilities in that regard, and she was failing most of them quite deliberately.

They sat down in the morning room, a cozy space for just the two of them, and enjoyed Cook's decadent breakfast. The one thing Mercy wholeheartedly enjoyed about being a duchess was how terribly spoiled her tastes had become. With a well-supplied pantry, Mercy's cook was a genius.

When no lecture was forthcoming immediately, Mercy thought it safe to resume conversation on another matter. "What are your plans for the day, dearest?" Mercy asked as she patted her napkin to her mouth, replete after a sumptuous feast.

Blythe shrugged and set her fork down after barely touching

anything on her plate. "There is nothing at Walden Hall that requires my supervision today. I had not thought to return till the afternoon, unless I am in the way here."

Mercy sighed in relief. She and Edwin wouldn't be left alone just yet. "Then you will stay and, if I can convince you to remain tonight, I will be a very happy woman. It has been an age since we stayed up late as we did as girls. Remember how Mama used to get so cross at our late-night giggling?"

"We should have listened to her better. She meant the best for us and now we have the lines on our faces to reveal our age. If I had a dau—" Blythe's words stuck in her throat suddenly. Her mouth sealed tight over her unfinished wishes.

Poor Blythe. She had been married first, and had nothing to show for her marriage now. She had lost her husband when she'd lost her son to a terrible fever that had swept the district. Even after these two years of widowhood, it was a subject that always changed her mood. Only Edwin's company seemed to jolly her into a better frame of mind.

Blythe dragged in a shuddering breath. "What are your plans today?"

"Well," Mercy stood, and drew Blythe with her, "I thought we might visit the library, find a horrid novel each, and spend the day alternately reading and playing with Edwin. Could we do that?"

The idea of lounging safely tucked away in her son's playroom was vastly appealing. If Blythe could be convinced to remain idle, and not fuss over Edwin too much, she might never think about her concerns again today.

Blythe frowned. "We can do anything you wish, Your Grace. This is your house."

"But you are my sister, so we will both decide on the entertainments of the day." She carefully tucked a stray lock of her sister's hair behind her ear. "I do not like to order people about, I most especially dislike that you think I should be bossy with *you*. What would you prefer to do, Blythe?"

Blythe smiled suddenly. "What you propose is perfect. I should like to spend time with Edwin very much. He is such a dear little lad."

Mercy held in a sigh of relief. "Good. Let's see what Hamilton and Gambrill Booksellers have sent to us. It was a very large crate that arrived yesterday, wasn't it?"

Blythe smiled, too.

Yet, as Mercy sorted through the stacks of books arranged in the library for her perusal, she could not help but wonder what thoughts swirled inside Blythe's mind.

Blythe had once been a daring, vivacious, and determined young woman. Out of all the Hunt girls—Mercy, Blythe, and their younger sister, Patience—Blythe had married first at just sixteen years of age. She had accepted a proposal of marriage from the darkly handsome widower, Lord Venables, a man seventeen years her senior. The match had set tongues wagging in decided shock.

Despite all the whispers about the match, Mercy had liked Lord Venable because he had doted on his second wife quite sincerely. He had enjoyed a good laugh with their family, too. But Blythe did not laugh now, and Mercy fervently hoped that the woman she once was still lurked beneath her grief.

Selections made and arms stacked with new entertainments, they retreated to Edwin's playroom.

"Auntie Bly, Aunty Bly," Edwin called as he ran across the room, all arms and wildly swinging legs. "Did you not go home today?"

Blythe dropped her books and scooped Edwin up into her arms. "There you are, my little duke. How could I leave you for long?"

Edwin kissed her cheek noisily and then wriggled to get down. "Come see what I did. Wilcox said I was very clever and even helped me knock down the tower we built. He's genius."

Mercy rolled her eyes at her son's language as he dragged Blythe away to the far side of the chamber to admire the messy corner of toys. He was growing up so fast that she could almost see him grow out of his clothes.

Blythe set her hands on her hips, foot tapping. "*That* is a mess. Clean it up, Your Grace."

Edwin's eyes widened but then he stomped his foot. "No. I'm still playing."

"Now, Your Grace. You cannot expect others to clean up everything after you." Blythe gestured to the toy-strewn floor. "You can play without making a mess. Be good for your mother."

Edwin peered at Mercy from around his aunt. "I *am* being good, Mama."

Mercy grinned. "I can see that. But you will tidy them up later, won't you, and not rely on Wilcox to do it? The butler has other work than cleaning up after one messy boy."

Wilcox was indispensable. But Edwin was coming to rely on him too much. Her son shuffled uncomfortably. "Do I have to?"

Mercy nodded. "Yes, but it can wait a while."

Edwin reluctantly nodded and then dropped to the floor to return to his play.

Blythe crossed the chamber, picked up her books, and chose one. "You spoil him."

Mercy settled on the chaise and lifted her feet to the cushions so she could stretch out comfortably. "He is my child to spoil. I will be the one to decide what needs to be done, and when, Blythe. Which book are you going to read?"

"I picked up *Fabulous Histories* by Miss Sarah Trimmer. I want to see if it will be suitable for Edwin's studies," Blythe murmured. "I think he needs educating rather than spoiling, and allowing him to make a mess from such a young age is setting us all up for trouble. One day you will see that I am correct."

One day, with luck, Blythe would have her own family to fuss over again. That day could not come soon enough for Mercy.

Chapter Three

Leopold did his best to settle his nerves as he set off for the abbey alone. This time he would not be denied the information he sought. This time he would argue until he received exactly what he had come here for.

He followed the road until he reached the entrance to Romsey, pausing as a grand carriage rattled through the vast gates. The occupants scowled at him, but Leopold was used to the ill-mannered guests of the Duke of Romsey and put them from his mind easily.

As he resumed his ride, a hundred memories assailed him. He held his mount to a walk as he rode along the tree-lined drive. So many memories—good, bad, and wavering in-between. The stream where he'd fished as a boy with his brothers, defying the old duke's wishes, was choked with reeds. He gritted his teeth. Of all the old duke's many edicts, presenting a formidable image to society at large was high on his list of expectations. Did the duchess have no sense of duty?

He broke from the trees and pulled up sharply. Before him, the abbey rose like a sinister beast, glowing golden now in full sunlight with the imitation of purity. Leopold knew better. The home of the Dukes of Romsey was nothing short of evil.

At least the forecourt was presentable to travelers. He rode up to the building and swung down from the saddle. His mount, no doubt frustrated by the less-than-energetic ride, pawed at the gravel drive until Leopold lay his gloved hand over his nose. "Steady. We'll be free and run against the wind as soon as we're done here."

When no groom arrived to take his horse, Leopold dropped the reins, stalked up the short flight of steps to pound upon the wide doors, and then returned to his horse to wait.

The doors creaked open, and he turned only his head to pin the butler with a stare designed to show his displeasure.

The old man blinked. "Master Leopold?"

"Wilcox."

Leopold continued to stroke his horse until the startled butler summoned grooms. Their mode of dress, when they finally arrived, fell so far below the expected standard of formality that he scowled at them.

Although he could rebuke them aloud, he saved his breath. His silence would have a greater effect than voicing his displeasure. That was the only useful trait he had adopted from the Duke of Romsey. Word of his presence would spread like fire on dry parchment until every servant knew that a Randall had returned. One who, while known for his even temper, would expect the same standards as the past Dukes of Romsey themselves.

As they led his horse away, Leopold turned to Wilcox. At least here was a man who held to familiar standards. And although the loss of Wilcox's hairpiece was a departure from previous tradition, Leopold couldn't be sorry for it. As boys, he and his brother, Oliver, had debated whether Wilcox had hair beneath his powdered wig. It was good to see Oliver's obsessive calculations about hair loss in grown men had been proved wrong in this instance. Wilcox still had a good head of iron-gray hair on display. Oliver had insisted that Wilcox must be bald.

"Sir, it is good to see you return." Wilcox ushered him inside with a wide grin. "Welcome home. Welcome home. No doubt you wish to pay your respects to the young duke and his mother."

Leopold glanced around the entrance hall, pleased that the space remained how he remembered. In the long years of his exile, this was the one part of the abbey featuring the last good memories he retained. It was the last place he'd seen his family all together before the old duke had separated them.

"If I could request an audience with Her Grace, I would be most obliged."

The butler took his hat, gloves, and greatcoat before leading him into the blue drawing room. "I will inform Her Grace that you have returned."

"Thank you, Wilcox."

The butler pulled the doors closed, leaving Leopold alone with the grandeur that was the Romsey's formal drawing room. Leopold hated the chamber. Last time he'd stood here in near darkness, he'd made a bargain with the devil himself. A bargain that, despite the sweetness of the moment, had sickened him for the deception he'd become a party to.

He glanced up at the walls and let his gaze rest on the old Duke of Romsey. The portrait of his father's cousin held pride of place above the grand hearth, smiling with deceptive smugness. How often had he seen that self-same smile aimed at him?

More times than he cared to remember.

At the far end of the room hung another portrait, a new addition to the chamber since his last visit. His second cousin, the late Edwin Randall, sat in regal splendor on a throne-like chair—the very image of health and vigor. A pity reality hadn't matched the portrait. Edwin, the fifth Duke of Romsey, had not enjoyed a long tenure as duke or the best of health. In fact, given the precarious strength of Edwin's heart, it surprised Leopold that he'd lasted until his heir arrived. But, since he'd not produced another son before his early death, that meant Leopold was next in line for the title.

The thought didn't please him. He wanted none of the pomp and certainly none of the intrigue that went hand in hand with the title. He had wealth enough to last a lifetime and wanted nothing from this place but answers.

He shifted his gaze to the portrait of a woman holding an expressionless newborn child across her knees. The current duchess appeared a formidable woman. Dark haired and grave in manner. He hoped the child, named Edwin after his father, received a glimmer of parental affection from her. Or perhaps, as often was the case with the Duchesses of Romsey, she left the care of her child in the hands of servants and never saw him.

Poor child.

Edwin Randall, the sixth Duke of Romsey, had Leopold's pity.

He'd never be as free to laugh as Leopold and his brothers and sister had been. Perhaps that was the benefit of not being the heir. Leopold's childhood had been a happy one—loud and rough rather than refined and sequestered in this place. But Leopold was incredibly curious about young Edwin's health. Did he have a weak heart like his father, too?

Rapid footsteps sounded in the hall, and he turned toward the door. After a moment or two of hushed consultation outside, a woman swept in—flanked by two footmen and a darkly dressed attendant.

The Duchess of Romsey shocked Leopold to his core. Where he had expected haughty civility, he sensed uncertainty. Where he expected grave regard, he sensed youth and unease.

This was the Duchess of Romsey?

He risked a quick glance at the portrait. The artist had only captured the tiniest portion of the real woman, and Leopold hastily produced a courtly bow to cover his surprise.

When he took a step forward, her two footmen moved to stand between him and the duchess. The action told him all he needed to know. The old duke had poisoned her mind toward him and his family. Getting what he wanted from her might take some time.

"Your Grace, forgive me for not calling on you sooner. My affairs have kept me abroad much longer than I anticipated. Please accept my condolences on the loss of your husband and his father. It is a great loss to the family to lose both of them in so short a time."

Actually, Leopold didn't believe their deaths a tragedy for the family at all. His cousin Edwin may have been as much a pawn as Leopold had been in the old duke's intrigues, but there had been no love between them. There was nothing about the fifth Duke of Romsey to miss. But to this day, he did not know if his cousin had a hand in the fate of his family. The loss of the old duke pained Leopold only because he was the one behind it all.

"Thank you," Her Grace murmured softly. "I had not expected visitors at Romsey today. Your arrival is a surprise and has caught us unprepared. I am sorry to have kept you waiting so long."

Blunt. Leopold preferred plain speaking to honey-coated pleasantries. Perhaps he and the duchess could deal well with each other. "It was hardly any time to wait at all. My return is a temporary diversion on a much longer journey. I'll not be a burden on the estate if that is what you fear." He glanced at both footmen to show he recognized the attempt at protection. He hoped the duchess could see it was unnecessary. He wanted nothing from her but information.

The duchess frowned and, after a moment of hesitation, signaled her footmen to step aside. Her attendant, a dour woman of indeterminate age, moved to flank her as she swept forward in a rustle of burgundy silk to sit on a wide chair. "Please, do be seated."

The duchess' soft, melodious voice was another shock to his senses. She was certainly not the woman he had expected to meet. Her voice brought to mind sweaty midnight pleasures— panting, grasping ecstasy that consumed the mind.

Leopold brutally pushed those thoughts from his head as he sank into an opposite chair.

A commotion occurred at the door and he turned, noticing the appearance of tea. Such considerations were rare in his presence, but very much appreciated. If the duchess relaxed enough, she might be more amenable to his request. The duchess' companion poured the tea without uttering a word and he took his cup, taking a sip while he considered how best to deal with her.

The duchess set her teacup upon the saucer with exquisite care and looked at him expectantly. "You mentioned you'd been abroad, Mr. Randall. Might we know how you occupied your time while away from Romsey?"

Leopold glanced at her hands. Despite her calm words, her tense fingers hinted she wasn't altogether certain he was not about to mount an immediate attack on her person. Blast the Dukes of Romsey to hell and back. "I've just returned from India. I earn my way as a silk merchant."

Her Grace's pretty green eyes widened. "Really?"

"Yes, since I left England ten years ago."

Perhaps unconsciously, the duchess' palm slid over the silk of her gown. A silk that he'd purchased and sent directly here, if memory served. Only the best for Romsey. The old duke had demanded it as part of their bargain and had kept a strict accounting of their transactions.

Noticing the direction of his gaze, her hands stilled. "You?"

Leopold nodded, but he was uncertain what to make of her

interest. By rights, she should disdain a member of the family who sullied his hands in trade. But he'd had little choice in the matter. He'd had to survive. He'd had to agree to the old duke's bargain to ensure his siblings had a similar chance for a good life.

"Thank you." The duchess glanced up at the woman beside her. "May I present Lady Venables, my younger sister?"

Leopold shifted his gaze to the other woman, doing his best to hide his surprise. The younger sister's appearance hinted at a far greater age. As he considered her, he realized the darker tone of her gown and the sober expression might reflect a state of mourning. "Lady Venables, a pleasure."

She inclined her head, but kept her lips pressed together, her expression wary. The mousy-haired, reed-thin woman dressed in priggish navy muslin seemed wound as tightly as a bowstring.

Leopold took another sip of his tea and let some of his tension fall away. Clearly all was not as expected at Romsey, but he should not anticipate the worst from these women. They undoubtedly had their own problems to deal with, it seemed. Lady Venables might be less than friendly, but he had wrongly anticipated the duchess' contempt. So far all he sensed was curiosity from her.

"Wilcox mentioned that it has been many years since you've been at Romsey. I must confess, I cannot recall my husband ever mentioning you. Are you greatly estranged from the ducal line?"

"His Grace and I were second cousins."

The duchess gasped. "Second cousins? But why would he never mention you? You must have been his heir? My son's heir now."

Leopold was very good at reading the lies people tried to hide. Her wide-eyed, innocent questioning caused a flutter in his chest. She wasn't lying in any way. She honestly hadn't known of his existence before today. No wonder she had been wary of him. The thought settled in his stomach like a rock. If she had not known of him then it stood to reason that she might not even know the whereabouts of his family.

Although his heart pounded, Leopold shrugged as if his potential elevation in rank meant nothing. And it didn't make the slightest difference to his plans. He had never wanted to be Romsey. "My father fell out with the old duke, his cousin, some years back. Family affairs have been tense ever since."

The duchess glanced up at her sister. A silent communication seemed to pass between them, and then Lady Venable gave a tiny shake of her head. Her Grace bit her lip then set her teacup away from her once more. "Well then, that is all in the past. We are glad you have returned to Romsey. Wilcox, please have a room prepared for our cousin."

Stunned by the unexpected gesture, Leopold set his cup aside and held up his hand. "Your Grace is far too kind. I have already secured lodgings in the village for the extent of my stay. I would never impose upon the hospitality of Romsey Abbey."

Her mouth fell open, but she quickly recovered. "Well then."

Silence thickened. He couldn't ask his questions now. Clearly, she knew nothing of his family, or she was more of an accomplished liar than he'd first thought. He needed time to think, to regroup and determine a new strategy of how to broach the subject. He couldn't scare her off with his knowledge of the old duke's treachery. Instead, Leopold offered a half smile. "Thank you for agreeing to meet with me, Your Grace, but I should not monopolize your time. Perhaps I might call upon you another day soon?"

The duchess inclined her head, but her expression betrayed her confusion at his rather abrupt leave-taking. "That would be acceptable. Perhaps you would join us for luncheon tomorrow. No doubt you would like to meet the duke."

Leopold's heart thumped painfully, but he managed to nod, climb to his feet, and leave her presence. As he crossed the entrance hall to collect his hat, he briefly regretted his decision not to press for information today. He didn't want to remain in this district longer than he had to, where loneliness for his family would only build in strength. He would avoid the usual haunts he and his brothers frequented and keep the memories of old close to his chest for another night.

But tomorrow, he would come to dine and meet the infant duke. Tomorrow, he would meet his last-known living relation.

Chapter Four

Despite the shocking impropriety, Mercy's joyous shriek echoed around the drawing room, bouncing off the formal portraits of the Dukes of Romsey quite nicely. Satisfied beyond measure, Mercy settled back into her chair and turned her head. "See, I told you we would be perfectly safe."

Blythe sat where Leopold Randall had been moments before, but her expression hinted there would be a lecture coming. "You must keep up your guard at all times. He is an ambitious man by all accounts."

Mercy threw her hands up to stop her words. "Oh, posh. Mr. Randall wouldn't hurt anyone. He seems much too nice for all the evil you've just told me."

Blythe scowled. "I merely repeat what I overheard your husband mentioning to mine years ago, when he asked about the lack of family in the Romsey line. If you had been at his side as you should, then you would heed the warnings. You must be on your guard from now on."

Mercy chose to ignore the fact that Blythe had known about Leopold Randall's existence before today and not told her about him. However, she honed in on the comment that she'd been a poor wife to her husband to have ever left his side. Blythe had doted on her husband. Yet Mercy had not had that kind of marriage. They had sometimes gone a whole week without speaking more than a few words together. It had stung, at first, but Edwin had made it clear that he preferred his privacy to her company.

She raised her hand toward Blythe to end her prattle. "Edwin had his physician on hand to care for him. Everything that could be done was done. Should I have left my son in the care of servants during that terrible time of illness? I could not have borne it."

Blythe's face grew taut with strain. "The nurse I recommended would have spared you the necessity so you could be at your husband's side during his last days. You knew he had never fully recovered after the fever that took my Raphael and Adam." Blythe's voice cracked at the mention of her son's name. Little Adam's death was still a sharp loss for her sister.

Mercy pressed her lips together. They'd been down this road before, arguing over every small detail of wifely responsibility, and Mercy's failures. She was so sick of feeling her younger sister's censure. Blythe had had a marriage to make a woman envious. Mercy had not. But because of Blythe's grief, she often held back from saying exactly what she thought of her sister's advice on the subject of husbands.

It took two willing people to make a marriage perfect. Mercy had been willing, Edwin had not.

She ran her hand over the silk of her gown, thinking of Leopold Randall's visit. "He is handsome, don't you think?"

Blythe fussed with the folds of her own gown, heightening her appearance of prim respectability. "I hardly think a duchess should notice those things about men."

Oh, Mercy noticed. Yet she'd never met a man to put such thoughts into her head so quickly. Mr. Randall's sun-kissed complexion, his obvious good health and virility, appealed. "Duchess I may be, but I think Mr. Randall is quite attractive. Do you think he spent many years in India?"

Blythe shuddered. "By his own words, he suggested as much. But I am not interested in speculating about such heathen places. We have more important things to discuss."

Mercy couldn't imagine what they might be. The life of a duchess was just plain dull, especially now that Blythe had lost her sense of fun. She had once been Mercy's best friend, a trusted companion she could tell her deepest, most scandalous secrets to. But that was before Mercy had married and learned there were some matters she couldn't discuss with anyone. Since becoming a widow, Blythe's manner had grown so stiff with propriety that Mercy feared she never could confide in her again.

She slapped her hands onto the arms of her chair as a marvelous idea came to her. "The book." Mercy dashed from the room, leaving her no-doubt disapproving sister to trail along at a proper snail's pace.

The book was her savior. The book was a secret. At least, from the past Dukes of Romsey, that was.

When she'd first married Edwin, he'd given her a gift belonging to his late mother. At the time she'd smiled, accepted the unexceptional jewel case from a woman long dead, and ignored it. But on a day when the wind blew heavy with rain, and boredom had led her to play with the pretty baubles she'd inherited, she uncovered a secret compartment.

The journal, a diary begun by her predecessors, contained the sort of gossip that the dukes always tried to hide—who they had wronged.

Mercy found the goings-on in the family she'd married into fascinatingly evil.

So far, she'd added nothing to it. Her late husband, given his fragile state of health, had been somewhat of a recluse. But the book might tell her of the falling out prior to her marriage.

She hurried to her chamber, pulling her keys from her pocket as she went. With one quick turn of the lock, she retrieved the book and sank into a deep chair beside the window. She flicked through pages, eagerly searching for the last duchess' remembrances until Blythe arrived. "Nothing yet."

Since Blythe disapproved of the book, Mercy ignored her gasp.

"Mercy, please put the book down and come with me."

Mercy tapped the page. No, this was the wrong duchess. She flicked the pages in rapid succession until she found a more likely date.

I suspect my husband disapproves of his cousin's wife not because she is so comely but because she has birthed yet another son, while I have but one.

Hmm, could that be the reason for the fallout? The production of heirs was of paramount importance to every great family. Not everyone wanted a cousin to inherit. She knew from her sister's experience that seemingly healthy children didn't always live to adulthood. Had fear been the reason for discord?

"Mercy!"

Oh, could Blythe ever be quiet when she was in one of her scolding moods? Perhaps enough time had passed for her sister to put her grieving aside. Really, Blythe should be listening to her, not the other way round.

With every intention of putting her younger—and lower-ranked—sister in her place, Mercy stood and crossed to her. But Blythe's pale complexion stilled the cutting retort she wanted to utter. Her sister appeared about to cast up her accounts.

"My dear, are you all right?"

Blythe shook her head and took a step back. When her arm rose to point at the bed, Mercy turned to see what she stared at.

Atop her bed, blood spattered in a wide arc on her favorite comforter, sat a poor dead rabbit.

Mercy gagged and rushed for the chamber pot.

Once she had retched until her sides ached, Mercy returned to find her sister—though still pale—examining the poor dead creature. Mercy thought she might be sick again. "Blythe, come away from that."

To Mercy's horror, Blythe's hand reached out as if to touch the pelt.

Mercy grasped her sister's arm and dragged her out into the corridor.

Blythe blinked as if dazed, and then her features hardened. "This has to stop."

Mercy ran her hands up and down her arms to try to bring warmth back into her body. She did not know how to stop these special "gifts" being left upon her doorstep, her chair, and now, it appeared, on the very bed she slept in. And whoever sent them, they were getting bolder, too. Thankfully, Edwin had seen nothing of them yet.

"I'll call Wilcox to take the mess away," Blythe said.

Mercy swallowed down the bile rising in her throat. "Thank you, Blythe," she whispered.

When Blythe hurried away, Mercy collapsed against the wall.

She didn't understand. She'd done nothing, offended no one. Yet somewhere out there was someone with a very peculiar notion of her needs. She did not need threatening letters delivered with the morning mail. But she had managed to ignore them. It was a little harder to ignore the dead gifts recently delivered at irregular intervals to her.

Wilcox and a footman scurried past her and entered her bedchamber. She didn't watch the grim business of removing the mess, but she listened and heard her butler's outrage about the oddities at Romsey Abbey.

When he'd handed the mess off to the footman with instructions to burn the lot, Wilcox approached her. "If I might be so bold, Your Grace, I believe it would be prudent to seek family counsel on how to put a stop to these despicable acts."

Mercy considered his words, but she didn't know what to do. This matter was slowly escalating beyond her understanding. "You think I should write to my brother for his advice?"

Wilcox shook his head. "No, Your Grace. I thought it prudent to seek Mr. Randall's assistance. He has returned at a fortuitous time it seems."

Mercy frowned, thinking the matter through. She didn't know Mr. Randall well enough to confide in him. Not yet at any rate.

"Why would you think Her Grace should confide in Mr. Randall?" Blythe asked as she rejoined them. "Is it not suspicious that he would return at just such a moment?"

Mercy startled at her sister's suggestion.

"He would never threaten a woman," Wilcox blurted out in Randall's defense, but then his cheeks darkened with embarrassment. He rarely contradicted Blythe, although Mercy had given him leave to speak his mind should he feel strongly about any matter. Rather than let a servant feel the wrath of her sister's sharp tongue, Mercy waved Wilcox away. He bowed and moved off.

Mercy read the disgruntled look in her sister's eye. "Why would you think Mr. Randall involved?" she asked, trying to turn Blythe's tide of anger before she suggested Wilcox be dismissed for insolence yet again. "He has only just returned from India."

"So he says." Blythe looked away. "We know so little about him."

Really, why was everyone so eager to label Mr. Randall a troublemaker? Mercy had a good feeling about him. One glance into those dark, smoldering eyes had promised her that here was a man she could rely upon. It had absolutely nothing to do with the way her pulse leapt at his brief smile. The man had revealed a pair of delightful dimples. No one with dimples could be truly evil.

Mercy stood tall. "Well, we shall learn more when he comes to dine tomorrow. In the meantime, we cannot condemn him without cause."

"Then what *shall* we do?"

Mercy grinned. "We shall go along and smother my son with kisses and then tell him he has a cousin. He'll be wondering where we are."

Leopold settled into a vacant corner of the Vulture's taproom and kept his eye on the crowd. The low-beamed inn thrummed with locals, all easing the day's aches over a tankard or two of dark ale. Gradually, Leopold grew accustomed to the competing noise of English voices, and the smell. India, with her cloying spices permeating the air, had made England the foreign country to his senses. But like India, he'd grow used to the difference if given enough time.

One by one, each patron whispered into each another's ears until the whole room knew of his return. More than one local tipped his cap to Leopold in respect. During their time here, his family had been well liked. They considered him one of them still, even if he stood next in line for the title.

A tankard slid across the battered table. "Here you are, Mr. Randall. Just the way you liked it when you were young. Put hair on your chest, that will."

He glanced up and found Eamon Murphy, the biggest gossip in the district, hovering at his elbow. "Eamon. Are you still knocking about these parts?"

Eamon grinned. "Nowhere else in the world like Romsey. Why would I leave?"

Leopold clapped him on the arm. "I seem to recall you had taken a fancy to a girl who lived a few miles away from Romsey. I thought you'd have taken over her father's farm by now and moved away."

Eamon scowled. "Haughty witch, that one. She got only her airs to keep her company nowadays. No one else would have her. But look at you. You're a real gentleman now. Too fancy to be hanging about with the likes of us. Why are you not up at the abbey with the duchess?"

Leopold forced a smile to his face, but kept the whys of his presence to himself. "What's afoot, Eamon?"

A cunning smile lit Eamon's face as he slid into the opposite seat. He leaned across the table toward Leopold. "What do you fancy?"

Leopold leaned forward too, enjoying the familiar banter. "What is the latest entertainment?"

"Heard tell of a cock fight over Crampmoor way. Rough crowd, but that's not unusual. There's a brothel up at Timsbury now. New one. Expensive. Caters to well turned out gentlemen such as yourself. But you've been in India. Bet you're after some of the white smoke?" Eamon's eyes glittered, as if he'd delivered Leopold an early Christmas gift.

Leopold did not partake of opium. He liked to keep his wits about him. When he shook his head, Eamon slumped. "The white smoke ruins a man, Eamon. Best not to start at all."

Opium might make a man forget home, but he merely traded one yearning for another. Leopold had seen enough of that sickness among the English in India to last him a lifetime.

Eamon sat back and scrubbed a hand over his face. "Only other thing is the duchess herself, and there are plenty of men wagering on her taking a lover soon. Odds are on Lord Shaw, but he's chasing the skirts of a *few* noble ladies, so it's hard to judge who'd have the best chance. But the earl's been calling on the duchess pretty regular. He's the favorite to make it a permanent arrangement by marrying her."

"Is that so?" Anger ripped through him. Gods, a Shaw couldn't gain control of Romsey. Even as a boy he'd heard tales about the family, none of them very complimentary.

Although Leopold had attempted to keep the disgust from his tone, Eamon must have picked up on his tension. The man straightened. "That's what I heard. Might be nothing more than gossip. Now you're home, the odds will change. She'd be wise to take your advice on."

Leopold picked up his tankard and took a swallow. Did people really think he could have any influence where the Duchess of Romsey was concerned? He wiped his hand across the back of his mouth before he dared to speak. "As good as I remember. Do you know they can't make a decent drop in India? Must be why the white smoke is so popular."

"Ain't nowhere like Romsey. Welcome home." Eamon smiled cheekily as he slipped away from the table.

So, the duchess, for all her prim innocence, had lovers lining up. Knowing her weaknesses could only help his chances of finding Oliver, Rosemary, and Tobias. If Leopold learned enough about her faults, he could use the information for leverage should she prove resistant to helping him. He'd use every trick he knew to get his way this time. The warm spark of mischief in her eyes wouldn't deter him.

Leopold smiled and took another drink while he watched Eamon working the room, wringing every last shred of gossip from the locals. Given enough time, Eamon would tell him everything he needed to know. He might even let slip some things he didn't know he knew, too, and help put Leopold's family back together.

Chapter Five

Leopold Randall was prompt, polite and, to Mercy's way of thinking, even more handsome than yesterday. After some initial awkwardness in his greeting, the dark-suited gentleman had sat down to luncheon, displaying exquisite manners—far more than Blythe had assured her he would possess—and kept up a lively conversation about his travels.

But there wasn't the faintest hint of those dimples, and Mercy was extremely conscious of her disappointment. "Tell me, Mr. Randall, have you married?"

She'd dreamed of him last night. A disturbing and exciting fantasy that she feared might be impossible to forget when he was near.

Randall coughed, appearing in danger of choking. "No, Your Grace."

"Really? I cannot imagine why." Mercy pressed her napkin to her mouth to hide the unexpected surge of happiness that came over her. She'd been pondering her handsome companion all through the meal and now luncheon was over, she was gripped with restlessness. She climbed to her feet and moved away from the dining table while she regained control of her emotions. "You appear too young a man to have given up on making a match. How old are you?"

Randall stood, chair scraping across the floor in his hurry. A raw, desperate tingle rushed up her arms as he moved to stand behind her. Mercy rubbed her hands across her bare skin to dispel the sensation.

"I'm not yet thirty." Randall's voice skittered across her nerves and when she glanced over her shoulder, his gaze inspected her from head to toe. Mercy quaked at the intense pleasure she found in knowing she'd caught him in an unguarded moment. He set his hands to his hips. "And may I be bold in return and ask yours, Your Grace?"

"Of course. I've reached the grand old age of six and twenty." As Mr. Randall nodded, his lips compressed tightly, and then his gaze slid down her gown again. Mercy's heartbeat romped out of control. "I assume you've a sweetheart waiting for you somewhere."

It was probably good that her sister had declined to join them. Blythe would be shocked to the tips of her dainty slippers by this brazen interrogation. But the need to know his secrets had loosened her tongue.

Mr. Randall offered a half smile. "Perhaps."

"Ah, a gentleman of discretion. Commendable."

And a great pity. If Randall's affections had clearly been uninvolved, he'd have made a pleasing companion. She enjoyed his conversation so far, and hoped to hear more of his exciting travels. But if there was a sweetheart waiting for him elsewhere, Mercy couldn't detain him here for long. She hoped he would stay a little longer though. The sound of his voice, the drift of his gaze over her skin, reminded her that she was an unattached woman with normal needs.

Her reaction to him shocked her. She should not be thinking of him on such intimate terms. With luck, Mr. Randall could turn out to be a much-needed advisor; at worst, an ambitious danger to her son. But she really didn't think him a danger.

Randall moved to stand at her side, although his position kept him a respectful pace behind. "Have I satisfied your curiosity enough for one day, Your Grace?"

Mercy turned, almost believing that Randall was teasing her. But his serious gaze showed no hint of amusement. "You have been more than candid for one day. Someone should have warned you that I tend to be a trifle blunt in conversation, an appalling habit that has survived my elevation in rank."

Randall's face softened. "As ever, I am your servant."

Mercy held his gaze, aware of the urge to move forward and lay her hands upon his chest but determined to ignore it. She took a step back. "The duke is waiting."

She skirted around Randall, trying to understand her desire to feel his hands upon her skin. She'd never had that urge before, and there had been dozens of men vying for an invitation to share her bed, during and after her marriage. Most men failed to hide their interest now that her husband had passed away.

Perhaps that was what troubled her most. She sensed no such intentions from Randall. Although he looked at her a great deal, he seemed to have no interest in touching her at all.

Without waiting to see if he followed, Mercy pushed through the doors connecting the dining room to a long corridor that led to the room where Edwin waited. Behind her, Randall's heavier footsteps followed, sending her nerves skittering once more. She couldn't understand why Leopold Randall left her breathless when he offered her no encouragement. Her reaction to him was unprecedented, but she would make herself behave as a duchess should.

She forced a grateful smile for Edwin's footmen as they opened the doors. A childish squeal filled the air, and she rushed forward to wrap Edwin in her arms.

He squeezed her tight about the neck. "Mama, Mama."

Mercy buried her face in his neck. "Hello, my darling boy, have you missed me?"

His little chin rose and she rained kisses on his cheeks until he wriggled. "Where have you been, Mama? Come and play."

Mercy chuckled. "Not yet, there is someone important you must meet first." She turned and set her son on his feet. "Edwin, this is your cousin, Leopold Randall. Mr. Randall, this is my son, Edwin."

Although her father-in-law had insisted that introductions involving her son be handled with a certain level of pomp and circumstance, Mercy had seriously disagreed, preferring infor-mality around Edwin.

Leopold Randall's face had lost all color, so much so that she wondered if he was offended by her casual introduction, or about to faint.

Randall recovered quickly and bowed deeply to her son. "Your Grace."

"Your Grace," Edwin mimicked, then copied Randall's bow.

Mercy couldn't help but laugh at her child's mistake. She knelt beside her son. "No, Edwin, you must use his name. Say *Randall* and then nod."

Edwin tried again and did the greeting perfectly. Mercy beamed. "Well done, Your Grace."

Edwin giggled and threw himself into her arms, but peered around her shoulder to see what Leopold Randall was doing. He'd had so little to do with gentlemen, other than servants, that he appeared as fascinated as Mercy by the tall, dark man before him. Randall's large size and dark suiting did overwhelm the room. However, true to his young nature, Edwin's curiosity didn't last very long. A toy caught his attention and he rushed off to play.

As Mercy began to rise, Randall caught her elbow to steady her ascent. The rush of heat across her bare skin overwhelmed her, and she looked up into his face. So close to him, she noticed just how dark brown his eyes were. The long sweep of his lashes against his skin as delightful a surprise as his dimples. But what she particularly noted was how quickly his gaze dropped from hers. With his gaze lowered, Mercy couldn't tell what he thought. That missing knowledge disturbed her.

"He is smaller than I imagined." His breath whispered across her cheek, sending a thrill along her spine despite the criticism in his words.

"Come now, he is only four years of age. He will grow into the title." Perhaps she responded a trifle defensively. Blythe always seemed to offer suggestions for Edwin's upbringing that were not quite sympathetic to Mercy's ideals. But she would not hear disapproval of her son from Leopold Randall.

"I thought he was older than four," he said. "When exactly was the duke born?"

She looked up into Mr. Randall's face and smiled. "May seventh, eighteen hundred and ten."

"Eighteen-ten." Randall's eyes widened. His fingers fell away from her arm as he glanced at Edwin again. He shook his head as if surprised, but then smiled apologetically. "It's been so long since I've been around a small child. I'd quite confused how big he'd be."

Mercy glanced to where her son played happily with his toys and let her tension slip away. He hadn't meant to criticize. He'd obviously heard some wrong information regarding her son's age and she could forgive him easily enough for his confusion. But he had let slip another small insight into his life that Mercy was curious about. "When were you near a young child last?"

Randall's harsh exhalation sent her pulse racing again. She glanced up at him, his expression weary.

"My younger brother, Tobias," he said softly.

"Are you close?"

"We were once." A flicker of a dimple appeared on Randall's cheek as his gaze sharpened on Edwin. "I was the eldest. He was my responsibility. I spoiled him."

Mercy laughed. "Then you are a better brother than most. Mine was quite joyful to be rid of me when I married."

"I imagine having one's sister become a duchess is cause for celebration."

"That wasn't what he celebrated," Mercy grumbled. "He celebrated getting me out from under his feet so he might return to his debauchery without facing my disapproval over breakfast."

There, finally, a dimple.

"Ah, I believe most men would experience a similar feeling." Randall's dimple deepened.

Mercy set her hands to her hips. "What is it about men and wenching? Can you not do without?"

When he didn't respond, Mercy decided her blunt question had flummoxed him. She waved her hands. "Ignore my question."

"As you wish, Your Grace," he said hastily.

Randall's speedy response didn't surprise her. Since she'd become a duchess, people rarely contradicted her, except for Blythe. But she'd hoped Randall would be different. Disappointed to be faced with another person prepared to let her gaffes pass unchallenged, Mercy moved to sit by the window, closer to her son.

Her companion cleared his throat. "Most men are influenced by their peers. To be seen as an accomplished seducer is to be accepted without question by your fellow man. But from all I've seen, ladies attempting to satisfy those same desires are not treated so kindly."

Mercy met his gaze. "You must rank quite high among your acquaintances. The stories you could tell of your travels, and companions, boggles the mind. The ladies must swoon at the sight of you."

Instantly, she regretted her observation. She sounded peevish even to her own ears. She should not be thinking of him in those terms, and she certainly shouldn't be letting him know that she thought him irresistible. Men tended to think too well of themselves when flattered.

Randall's face darkened. "*Most* men chase the ladies, Your Grace. Not all."

He left her abruptly and moved to the other side of the chamber, passing her son with the barest of glances. What was it about him that made her want to question him, to dig beneath that polite façade and discover his real opinions? Perhaps she'd been too long alone. Her late husband might not have been a perfect man, but they'd rubbed along together well enough, she supposed. However, she'd never needed to see into his soul like this. She'd never wanted to know what her husband had done when they had been apart.

"He has your eyes," Randall noted, returning to sit across from her.

"But not my temper," Mercy added with a laugh. "He is a vastly agreeable child."

Mercy let out a relieved breath at the return to a much safer topic of conversation. She could talk of Edwin for hours and never be discontent. Speaking of her son might even banish her foolish thoughts about the man sitting opposite, and that could only be a good thing.

But then Leopold Randall's gaze fixed upon hers, and she couldn't look away. He'd not done that before, she realized. He'd not offered more than the briefest of glances. Whatever emotion she'd stirred within him by her talk of his paramours had been conquered and hidden again. Randall puzzled her immensely. Did he not like women?

A wild surge of rebellion stirred within her. She wanted to find out exactly what he *did* like, and damn the consequences of that discovery.

His dark-eyed stare provoked an irrational longing to move closer. Hot color stole up her face, and Mercy was the first to break. She looked to her son again. "I am truly lucky to have him."

"Were there complications?" he asked suddenly.

The blunt question into matters most men wouldn't think to enquire after pleased her.

"I carried him easily. The birth was arduous, but quicker than I was led to believe. I was blessed. Some women have a much harder time."

Randall's breath hissed out, and she had to wonder why he'd held it in the first place. "I believe my mother's labors grew shorter each time. My youngest brother, Tobias—her fourth child—arrived before she'd made it to the birthing chamber."

Mercy snorted a laugh, and then quickly covered her mouth to pretend the unladylike sound hadn't escaped her control. "Oh dear, I am glad Edwin took a little longer than that. How positively embarrassed your dear mama must have been."

"Mother always hinted her children needed more patience." Randall grew silent again, his gaze fixed on his fingers.

Mercy leaned forward. "You miss her?"

"Every day." His glance pinned her in place. "My mother was an angel. Spontaneous. Always smiling. Happiest when her family rumbled under her feet. My father was devoted to keeping her happy, despite the difficulties of living here."

"I'm told they died in a carriage accident? I'm so sorry." At his arched brow, Mercy rushed to explain. "Wilcox has been advising me on family matters I was previously unaware of. You must have been devastated to lose them both on the same day."

Randall kept silent, lips pressed tight together, his expression unreadable. After a long moment, his jaw unclenched. "He *claimed* it was an accident."

"He?"

"The old duke wrote a short note to the school so they might inform my brother and me of our orphaned state."

Mercy blinked. "Oh, that was kind of him."

And utterly impersonal.

Randall scowled and turned his face away. Judging by the high color in his cheeks, he was angry, possibly furious. Before she could question him, Edwin hurried over and pushed a small wooden horse into Randall's hands.

He appeared startled, but then his fist closed over it. The small, carved piece disappeared from view and when he opened his hand again, Edwin smiled in encouragement. Clearly her son had decided he liked his older second cousin. When Randall began to play, prancing the horse for her son's amusement, Mercy leaned back and watched them.

Edwin accepted strangers so easily. Perhaps too easily, yet she couldn't be sorry that he and his cousin had become acquainted. The boy would need male guidance later in life. Who better to show him the way than an elder relation?

When Randall handed the horse back to Edwin, her son hurried to her side. He fell into her lap, prancing the horse as Randall had shown him, up along her arm and into her neck.

"Play, Mama. Please!"

She pressed a brief kiss to her son's raised lips and pushed him toward his toys. "I'll be there soon."

Mercy stood and pulled the bell to summon food for her son then turned to face Mr. Randall. He regarded her with a bemused expression—and Mercy hoped that what she was about to do wouldn't send him running from the estate.

"I'm about to do something shocking again, Mr. Randall. Prepare yourself."

Chapter Six

Leopold didn't think he could be any more surprised by the Duchess of Romsey. He had the distinct feeling he was engaged in a battle of wits with a formidable enemy and was scrambling to defend himself from this slight woman. Her informality was chipping away at his hostility. She seemed nice, lovely even, but he could not think that way about her. He had to keep her at arm's length until he achieved his goal.

She glided across the room and then settled to the floor with her skirts bunched around her. Sitting next to her son, the image was so pure and good that his heart stuttered. He had never expected to be so moved by the appearance of Edwin Randall or his mother.

He pressed his hands to his knees, fighting his softer emotions. His own mother had played with her children in just such a way. The reminder chipped away a little more of his defenses. At least the duke was loved, so there was some hope for the future. It was clear to him that Edwin was the center of the duchess' world.

Leopold looked about the room for something to do other than stare. The chamber was filled to the brim with entertainments, but the wealth around him paled in comparison to the duchess' attempts to make the little boy happy. She wriggled around on the thick carpet until she lay flat on her belly. From the angle Leopold sat, he had a good view—perhaps too good a view—of her calves and tiny feet. Her legs were restless as she played with her son, and Leopold had a hard time ignoring their movements. Good God, she was dangerous to him and his sanity.

The boy, too, would bring him to his knees.

He studied the child. Dark hair, lanky build, small dimple in his left cheek when he laughed, which was often. Leopold lifted his hand to his cheek and stroked over the same spot. If he smiled broadly, his own dimples would show…and that might lead to questions he didn't want to consider. Not yet, at any rate. He simply had to hide behind formality, find nothing agreeable enough to make him smile, until he discovered the fate of his remaining family.

Yet the child interested him on a deeper level.

Despite the improbability, this boy, this duke, may very well be his own son.

His age was about right for the night Leopold came here to fulfill the duke's last despicable demand.

If his brother Oliver were present, he would have the percentages and reassuring calculations to prove that Leopold's fears were groundless and the child could not possibly be of his making. But he could count as well as any man. He knew when he'd come to Romsey Abbey last, and he knew when the child, Edwin, had been born.

Nine months later.

He covered his mouth. The consequence of his actions five years ago had never truly seemed dangerous until now.

On his last visit, the old duke had demanded he bed a woman in the dark of night, another deed to be performed in the duke's service to keep his brothers and sister safe. Fool that he was, he'd never considered he might have bedded his cousins wife—and that this could be the consequence.

But why had Edwin allowed it? Had his cousin been unable to bed his own wife and sire a child due to his weakened heart?

What he remembered of that night was a blur. Despite the initial awkwardness, performing for the duke had not been difficult that night. His midnight lover had been worth the sacrifice of his time and energy. She had been irresistible, insatiable, and he had made sure she thoroughly enjoyed their many couplings.

But he had never seen her clearly, or even asked her name.

He should have asked. He should have demanded to know every detail of the bargain he'd made to have spared himself the shock now.

Leopold sat back, crossing one leg over the other as he dipped his hand into his coat pocket. He extracted his notebook and charcoal and without thinking too much about it, or asking if the duchess objected, he scratched out the scene before him on a fresh page. The familiar activity calmed him. While he sketched, he didn't need to think or act on anything but what he witnessed at that moment. He could rid his mind of guilt and pretend all was right with his world.

Despite his misgivings, the duchess was lovely. As he neared completion of the outline, the duchess lifted her feet from the floor and crossed them at the ankles. They rocked backward and forward slowly in the air, and Leopold hurried to capture the unguarded pose. He looked up as the boy laughed.

Two deep dimples—just like his.

The young Duke of Romsey was a happy child. Perhaps, without the old duke's influence, he would grow to be an honorable man one day. Leopold hoped so. His child or not, the boy was the only family he had left. He would not like to be constantly checking over his shoulder a few years down the track when the boy was grown and corrupted to resent his existence.

With the sketch complete, Leopold slid the notebook away before he was noticed and dropped his hands to his knees. He'd add it to the many he carried with him to fill the void of emptiness his life had become.

But he had to wonder what the duchess would think if she learned he'd keep their images with him long after he'd left Romsey? Would she be pleased to know he'd never forget her?

Leopold Randall was a captivating man. He watched them without speaking, but his gaze followed their every gesture. For the half hour she'd played with her son and his toys, jumping make-believe fences, mimicking the animals of the farm, positioning his infantry about the toy-sized estate, Leopold hadn't spoken.

He'd sat silent and motionless, so much so that she peeked to check whether he was still with them. But he sat with his hands clenched on his lap, an unreadable expression on his features as he watched her son. When his gaze slipped sideways, and he caught her looking at him, heat stole up her cheeks.

Too handsome.

A slow smile grew on his face, warming his eyes to a brighter brown.

Mercy turned away, heart thumping fast. That look in his eyes made her body thrum with excitement and she struggled to gather her wits. Luckily, she was saved by the distraction of a knock on the door. A servant arrived with little cakes for Edwin, and placed them on a nearby side table. Between bites, Edwin continued to play and demand her attention until his eyes grew drowsy. When he fell asleep on the floor, she pushed his dark hair from his eyes.

So precious. So perfect. Her angel boy. So sweet in his dreams.

She placed her hands to the floor and pushed to stand up. Randall crossed the room, caught her elbow, and helped her regain her feet.

As she thanked him, her foot landed on a farm animal, causing her to wobble and fall into his arms. Delicious heat washed over her as he caught her tightly against him. She kicked away the offending toy, wriggling against the man holding her so silently. When she looked up, his face was inches from hers. The urge to rise on her toes and kiss him overwhelmed her. Those dark brown eyes filled her vision; his harsh unsmiling mouth tempted her to please him.

The scent of him caught her completely unprepared. Warm sandalwood, enticing and wickedly delightful, reminded her of a long-forgotten night of pleasure. The memory was from so long ago that sometimes she wondered if the occasion had been real or a product of her lonely mind. She was lonely now, and so very attracted to him. Was it wrong to indulge in a small moment of physical pleasure?

Ignoring the need for decorum in Edwin's presence, Mercy rose to the balls of her feet, stretching as far as she was able, to press her lips against Randall's.

The light, teasing brush brought a burst of desire to her blood in a shocking rush. But when she angled her head to deepen the kiss for more, he stepped back, far out of reach.

"Your Grace?" Randall didn't smile, and the formality of his question suggested to her that what she'd just done was not welcomed. She wasn't so grand that she could throw herself at any man she found attractive and expect him to feel the same. It was unfortunate he seemed the only man so far to tempt her in that way.

"I just meant to thank you," she whispered. Humiliation at his reaction cut into her soul, and she turned away to hide her disappointment and shame. What could one say at such a moment? Should she explain herself? Assure him that it was an impulse born of the moment and loneliness, or ignore what had happened completely?

Mercy chose to ignore it.

She knelt at her son's side and gathered him into her arms. His weight was slight enough that she could still negotiate the long dress and rise, but she wouldn't be able to do it much longer.

Randall's hands slid about her waist to steady her ascent. She blushed again, but not with embarrassment. She really had wanted that kiss to continue.

"Where are you taking him? Shall I open a door?" Randall asked, his tone soft, deep and altogether reminding her that she wanted to feel his breath across her skin again. His hands circling her waist still caused all sorts of problems for her breathing.

Mercy swallowed nervously. "There is no need." His hands slid slowly from her waist as she moved away toward a thickly padded window seat. She missed the touch immediately, but she had to be a mother now to Edwin. He would always come first in her world.

Edwin settled easily enough, snuggling into the light blanket and pillow that awaited his afternoon nap. She leaned down, pressed a kiss to his brow and sat quietly at his side. "We spend most afternoons here, Mr. Randall," she said softly. "Would you ring the bell again for the servants to bring a tea tray for us now?"

"Of course, Your Grace."

With Randall no longer hovering so close, Mercy could breathe again. She smoothed Edwin's hair once more, and when she couldn't bear the silence any longer, she turned to face her guest. But he wasn't watching her, condemning her actions with those dark eyes. He'd fixed his gaze on the outside world.

Knowing her unseemly behavior would always lurk between

them, she approached until she could see the side of his face. She should really clear the air or her unforgivable lapse in decorum would always be a discomfort between them. She usually didn't try to kiss every handsome man that called at Romsey Abbey. So far, only he affected her that way.

Randall's head turned after a long moment. "Does he sleep well? Deeply?"

Mercy drowned in his dark-eyed stare. Her breath caught. She let it go in a rush before he noticed. "You could drop a pail of coals beside his sleeping form and he'd not wake."

A dimple appeared. "He will grow out of that as he becomes older."

Mercy nodded, unsure how he could be so certain, but accepting that with two younger male siblings, he might have an idea of what he was talking about. Her brother, Constantine, was older but disliked answering her questions. He said she fussed too much.

Randall turned to face her. "You are a good mother, never doubt that." He curled his hand around the back of her skull, pulling her forward and into his arms. His lips pressed briefly, and then he angled his head to deepen the kiss.

Mercy curled her fingers into the lapels of his coat and savored the moment, to hold someone desirable and warm against her body. It had been an age since she'd been kissed with such passion. With such tender desire evident in the hungry merging of their mouths. Mercy opened to him fully. His tongue invaded, setting her nerves alight with long-dormant desire. She slid her hands upward to curl behind his head and lay her body along his. Randall's hands firmed on her back, tucking them close together until she blazed with need.

But then he stopped, pushing her away gently and retreating until a respectable distance stood between them.

Dazed, Mercy could think of nothing to say. She blinked at the space he had stood in just moments before. She set a hand to her mouth, overcome with wonder.

A knock rattled the door.

Mercy took a deep breath, and then another. She must have missed the first knock by her servant, unlike Randall. She glanced at him, but he had turned his back to her and wouldn't meet her gaze.

"Come in," she called nervously, but she wished that servant to the very devil for disturbing what could have been the best kiss of her life.

Chapter Seven

Leopold was in hell and unlikely to ever return. He hadn't meant to kiss the duchess, or hurt her feelings by avoiding her first attempt. But the desire simmering behind her gaze proved impossible to ignore. He was only human, fallible, and fast losing his mind. She was the Duchess of Romsey, his superior, and a relation by marriage to boot, even if the connection was far enough removed not to be improper. He should not be having such lustful thoughts about her, especially when the child was in the same room.

But in all fairness, she'd started it.

Only, he was aware of how unwise it truly was.

Waiting for the tea tray to be settled helped to douse his lust because the duchess stopped gazing at him with such wanting eyes. Did she know that men would fight to the death for such warm appraisal, for the touch of her hand upon their sleeves? Given her heightened color, she was affected by that kiss, so at least he wasn't alone with his impossible thoughts. But he had to ensure such a lapse never occurred again. He could not become any further involved in her life. He was merely passing through on his way to make his own future. He could not act on his desires again without the risk of discovery.

When the duchess passed over his teacup, he was very careful not to touch her fingers. Another brush of her skin, coming so close on the heels of their kiss, would be unwise. He didn't trust himself in her presence, and he wasn't certain whether to trust her either. The fact that she had initiated a kiss of her own made him wonder just how she'd been spending the year since his cousin's death. The gossip could be wrong. Had she taken lovers already?

The thought made him sick to his stomach.

After a few hasty sips, he put the cup down. Better to get his inquiries over and done with and be on his way before he did something stupid. There was no cause for him to linger.

He cleared his throat. "The reason I returned to Romsey was to make enquiries about the location of my three younger siblings, Oliver, Rosemary, and Tobias. They have been lost to me for many years. I'd like to know what's become of them."

The duchess' cup rattled to the table between them. "You mean you don't know where they are? But you sound for all the world like a man who's seen them every day of his life."

The last decade had been unbearably empty without his family. He'd noticed their absence more with each passing day. He touched his head, and then his heart. "All I have of them reside here."

"Oh. That is so sad." The duchess dabbed at her eyes as they turned glassy bright with unshed tears. "But why come here looking for them? We have no guests staying at the abbey."

Here was the gamble. Was she as innocent as she seemed? There was no way to be completely sure, unless you were like Oliver and could make a rapid calculation. He had to take the chance and trust her with the truth. "The old duke, your father-in-law, knew what became of them."

"Really?" she squeaked. "How extraordinary. But I promise you, I knew nothing of their existence, or yours, before yesterday. What did he say of them?"

Acid curled in Leopold's stomach as he recalled the old duke's words. He had turned the phrases over and over in his mind, searching for clues to their location. He had found none. "That they would be well cared for if I did as he requested, no matter how distasteful the task he demanded, or the risks I faced in my business dealings away from England. All he cared about was his own needs, and that of the duchy. I had to protect my family in any way I could. I did as he asked, even avoided England when he demanded I stay away. Now he's dead, I want to find my family. I will not rest until I discover their fate."

The duchess' skin blazed a fiery red. "Of course you want them back. How can I help?"

He had not expected that kind of response. From the start,

he'd assumed the duchess would be a cold woman. How indignant she seemed right now on his behalf.

Leopold sat forward, praying her expression remained that way after he made his next request. "Perhaps you might allow me to see some of the duke's papers. He may have left clues as to their whereabouts in a journal perhaps."

A frown line appeared on her brow. She bit her lip as she considered his request. Asking for this, to invade the sanctity of the ducal domain, was a risk. But if the duchess had no knowledge of his family then his only hope was to find a reference written down somewhere in the old duke's papers. And perhaps in her husband's papers, too. He doubted the details about Oliver, Rosemary, and Tobias would be in an obvious place.

The duchess sat in silence for a long time, and Leopold feared she would refuse. But then her gaze refocused on him. "The old duke was not an avid diarist, so it may be difficult to find any information you seek quickly. Perhaps a room-by-room search would be best. If we start in his former bedchamber, which has stood untouched since his death, we might have some luck."

Leopold sat back, stunned. "We, Your Grace?"

The duchess stood. "Of course. I am going to do everything I can to help you find my son's cousins. It is positively scandalous that the duke has removed them. Come this way."

She had bustled to the door before Leopold realized she meant to start the search now. He glanced at the sleeping child, so small and innocent and defenseless.

A wave of protectiveness swamped him. At least the boy was free of the old duke's evil. He would grow up safe and secure and happy. The duchess' obvious love proved that.

Her Grace directed a maid to stay with her son, and then gestured for Leopold to follow her out of the room. "The apartment is largely unchanged. Aside from closing it up when the duke died, I've not been there since. Perhaps he kept the information closest to him. He spent the last year of his life giving orders and writing his correspondence from his bed."

"If you think that the best place to start then I am grateful."

As they headed for the main staircase, the butler rounded the corner and approached. "Excuse me, Your Grace," Wilcox said.

"You have a gentleman caller." Given that Wilcox's lips twisted over the word "gentleman," Leopold's curiosity increased.

Wilcox pushed a silver salver toward the duchess. It held a single calling card. Discreetly, Leopold inched closer and scanned it over her shoulder. *Lord Shaw.*

Leopold revolted at the notion of that man calling on the duchess, too, but he held his tongue while the duchess decided what to do about the interruption.

She pushed the salver back at Wilcox and said softly, "Would you please thank Lord Shaw for his visit, but inform him that I am otherwise engaged today?"

The duchess smiled wearily at Leopold and urged him away from the main staircase. "Perhaps we'll take the servants' stairs just this once." She turned and opened a discreet panel halfway along the hall and disappeared.

The familiar, dark staircase brought back unpleasant memories for Leopold, but he instinctively caught the duchess' elbow for the long climb up the stairs. Since she moved in something of a hurry, she didn't appear to notice his assistance. But as they reached the upper corridor, she murmured her thanks before leading him to the old duke's chambers.

The door swung wide and stale, dusty air washed over him. He coughed, then hurried across the room to throw open the drapes and a window to fill the chamber with fresher air.

The duchess covered her mouth. "I never dreamed the room would be so bad."

Leopold's disgust rose at the state of the apartment. Dust covered every surface in a thick blanket and swirled on the current of air that they had disturbed. "The housekeeper should have attended to the cleaning of this room without being instructed to do so."

She grimaced but didn't comment.

Leopold considered the room, wondering where the old duke might have kept his secrets. He wouldn't want just anybody to stumble upon them. Would the scoundrel want the hiding place in clear sight of his bed or hidden from view?

Leopold checked behind every painting and mirror on the walls, looking for hidden compartments opposite the bed, while the duchess checked the drawer contents. Since there could be room to hide paper behind each drawer, Leopold moved to the duchess' side and worked with her, removing the heavy drawers completely and peering behind them.

"Just think, my father-in-law would be spinning in his grave about now. I had my suspicions about his nature, but never completely believed he was so evil until now. What did you do to be banished from England?"

His heart had beat too strongly for the old duke's comfort...or he'd never wanted Leopold to learn he'd fathered the current duke.

Both were probably good reasons for the old duke's actions, but he couldn't very well confess the latter to the duchess. Leopold shook his head. "It's an uncomfortable story."

The duchess sat back on her heels and regarded him. From the light in her eyes, he gathered she was preparing arguments to pry the secret from him. But, until he learned the fate of his siblings, he couldn't risk telling her the truth about his life. She'd send him away for certain if she found out.

The duchess knocked the dust from her fingers. "Another time, perhaps. When you've come to trust me. I should like to right the wrongs done to your family. You are our family as well, now."

Leopold swallowed hard, feeling the worst sort of cad. Neither of them trusted the other completely yet, and she certainly *shouldn't* trust him. Something she said, though, made him uneasy. The duchess and her son were indeed part of his family; family he didn't want to have and one relationship he could never acknowledge openly.

Leopold shrugged off his discomfort and turned back to the task at hand. Despite the kiss, and their possible past, Leopold had best remember that she was someone he had to keep a distance from.

When they had exhausted all obvious possibilities, he moved to the bed. The solid mahogany behemoth, another symbol of the duke's power, took up most of the space. Determined not to be intimidated, Leopold tossed the mattress, and then crawled into the space beneath to check for hidden compartments. He couldn't imagine the duke on his hands and knees hiding anything, but it was best to discount all possibilities. He rapped his knuckles against the paneling, searching for oddities in the construction of the piece.

The duchess poked her head under just as he was finishing. "Did you find anything?"

Their eyes met in the shadowed half-light, and his heart lurched at her soft smile. "No. Not one blasted thing."

She reached out her hand to help him up and at the light touch, her skin pinked. "Come, up off the floor with you. You're covered with dust."

Although his first instinct was to stand unaided, he allowed her to tug him to his feet. A cobweb of dust hung from her dark hair, and he lifted his hand to remove it. The duchess shifted her weight from foot to foot, and the urge to draw her close again overpowered him. He dropped his hand away from the temptation.

But the duchess was a dangerously persistent woman. Her hands rose to his coat and she swiped ineffectually at the dust on his shoulders. "It's getting late," she whispered, inching closer.

Leopold glanced at the window. Night was closing in. Since the new moon had just passed, he needed to leave now while he could easily see his way back to the Vulture, and return early tomorrow, if she was sincere in her wish to allow him to continue. God alone knew if he would get a wink of sleep tonight after kissing her today. He had to get away.

The duchess' hands settled on his arms. "Will you dine with me?"

Her question surprised him. He'd not expected to be here all day. He'd been waiting for her to give up and declare it hopeless after the first hour. An invitation to dine was not a good idea when she tempted him so badly.

The duchess bit her lip, an enticing sight that stirred him to new levels of pain.

Damn it. He should not have come to the abbey, even though his need was great. He should have been wise and sent runners to act on his behalf. But he hadn't imagined then what he suspected now. Despite the loveliness of the duchess and the appearance of her son, there was nothing for him here, no future, nothing but lies and heartbreak.

Thankfully, he had a valid excuse to refuse her invitation.

"Unfortunately, I have other plans for dinner this evening that I should not neglect. I may be unforgivably late, as it is. I should not like to disappoint my," he searched for the appropriate word to describe the man he needed to interrogate tonight, "friend."

Eamon Murphy was not exactly *his* friend, but the term would do for now. When they were young, Eamon had been closer to Oliver, as impossible as that might seem. He had always had a knack for knocking sense into Oliver when he was being insufferably clever with his brilliance.

The duchess drew back, a bright blush on her cheeks. "I'm sure your friend will understand your delay. Have a pleasant evening, Mr. Randall. You may return as early as seven. The duke is an early riser, so you need not fear calling at that hour."

Leopold knew a dismissal when he heard one. He bowed, turned on his heel, and hurried out before the duchess changed her mind about helping him tomorrow.

Chapter Eight

Mercy kicked the pillow clear across the room. How stupid and desperate she must seem to a worldly man like Mr. Randall. Regardless of what he'd said previously, he probably had a string of willing women waiting for his return wherever he stayed at night.

The dove-gray pillow halted her furious pacing. She reached down, picked it up, and threw it at the wall. *Numbskull!* God, she hoped he would not return tomorrow. She couldn't stand to see Mr. Randall's satisfied bearing the morning after he'd met with his light-skirt to have his pleasures satisfied for a fee.

Mercy started at a tap on the door. She looked at the pillow, gave it one last kick, and then composed herself to receive her servant. "Come in."

Her butler peeked around the door before he entered her chamber. "Your Grace, I thought you might like a glass of sherry with your late correspondence." Wilcox laid out the contents of his tray, wisely ignoring the destruction littered around them.

Knowing further displays of pique were unsatisfying in front of disapproving witnesses, Mercy placed the pillow back on the lounge, and then sat at her writing desk.

Instead of the correspondence, Mercy picked up the glass first, staring into space. She wished the day she'd just had could disappear. But there were parts of it that were pleasant. Despite his obvious disinterest, Mercy had enjoyed her conversation with Leopold Randall. When she was not attempting to kiss him, they worked well together. Come tomorrow, she'd have to behave as a proper duchess would.

If only she could work out how to maintain *that* charade longer than a minute in his presence.

Wilcox cleared his throat. "I trust your time with Mr. Randall went well."

Mercy picked up a letter with deliberate care, schooling her features to show only minor interest in the topic and the man in question. "Yes, he was pleasant company. The idea of finding information about his siblings is quite diverting. I had no idea the old duke was such a scoundrel."

Well, she'd had some idea. He'd always gotten what he wanted for the duchy in the end. Her speedy marriage to Edwin and his concerns for the production of Edwin's first child were proof of his demanding nature. Those long, assessing glances when she rejoined them after her courses had run its natural length still remained clear in her mind. The worst mortifying interview, over the lack of childbearing, she'd blotted from her memory.

The fire popped as Wilcox tossed another log on the fire, and she jumped. That part of her life was over. The past had no power over her anymore. She had produced the required son and could be content. All she had to do was preserve the estate until he was fully grown.

Mercy broke open the seal of her first note as Wilcox dusted off his hands. "The village is all abuzz for Mr. Randall's return. According to Eamon Murphy, he's done right by the widow Turner, too."

Mercy snorted. Well, that explained whose arms Leopold had hurried to tonight. Probably charmed his way into her cottage and into the woman's bed well before he ever came here to kiss *her*. She pinched the bridge of her nose as mortification assailed her.

Wilcox, unaware she was only half listening, rambled on, "Her husband was a great friend of his, if memory serves, when they were lads. Mr. Randall has employed more than one of the villagers to fix her place, Eamon says. Brown, at the Vulture, reports he arrived with just the one servant, but pays his way with hard coin, and his possessions are first rate."

Mercy wanted to continue to think unkind thoughts, but Wilcox's recounting of Randall's charity made that extremely difficult. And he was a rich man. The first one she'd encountered who hadn't given himself airs above his station.

"It's very good of him, really," Wilcox continued. "He's had no ties here since his parents died, but they say he'll be setting the boy up with a tutor so he might make something of himself. The valet

let that slip to Mr. Brown, who told Eamon Murphy, who is now telling everyone who will listen."

"I know how the village grapevine works." Mercy unfolded her letter. "You make Randall sound like a saint."

"Not a saint. Hardly that. But he is a decent man, like his father, and an honorable one. He'd be a worthy advisor, given all that Eamon has discovered about his time in India."

Was he a decent man? Mercy dropped her gaze to the letter, ignoring the way her heart pounded at the thought of that decent man's kisses. She definitely needed to forget those.

I'm coming for you, Your Grace.

Mercy dropped the paper onto the table as a chill swept through her body. She put the chair between her and the letter for good measure, wishing she hadn't read her correspondence.

Wilcox appeared at her elbow, concern writ large on his face. "Your Grace?"

Mercy closed her eyes and forced her heart to settle. They were just words. "Another." But those words terrified her at night.

Wilcox read the letter swiftly. His free hand curled into a fist. "We need that help now, Your Grace. If you won't flee to London, I beg you to confide in Leopold Randall. He will know how best to treat this matter and ensure your safety. He'd never allow anyone to hurt the duke."

Mercy paced the chamber. "Could it be true what my sister suggested, that he might be responsible for the threats?"

Wilcox snorted. "Never. Besides, he was with you and His Grace this afternoon, and could easily have harmed you and the boy before anyone could have intervened. Lady Venables is quite wrong to think him capable of causing such mischief. She doesn't know him."

"And you do?"

"There is no way Leopold Randall would hurt your child. The boy is a Randall to his fingertips." The butler's earnest expression hinted that Mercy should believe in Leopold as strongly as he did.

The problem was that Mercy thought Leopold Randall wasn't being completely honest with her. He had secrets he feared to share. But, given she held no power over him, she had to wonder what stopped him confiding. A widowed duchess buried in the country posed no threat to a man of his means. Given the fortune he was reputed to possess, he could disappear without a trace. That thought didn't appeal at all.

Mercy tapped her fingers against her lips. Fear, a near constant shadow, bubbled up inside her and wrapped around her heart like a tight vise. She didn't know what to do about the threats, but she'd sleep in Edwin's room again tonight. She'd never rest otherwise.

Whoever it was who'd threatened them by letter for months and months was coming to Romsey, and she didn't know what to do.

Eamon Murphy staggered and fell to the ground in an untidy heap outside the Vulture Inn. "Damn me, but you've developed a cast iron constitution. Why aren't you drunk, too, you devil?"

Luckily, at this late hour, there was no one else about to see or overhear their conversation unless Eamon got too loud. Leopold pulled him up to a sitting position against the low stone wall, glad of the distance between them and the inn's few remaining patrons. "India made a man of me."

"Can see that." Eamon nodded sagely. "The ladies are drooling over you every time I turn around." He tugged at his waistcoat, attempting to put himself back to order, but he was so jug-bitten that he merely rumpled himself further.

Leopold squatted down beside the inebriated man with a sigh. He didn't want the ladies. He just wanted his family back. "I'll leave them for you. Now, answer my question. What do you remember?"

Eamon squinted. "I liked Ollie. Could use his predictions these days to improve my chances of taking the pot. Everyone said he was mad, but we would make a killing at the tables, now I know the ropes. He was good at calculating my chances of winning when we were young."

Oliver's oddity was also damned annoying. Who wanted to

hear they had less than ten percent chance of getting more than a kiss from the housemaid? Despite the likelihood of Oliver continuing his little pronouncements, and making everyone damn uncomfortable in the process, Leopold still wanted him back so he could hear them all over again. "I'll be sure to clue him in on his usefulness to you once I find him, but I have to discover where he is first."

"I don't miss that little upstart, Toby. Never met a child so nosey," Eamon sang off-key.

Leopold sighed. The conversation had been spinning in circles all night. He'd thought dragging Eamon outside for some fresh air might have loosened his tongue. It had, but not in the way he liked.

Disheartened, Leopold sat beside Eamon and stared at the distant abbey. A single light glowed in an upper window, somewhere inside the family wing. He couldn't help but feel fate was laughing at him. Were his best chances of success to be found within the abbey walls?

"Now that sister of yours, well, she was something else. Even at eleven, she had heads turning. Unfortunately, she'd then open her mouth and we'd all run away again with our ears ringing. Well, except for His Grace. He had his eye on her, even if she were just a child at the time."

Leopold stilled. "The old duke?"

"No. The younger one. The duchess' husband wanted the vixen bad."

Eamon lurched across Leopold's lap suddenly, snatched the bottle of rum lying beside them unattended, and then sat up again. He wiped the top with exaggerated care and took a long pull. Leopold ignored the slow dribble of rum that spilled onto Eamon's shirt as he thought over that latest piece of information.

So Edwin had wanted his sister.

Disgusting. And perhaps a valuable clue, too. He'd now need to check through Edwin's papers as well. That is, if the duchess allowed him complete access to the abbey, of course.

"My word, you do the morning an injustice, Your Grace," a deep voice rumbled nearby.

Mercy pulled her mind from her heavy thoughts to find herself face to face with Lord Shaw in the entrance hall. The broad-shouldered man stood with his hat and riding crop in his hand. When she glanced around, she could find no trace of her butler to attend him.

After the endless circle of her fears last night, Mercy didn't approach. Although normally a generous and trusting person, her confidence in others was fast eroding with her nightmares. "I had no idea you'd come to call, my lord. What brings you to us so early in the day? Wait, I'll call my butler to attend you."

"I've no use for butlers, but pretty women are another thing entirely." His slow smile disturbed her as he came closer. "Must a man have an excuse to call on a beautiful woman?"

Botheration! He'd come hoping to seduce her again. She simply couldn't deal with flirtations after her sleepless night, and certainly not from Lord Shaw. "Usually, yes. Gentlemen frequently have an ulterior motive for the things they do in apparent innocence."

"My word, you're prickly this morning." Despite her attempt at evasion, he slipped an arm about her waist. "How about a kiss to brighten my day? I'm parched."

When he lowered his head, Mercy pushed hard to dislodge him, and gained a laugh to go along with her freedom. "I believe I have been as forthright as I may be. Kindly keep your hands to yourself, Lord Shaw, or I shall have Wilcox turn you away in the future."

Shaw didn't back down or move away. "You need a thorough tumble or two, and a man to run this place, Your Grace. I've offered you that repeatedly, and I know you're tempted by the pleasures of the flesh. You have bedroom eyes, and a woman like you needs to be serviced often to keep her happy."

Mercy stiffened at the vulgar insult. "Lord Shaw, I don't believe we have anything else to say to each other today. I have a gentleman waiting to meet with me about estate business, and I have no time to waste with you. Good day to you."

"You mean that insolent pup, Randall, is here ahead of me?"

Shaw sneered. "I'd heard he'd returned to the district. In fact, I'm told he held a pistol to a debt collector's head just two days ago. Dangerous man. You should be on your guard when he's around."

Although dismayed by Lord Shaw's intelligence, Mercy couldn't let her fear show. She had to get the scoundrel out of the abbey before he tried to kiss her again. "Good day, Lord Shaw," Mercy ground out.

Lord Shaw smacked his riding crop against his leg. "You know where to find me when you need a good ride. I'll always be up for it, Your Grace."

Mercy's stomach revolted at the image.

With a jaunty flip of his hat, Shaw let himself out. When the door closed behind his back, Mercy fled the hall for the safety of her study and the comforting presence of old leather and hidden pistols.

Damn it, Edwin. Why the hell did you die so young and leave me alone and unprotected?

She dragged in a ragged breath as the door opened again, but it was only Wilcox. "Forgive me, but I happened upon the end of your conversation with Lord Shaw. I could have sworn I secured the main door after Mr. Randall arrived. Are you all right, Your Grace?"

Mercy found strength again in the concerned gaze of her servant. She'd been right to mistrust the earl before, it seemed. Her heart slowed from its frantic beating and she drew in a full breath. Lord Shaw had become increasingly vulgar when he found her unattended. If not for the difficulties between her and her sister, Mercy would have unburdened her fears on Blythe long ago and sought guidance on a better means of deterring him. Not that her sister would completely believe her innocent of offering any encouragement to Lord Shaw. She tended to think Mercy was too free with her affections, even harmless ones. "I'm unharmed."

"But not quite ready to receive Mr. Randall yet, perhaps?"

"No. I'm all right. I just need a moment to find my balance again."

Her butler smiled. "I'm sure he will be just the distraction you need. I'll go fetch him. Slowly," he added as an afterthought.

Once Wilcox departed, Mercy fidgeted with her attire, nervous to see Leopold Randall again. It amazed her that not once had she feared Leopold Randall, even when so many people spoke badly of him. She thought of him as an old friend and ally already. A man she could trust.

Chapter Nine

Leopold tried his best to rein in his impatience as he waited for the duchess. Despite yesterday's assertion that she would be ready to receive visitors from seven in the morning, he'd been cooling his heels in the drawing room for the past hour. Waiting had never been Leopold's strong suit.

He stood again, paced to the window, peering at the ruin that was the abbey's side garden. Again, the estate showed obvious signs of neglect. Given the rate of decay, the property would be costly to repair within the next five years.

Scowling at the thought of the problems and unnecessary expense young Edwin would face later in his life, he turned his back on it all. The troubles of the duchy were not his concern. His only responsibility was to find his siblings. And once they were together again he would settle somewhere near them and consider the future. To Leopold, that future had never seemed so far away.

The clatter of horse hooves turned him back to the window. A horseman entered his line of sight, ambling away from the abbey. Although the man's back was to Leopold, the fine horse, and the way he sat in the saddle, hinted that the gentleman held considerable consequence in society. That he'd been born in the saddle as every lord was.

Unease stirred in Leopold's belly. Although he was here too, the hour was really too early for proper social calls. Any man leaving the abbey at this hour would be assumed to be leaving after a long night. And that night might have been spent in the duchess' bed. No wonder the gossips speculated about her love life.

Leopold should leave. He should never have come back.

Wilcox entered the drawing room as he rushed toward the door. "The duchess will see you now, Mr. Randall. Please come this way."

He groaned. Did he really want to see her after she'd entertained a man in her bed?

Who the hell was he kidding? He was a fool. Of course he did. Leopold hurried after the retreating butler, eager to get today over with and be on his way.

Wilcox stopped and turned around to face Leopold. "I fear I should warn you that the duchess is out of sorts this morning. She's had an unexpected early visitor and is, even now, greatly distressed by the conversation. It is my hope that she will be settled again soon." The butler looked about to say more, but suddenly closed his mouth.

Since servants rarely involved themselves so closely in their masters' lives, Leopold was surprised by Wilcox's candor. However, the intelligence that Her Grace's visitor was unexpected loosened the tension gripping him. "Of course, Wilcox, I shall attempt to distract her from her troubles."

Wilcox grinned. "You do that very well indeed, sir."

To his surprise, Leopold was shown to the ducal study—the beating heart of any estate. The duchess waited on the far side of the room. But between them lie a disaster of mammoth proportions. Papers littered every surface; piles had built up beneath chairs and toppled over. It appeared disorder stretched even to the interior of the abbey.

Where the hell was the steward in all this? If he'd worked for Leopold, he'd have rung a peal over his head and dismissed him.

"Good morning, Your Grace." Leopold bowed respectfully, determined to remember his place this time. What happened here was none of his business, except to find what he searched for. He had to remember that when dealing with the duchess.

No more touching, no more kissing.

No more thinking about satisfying physical needs.

"Mr. Randall, so good of you to call on us again." The duchess didn't offer a smile, and her clipped words made Leopold distinctly uneasy. Had she changed her mind about helping him?

Since the duchess remained on her feet, Leopold had no choice but to do the same. He shifted his weight from foot to foot, wondering what to say next.

The duchess cleared her throat a few times before she spoke

again. "It has occurred to me that we might be able to help each other, Mr. Randall."

Her words stirred uneasily between them, and Leopold wondered what mess he'd unwittingly stepped into. "How so, Your Grace?"

The duchess rubbed her fingers across her brow. "As you might have noticed, I am woefully unsuited to managing the estate alone. At one time, I had assistance. My husband's steward stayed a few months beyond his death, but I've had no luck finding a suitable replacement. Imagine my surprise when I stepped into this mess ten months ago. My brother, Lord Grayling, my son's guardian, will not stir himself from his own estate to guide me. However, it occurred to me that you seem to grasp the essentials of managing this estate far better than myself, even after being away so long."

Leopold stared. "Are you suggesting I enter into your service?" The request filled him with fury. Leopold set his hands to his hips and glared.

The duchess rubbed her brow again. "No. No. Of course I could not have you enter into my service. But I do need help." Her arm waved over the paper-strewn desk. "I do not know where to start, or who to hire to fill the position. I'm afraid I'm making a mess of everything." She covered her face with both hands and her shoulders shook with silent sobs.

Her obvious distress cooled Leopold's anger quicker than a dunking in a cold stream. He took a step forward.

He didn't understand what had brought on such a strong reaction to her difficulties, but he couldn't help but be concerned. Yesterday she had seemed content. What had happened overnight while he'd been away?

Although he'd promised moments ago not to touch her again, he crossed the room and set his hand to her shoulder.

The duchess turned and burrowed blindly into his chest.

Astounded by a Duchess of Romsey seeking comfort from him, he wrapped his arms about the sobbing woman to give her that. Her hands clutched at his chest as she dragged in great gulps of air. Leopold smoothed his hands along her back, bumping over her spine, and the softer womanly curves he shouldn't be thinking about.

Desire, urgent and insistent, swept over him and he tightened his grip a little more around the shaking woman. The duchess' scent invaded his senses, pushing his caution aside. He wanted to bury his face into the curve of her neck to taste the sweet skin there. He wanted to mold her body with his hands until she moaned. He wanted far more than he could have.

When her sobbing passed, Leopold continued to hold her loosely against him. "What exactly do you need from me, Your Grace?"

The duchess stiffened, but didn't pull away. She kept her head against his pounding heart. "I know you want to find your siblings, and to do so you need to search the abbey for information. What I ask is that you help me sort through this disaster as you go. Perhaps you'd consent to stay here as well so you make better progress in your endeavors."

Stay here?

Leopold gulped at the thought. He'd be able to search day and night. He could find his family far quicker than if he merely visited when allowed. But could he resist the temptation?

Leopold set the duchess away from him. She seemed as dazed as he by the loss of contact.

Could he trust himself not to be enticed by her?

Given she'd just been in his arms without a murmur of protest, Leopold had his doubts. "To help you return Romsey to order and employ a new steward?"

"Yes." Her watery gaze fastened on his. "But Romsey Abbey is a large estate. With just Edward and me in residence, the place feels empty. I want to offer you the opportunity to make your home here and, once you find your brothers and sister, to bring them here, too. It would be nice to have family about the place, even for a short while."

Any words he could have uttered lodged tight in his throat. He couldn't speak to accept or refuse. Dear God, as a lad he'd dreamed of living within these walls. But it had been a boy's foolish fantasy, a wish that had little chance of ever coming true.

Until now.

"I understand that my request may not be convenient, but the abbey is large enough that you need not fear for inviting your own acquaintances to call. The east wing is little used."

Leopold nodded, noticing the way the duchess bit her lip after each statement, and he tried not to think of kissing her cares away. "It was empty in my youth, too. However, I would not like to cause the staff additional work. I would not require considerable space."

The duchess' chin lifted. "So you will stay?"

Leopold nodded, and then had the wind knocked out of him as the duchess jumped into his arms.

"Thank you, thank you, thank you, Leopold!"

The duchess wound her arms about his neck tightly and hung with her feet dangling off the floor. He had little choice but to hold her close or else have them both topple over. Her lips pressed to his cheek, and then the duchess kissed him full on the mouth.

Startled, Leopold attempted to deny her again, but in opening his mouth to speak she invaded to deepen the kiss.

Lust flared at the touch of their tongues, obliterating his reasons for maintaining the proper distance between them. He cupped her bottom, pulling her hips hard against his. The duchess curled herself closer, fingers sliding into his hair as she devoured his mouth.

A storm of desire washed over Leopold at the duchess' unbridled need. It matched his completely. He gentled her kisses when she became frantic. She followed his lead, rubbing herself against his body provocatively. He cradled her in his arms, stunned that he'd fallen under her spell again but unable to find his good sense. His heart swelled with longing as he heard her soft whimpers. They echoed in his head painfully, reminding him of another night so long ago.

Reluctantly, Leopold ended the kiss and buried his face in her neck, panting hard. He hadn't expected this when he'd returned home. He hadn't expected this irresistible passion to spring up between them. It couldn't end well. It wouldn't.

The duchess' feet swung restlessly as her arms tightened about his shoulders. Her quick pants of desire stirred his lust to painful levels, yet she seemed in no hurry to leave his arms or continue what she'd started. Leopold gratefully held her close because, unfortunately, he had no idea what to say to her after this shocking lapse.

The duchess wriggled a little more and Leopold relaxed his grip. She slid down his body until her feet touched the floor, but she didn't look up. She didn't take her hands from him either.

After a moment, she patted his chest. "I'm very glad you're staying."

Despite the awkwardness of having kissed each other senseless just moments before, Leopold's lips lifted in amusement. "I did think you somewhat pleased, Your Grace."

At the formality of his words, she looked up. "Perhaps you should call me Mercy when we are alone. I should like that very much."

Leopold blinked. So Mercy was her real name, after all? He'd thought it a cruel nickname the first time he'd heard of it. "I should not be so familiar, Your Grace."

Mercy's fingers stroked over the fine silk of his waistcoat, smoothing the fabric in an unsettling and affectionate way. "Well, given that I cannot seem to stop kissing you, I would not like to be Your Grace all the time. It seems absurd."

She glanced up shyly, an impish grin lifting her lips at her wicked habit of kissing him. Leopold couldn't help but smile in return. As he did, her small hands rose to cup his face, one finger dipping into his cursed dimples on each side of his mouth.

Leopold moved out of her reach and let his smile fade away.

"I think your dimples make you appear very handsome. Quite rakish."

"I'm not a rake." But he was a prime idiot for being here still.

"No, I know. Everyone tells me you are a good man. I thought that the moment we met. You have a face that inspires trust."

Leopold turned to her, astonished by her candid observations. "Are you like this with all gentlemen who come to call?"

She leaned against the wall behind her. "What? Brazenly forward with my speech with no thought to my elevated rank? Of course I am. It sets my sister's teeth on edge, but I will not lose all of myself to the duchy."

"I was talking about the kissing."

Mercy stilled, a frown marred her brow. "No. No. Only you

have had to suffer the indignity of my scandalous advances. I don't know how you do it."

Only you. Leopold's heart pounded at the thought. Yet he must not forget his place again.

She drew closer. Her hands skimmed over his arms lightly, and then rose to adjust his cravat. Her deep green eyes held his gaze and she extended her tongue to lick her kiss-swollen lips.

Leopold's cock thickened.

"Do you know that I've never wanted another man to touch me, not since my husband died? Most men are so obvious about their ambition to bed me. I quite like watching your eyes darken with desire like that. It makes me feel all fluttery."

Leopold dragged in another desperate lungful of air and kept his hands by his side, curled into the tails of his coat. He would not touch her again. He didn't trust himself.

"But unlike most men, you have the restraint of ten."

She rose on her toes, brushing her lips lightly over his. Leopold growled, pushed to the edge of endurance by her teasing, and captured her wandering hands. "Enough, Your Grace, I'm not your plaything."

Mercy settled back to the ground with a huff. "I had not once considered you in those terms, Leopold. I just enjoy kissing you. But, as you wish. I will do my best to behave."

What *he* wished was to bury his face between the firm swells of her breasts and taste her soft skin. Ruthlessly, Leopold held himself in place.

Mercy glanced at her wrists, and he released her.

"As I said, the restraint of ten men." She sighed a little wistfully and stepped back a few paces. "Lady Venables is joining me this afternoon for luncheon. Would you care to join us on the terrace before you begin in here? It seems as if the day will be fair."

Leopold shook his head, even though she couldn't see him. "I believe I should get started in here immediately. There is a lot to be done, I fear."

Her green eyes met and held his a long moment. "That's what I thought you'd say. I truly do appreciate any help you can spare for my son and me. But I also understand that your first concern is finding your family, and that you will likely leave the moment you discover their location." She frowned. "Whenever that happens, I still want you to consider coming back here with them. If only so we may become acquainted. I'm sure we will all get along famously."

Mercy opened the door, but looked back at him one last time. Her gaze skimmed him from head to toe and back again, a smile tugging at her lips. The effect on his body was immediate. He shifted uncomfortably under her scrutiny.

Her lips curled into another impish smile. "I'll see you at supper. We dine at eight."

The door shut with a soft click.

Leopold continued to stare at the polished wood.

Dear God, the Duchess of Romsey appeared far more single-minded than her predecessors. Leopold very much feared he wouldn't be able to resist her come-hither looks for long. And when he did fall at her feet, he'd be utterly ruined.

Chapter Ten

Once Mercy stepped into the relative privacy of the hall, she gave in to her emotions and let out a satisfied huff. Yes, she and Leopold Randall would get along famously once he got over his shyness. Mercy just needed to be patient with him, and give him time to adjust to life at the abbey. She hoped he adjusted quickly because the man was truly delicious to look at, and especially to taste.

Fate had returned him to the abbey for a reason, and Mercy was only too happy to take advantage of it. She was supremely confident that her scandalous behavior was the result of finding a good man at long last. Why else would one glimpse of his dark eyes and taste of his firm lips make her act so shamelessly?

She had never behaved, or even felt, like this before.

Well, perhaps once before.

Just once.

Mercy frowned at the similarities in her behavior then and now.

Both occasions were entirely different. And yet…

She shook her head to dispel the remembrance. All that mattered was that she felt alive again, no longer weighed down by responsibilities beyond her strength. Leopold's steady presence would hopefully unravel the mess she'd created of the estate's affairs, while also keeping Lord Shaw at bay. Given his meticulous nature, she felt certain Leopold would find just the right man for the position of steward. Hopefully, Mercy would get along well enough with her new employee that the steward might stay to work for the duchy beyond Edwin reaching maturity.

Once the issue of running the estate was behind them, she planned to convince Leopold to make his home at the abbey. The very thought of accepting the man's passionate kisses, along with his confidences, made her heart pound eagerly. Even now, she yearned to return to him and feel his hands over her body, even when her embraces were hesitantly returned.

Patience. She must be patient.

Resolute, Mercy twirled on the spot, enjoying the caress of her silk gown as it slid against her legs. This was likely another gown made from the fabric Leopold had sent to the estate. She imagined the caress as if it was his fingers brushing over her skin. The impatient throb at the junction of her thighs returned, as persistent as when she'd been kissing Leopold earlier. Heavens! She really shouldn't imagine that just now. She'd never retain her mind.

When she was steady again, she looked up to find her butler watching her with an indulgent smile hovering on his lips. Embarrassed to be caught fantasizing, she hurried forward to meet with him.

His smile grew. "I take it the meeting with Mr. Randall was satisfactory to your needs, Your Grace?"

"Yes. Everything is perfect now." She smoothed her hands over her gown, hoping that she wasn't too rumpled from Leopold's embrace. "Can you see to it that the blue suite is aired and made ready for occupation today? Mr. Randall has consented to stay here indefinitely."

The butler's eyes widened. "Indefinitely?" A frown grew on his brow. "That is an unexpected development."

Mercy tapped her lips, ignoring Wilcox's confusion. "Randall undoubtedly has possessions at his lodgings at the Vulture. Be sure to have them sent for, and see to it that any servants he may have are housed accordingly."

Wilcox nodded slowly. "It will be done immediately, Your Grace."

"Excellent."

"I've heard he travels with only a valet attending him, Your Grace."

Of course he'd have only one servant attending him. From what she could tell, Leopold had simple tastes and needs. "He will also be assisting me with some estate business. See to it that all his requests are obeyed as if they were my own, and be sure to see to his every comfort. His work will likely keep him busy—he was looking at the account papers when I left him a moment ago."

Wilcox adjusted his cravat. "Of course. I shall inquire of his immediate needs and see to it that he is made very comfortable. Might I enquire also, Your Grace, what his routine will be with regard to His Grace? I know you are restrictive of whom may visit with the duke and when."

Mercy tapped her fingers against her lips again. Leopold *had* been more curious about the child than she'd expected but, like most men, she doubted he'd want much to do with him. Not at his current stage of life anyway. Perhaps later, when Edwin was older they might spend more time together. Edwin would need a man's guidance more than a mother's love as he aged.

However, because a duke must be protected from any possible harm, she was cautious with her son. Yet with Leopold, she couldn't imagine such measures would be required. However, it would be best to speak up now rather than face an uncomfortable scene later if a servant thought to deny him from visiting with her son.

"He may see the duke whenever he wishes, except during His Grace's naps. I shan't allow him to be disturbed from his rest for any purpose. But keep a servant with them at all times. Mr. Randall shouldn't be required to play nursemaid to my son's daily needs."

The butler appeared relieved. Had he really thought she would listen to her sister's nervous carping? "As is proper, Your Grace. I should also inform you that Lady Venables has arrived much earlier than anticipated. I've put her in the morning room and sent in a tea tray."

Although Mercy smiled for the butler's sake, she dreaded the discussion to come. Blythe would not be pleased to have a gentleman she trusted so little staying so close to Edwin. But, Mercy reasoned, it was her responsibility to look after her son's best interests. She had every confidence that Leopold would do very well for them both.

The butler held out a tray. "Your correspondence, Your Grace."

Mercy glanced at the heaped salver with distaste. "Would you leave all of that in the study? I'll look at it later. Oh, and be sure to provide Mr. Randall with a hearty luncheon tray. He will not be joining us on the terrace. He may have it either in the study or elsewhere if he desires. I require dinner at eight this evening. Mr. Randall will be joining me."

Sure that all the day's instructions had been given, Mercy hurried along the hall toward the morning room. There were days when she found the sheer vastness of the abbey annoying. To get anywhere quickly, one had to almost run. It was a good thing, she thought, that the activity of moving so quickly did not disagree with her as it did with so many highborn ladies. Blythe was forever pleading for Mercy to act with more decorum and walk at a snail's pace. But if she did that, she'd take all day to get from one side of the abbey to the other.

At the morning room door, Mercy stopped for a moment. She adjusted her gown, brushed her hands lightly over her hair to make sure most of it remained properly confined after her interlude with Leopold, and then put her hand on the knob. Light pressure swung the door open, and she caught a glimpse of her sister in an unguarded moment.

The fine lines radiating from around Blythe's mouth pulled at her heart. Her sister stared across the room with fixed attention on nothing at all. The tea tray remained untouched. Grief had aged her until she retained little resemblance to the youthful girl she had once been. Mercy had even detected the odd glimmer of gray strands in her elegant locks. Once upon a time, she might have teased Blythe about growing older. At one time they had both considered the terror of old age the ultimate horror. Yet, because Blythe still grieved so badly, Mercy held her tongue.

She missed her sister's former lightheartedness. Nowadays, her sister appeared exhausted, drained of life and vigor. Mercy had no idea how to change her sister's life back to lightness and merry, but it was something she wished for every day.

With a forced spring to her step, Mercy rushed into the room. Blythe's face soon smoothed into a refined expression as it always did. The swift change pained Mercy. "Good morning, my dear." She dropped onto the cushion beside her sister, threw her arm around her shoulders and pressed a kiss to her cheek, ignoring Blythe's stiffness as she squeezed. "Did you sleep well last night?"

Blythe nodded. "I've been thinking about your gowns. You will need new ones."

Mercy drew back, puzzled by the subject. "I do not need more gowns, I have a vast sufficiency. Far too many as it is for the country."

"Nevertheless, I've sent for the seamstress from London. She will replace your wardrobe as quickly as she can. We cannot have you wearing gowns created from material supplied by that man."

Mercy adjusted her seat so she could better see her sister's face. "Blythe, you shouldn't have sent for the seamstress without consulting me. I like the gowns I have now. The fabrics are so beautiful, and I can at least manage to furnish my own wardrobe. The gowns I wear most often are favorites of mine."

A knock sounded on the door and they both turned. "A light repast is ready to serve, Your Grace."

Wilcox was a lifesaver. He'd moved her morning meal forward to match her sister's arrival. She'd have to thank him with another bottle of her husband's best brandy when Blythe had gone for the day.

The butler crossed the room and set wide the doors to the terrace. The terrace was the perfect place to conduct an informal tête-à-tête. The gardens' wild, unkempt nature held lots to distract Blythe and, with the servant's hovering, she was less likely to continue her lectures.

Hopeful that she had been firm enough concerning her gowns, Mercy chewed slowly, savoring the delicious fare served up for her pleasure in relative silence. At least that was one area she had not failed at.

She had managed to hire, and keep, a fabulous French cook who delighted in the challenge of feeding the palettes of a single woman and inquisitive boy. Edwin loved the surprising treats Cook sent to him daily. If it were possible, her son would spend his days in the kitchen as chief sampler for the whole household. But he had another future in store for him.

The thought sent a shiver up her spine. She hoped she could prepare him adequately for his future as head of this estate.

While Mercy ate and engaged in polite conversations with her sister, she ran over the things she had to remember to do for her son. She'd had so little time with her husband and her father-in-law that she often feared she'd neglect something important from his education. However, with Leopold returned to the estate, she had an ally who might know more about raising a boy to become a duke, and a good man, than she did. At least, she hoped he did.

Mercy ran her fingers over the blue silk gently, thinking of Leopold's arms curling hard around her.

"I know that look. Stop it."

Mercy glanced guiltily at her sister, and then around the terrace to check for servants. They were alone again. Drat it. "I beg your pardon?"

Blythe pressed her napkin to her lips. "A lady should keep unrefined expressions off her face. You embarrass yourself and the family."

Astonished by the hiss of anger in her sister's voice, Mercy stood. "Who are you to tell me what I may or may not do? You are forgetting your position, Countess."

Blythe climbed to her feet, too. "No. You are forgetting yours. Is it necessary for you to behave like a bitch in heat because a man has visited your home? Look at you. The flush to your cheeks, the faraway gleam in your eye, you are thinking of matters best engaged in with a husband. Stop thinking of Lord Shaw that way."

Mercy took a careful step back. She'd never seen Blythe so angry. Miserable, yes, but not so furious her eyes gleamed with a wholly unfamiliar light. "I was considering my son's future, actually; a task that occupies a great deal of my thoughts actually. I do not think of Lord Shaw in those terms, or anybody else for that matter," she lied.

It was lucky for Mercy that she'd never confided yesterday's kiss with Leopold to Blythe, or else she'd be lashed by the sharp edge of her sister's tongue.

Blythe blinked. "Do you deny he was here this morning?"

"Lord Shaw?" When Blythe gave a terse nod, Mercy took a deep breath. "He was here this morning, but the hour was too early for calls and I sent him away, just as *you* would have done. I have spent most of the morning with Leopold Randall."

Blythe's breath hissed out. "You think of that scoundrel, too, in a manner wholly inappropriate for a lady of your station?"

Mercy shook her head. "Leopold Randall is hardly the scoundrel you make him out to be. He has been nothing but respectful in our dealings."

Blythe didn't need to know the exact details of her interactions with Leopold. And she didn't ever need to know about their kissing, either. Keeping her sister in the dark about any amorous adventures would be absolutely necessary in the future if this was how she went on without cause for her suspicions.

"He is a threat to your son's position and should be removed from the grounds once and for all before the worst comes to pass. I speak in the best interests of the duke."

Mercy set her fists on her hips. "That could not be best for my son. I need Randall to remain here and, in fact, I have requested his assistance with estate matters. He has promised to help me engage a new steward, someone who will not desert his post in unseemly haste like the last, and I hope he will guide me on matters of management that I do not currently understand. You know I was woefully unprepared to manage the abbey upon my husband's death. Edwin needs him here."

Blythe folded her arms across her chest and hugged herself. "Have you even considered a man like Randall is a definite threat to your son's future, too. If given the chance, would Mr. Randall make an attempt to claim all that belongs to Edwin. I don't trust him. He is only saying what you want to hear."

"Nonsense."

"He'll seduce you and take it all."

More likely Mercy would seduce him, but she did not admit that. "Calm yourself, sister."

Blythe squinted at her. "I've no patience with your reckless ways anymore. Don't expect to cry on my shoulder when he breaks your heart."

That wild look was back in Blythe's eyes again, frightening Mercy out of her wits. Surely Blythe didn't mean to sound critical or cold. They needed help and Leopold Randal was just the man to help them. "I promised to spend the morning with my son," Mercy murmured, wishing not to argue further today. She inclined her head to her sister. "Good day, Blythe."

Blythe curtsied, accepting the dismissal. "Good day, Your Grace."

Blythe departed, spine ramrod straight and proper. She kept an eye on Blythe until she reached the doors and when they closed behind her, Mercy hugged herself. She had never liked her sister's odd moods but today they worried her very much. Blythe had become a different woman, someone Mercy barely recognized sometimes.

Mercy sank into the nearest chair. She refused to believe Blythe meant her words today. Today's outburst was yet another emotional outburst, brought on by years of suffering and grief. She'd been alone for too long. Maybe Mercy should insist Blythe come to live at Romsey, too. Edwin's presence always raised her spirits. Usually Blythe was as gentle as a lamb.

And all of this on top of the threats, and Lord Shaw's ghastly visit this morning. The only bright point of her day had been securing Leopold's acceptance to remain here with her and Edwin. Now, more than ever, she needed someone she could depend upon. Yet it seemed that a total stranger might be the only one among her longer acquaintances who could provide the support she craved.

Determined to put the troubling conversation behind her, Mercy lifted her gaze to the gardens. She caught sight of a procession of servants coming from the far reaches of the estate and heading for the abbey. At first, she was puzzled, until she remembered she had left Leopold in the study on that side of the building.

Curious to know exactly why Leopold needed all her outdoor servants, Mercy climbed to her feet and crept toward the study to engage in some discreet eavesdropping.

Chapter Eleven

Leopold scratched off the name of the last Romsey servant on the cramped sheet and slid it under the desk blotter for safekeeping. By his calculation, the estate had far too few outdoor staff to manage the grounds, and not enough housemaids to keep the abbey pristine. No wonder important matters had become neglected. No wonder the dust was thick in the corners of every room.

"Your brandy, Mr. Randall," the butler said.

It had been a very long day for Leopold. "Thank you, Wilcox. Pour yourself a glass as well. You sound like you need one."

"Thank you, sir."

Leopold scowled. "Enough of that. We're alone."

The butler took a careful sip, and then another. "It won't do to relax the proprieties. You will need to appear in control of the whole household, including me, if you are to succeed quickly at setting the place to rights."

Leopold drained his glass. Being the nearest thing to lord of the abbey didn't sit well with him, but Wilcox was right. He had to show he was in control here, at least until the new steward was hired and settled in, in order to get what he wanted done quickly and without any further grumbling. The first way to do that was to raise everyone's wages.

He pressed his fingers against his brow rather than look at the mess piled high on the far side of the room. He had cleared a space earlier, but he had merely cleared the desk and chairs rather than deal with any of it. "Wilcox, might you direct me to the books of account. I'd like to know how the estate's finances currently stand."

Wilcox set down his glass, and moved to a nearby bookshelf. "From what I understand, the estate is financially sound. Very little has been spent to drain the coffers in the last few years besides keeping up the necessities. The duchess has never been given to extravagance, and there should not be any outstanding debts." He held out a narrow ledger.

"Thank you." Leopold opened the cover and began to flick through the first pages. "Do you by any chance know if this has been kept up to date?"

"I believe she did her best, sir, but she is unused to such matters and more than once grew frustrated with her lack of experience and knowledge. I believe she's kept all her correspondence from her London man of business and solicitors separate in the left-hand drawer since the steward left."

Leopold leaned to the side and yanked open the drawer. *Ah, neatness!* At least Mercy knew enough to keep the most important papers together. The drawer should contain details of his cousin's will, disbursements, as well as the guardianship details for young Edwin. Familiarizing himself with those important facets of the estate would be his next chore, quickly followed by checking the ledgers before he approached Mercy about increasing the wages of everyone employed on the estate. Given the skin-flint habits of the past dukes and their wives, he'd better have a firm grasp of the realities of the estate finances before he tried to convince her to dip into the family coffers.

Wilcox cleared his throat. "I've assigned a footman for your use. Jennings will be waiting outside whenever you require assistance. Dinner will be in an hour, sir, and your valet is awaiting you in the blue suite."

Leopold pinched the bridge of his nose to hide his surprise. God in heaven—not the blue suite! He'd never survive if he had to spend more than one night in there. But unfortunately he couldn't very well explain his reluctance to the butler tonight. Tomorrow he would assess the work required in the east wing and see if the space was in any way livable. Better far away than close to temptation.

"While I appreciate the thought, I do not require a footman to attend me. My man Colby provides all the assistance I need. Jennings can return to his usual duties. Thank you, Wilcox. I'll finish up here directly."

Once the butler disappeared, Leopold threw his quill to the desk. What a bloody mess the estate was in. One glance at the surly faces of the servants proved just how bad things had become for them. Money would smooth the way to a certain degree, but the young duke and duchess needed to be seen as generous by their people more often for his peace of mind.

There had been a level of dissatisfaction that had his senses prickling with unease. The groundsmen were bitter, at first. Less so once they understood that Leopold meant to make changes to improve their lives. But until those changes happened, he would have to be on hand to smooth the way. That meant he would probably have to accompany Mercy and Edwin on any outings, just to be certain they remained safe.

He'd hate to leave, only to find them in more trouble should he ever return.

Leopold dropped his head to his hands and ground his temple hard. He hated being at Mercy's beck and call. He hated that everyone would see him stand so close to the young duke and speculate about his ambitions to gain the title.

He didn't want any of this. He wanted Oliver, Rosemary, and Tobias to look after, just as he had when they were small.

A knock on the door brought a groan from his lips. He just needed a moment longer to curb his impatience before dealing with anyone yet. He couldn't engage in another skirmish with Mercy now. He'd likely give in and help himself to what she offered.

When the knock came again, Leopold groaned. "Come."

Colby's head poked around the door. "Am I disturbing you, Mr. Randall?"

The disappointment of seeing Colby, and not Mercy, at the door was momentarily unsettling. He pushed it away. "Yes. But the intrusion is welcome. Come closer."

His valet shut the door behind him and eyed the room. "Is it safe?"

A laugh escaped Leopold. Gods, he needed Colby's direct way of speaking to improve his mood. "There's nothing else alive in here. Nothing dead enough to stink up the place anyway. It's relatively safe."

Colby picked his way across the room until he reached the desk. "I hope I did the right thing by following the duchess' instructions today to move us to the abbey, sir. Her note was very insistent that you should be settled in here before nightfall."

"Yes, yes." Leopold waved his hand at the disaster around him. "I was somewhat preoccupied with all this and it slipped my mind to send a note myself. You did the right thing following Her Grace's instructions."

Colby picked up a desktop curio and rubbed the dust from the top. "Her Grace has a lovely way about her."

Leopold squinted at the younger man. "Don't tell me you're captivated by another highborn lady so quickly. We've only been in the district a few days."

An impish grin crossed Colby's face. "She wasn't anything like I expected a duchess to be. Very anxious about your comfort, she was. Her Grace came up to your bedchamber herself and wanted to be sure you were squared away properly. For a moment there, I was afraid she would supervise my unpacking."

Leopold pursed his lips, puzzled by Mercy's inquisitiveness. "Are we? Squared away, that is?"

"You are, sir. My quarters are on the floor above. I have a narrow chamber to myself with a view to the west gardens. Much better than our last quarters."

Leopold chuckled as he relaxed into the hard-backed chair. "Was the view of the pigsty from the Vulture windows unappealing?"

Colby said nothing, but neither of them would miss the stench. "I've arranged for hot water to be sent up to your chambers in half an hour, sir. Her Grace was most insistent that you be given ample leisure this evening to prepare for dinner. I think she must be very lonely here, sir. The staff below stairs are all in a rush with preparations for tonight."

Leopold choked. Mercy couldn't manage the estate, yet she fussed over his comfort and had arranged an unnecessarily extravagant dinner. Would an hour go by without her astonishing him? Leopold feared there wouldn't be. But then he remembered she'd been raised to be the perfect hostess. Why else would the old duke have arranged the match for his son to such an impetuous woman?

No matter how hard he tried, Leopold could not imagine cousin Edwin and Mercy married. Perhaps that woman in the painting fit the bill. But the woman he'd held in his arms this morning did not.

He closed his mind to the past, shut the journal carefully, and dropped it into the open desk drawer. "I'll come up now. No point continuing with anything at this hour."

"Very good, sir. Do you like it here in the abbey better than the palaces of India?"

Colby kept up a steady chatter as Leopold followed him upstairs and along the corridor to the family wing. His servant's curiosity about the abbey amused. Colby wanted to know who graced each painting, as if Leopold had a close connection with the contents of the house. He did know the details of some, simply because his father had pointed them out when they had visited. Leopold had committed those few to memory, but Romsey Abbey housed a great collection of art and furniture, dating back centuries. Only the old duke and his son would have known the stories of all.

As he passed one closed door, he heard young Edwin squeal with joy. Leopold gritted his teeth and turned into the blue suite. He didn't recognize anything in the chamber, but he knew the space well. The bed stood seven long paces from the door, and it squeaked.

"The duchess was curious about your other possessions, sir. Shall I have them sent up from Portsmouth?"

In the act of parting the drapes, Leopold turned. "No. I have no need of those items until we settle into our permanent accommodations."

Colby appeared ready to say more, but instead closed his mouth. It was clear the young man liked Romsey better than anywhere else they had traveled. But staying here brought too many complications for his peace of mind. He would find his family, organize things so Mercy and Edwin would be better prepared for the future, and then set up his own estate. Perhaps he could visit occasionally when time allowed. But those visits would be brief and far between.

While Colby hurried from wardrobe to bed and back again, Leopold told himself his decision was still the correct thing to do. Right for him, right for her, most especially right for Edwin.

The boy might never question his parentage if Leopold went away.

The deep bath and relaxation of his quiet chambers were just what he needed. He hadn't sat still behind a desk for that long in ages and his body ached from the strain. When he was clean, neat, and presentable, according to Colby's strict standards, he followed a footman down to the drawing room.

Mercy was already waiting for him.

For a brief, delicious moment, Leopold looked his fill. Tonight she had dressed in a simple pale green silk, cut low over her breasts with tiny slivers for sleeves. Leopold's mouth watered with the urge to rip the gown apart with his teeth. Yet he managed to cross the room, bowed respectfully, and kept his hands at his sides by sheer force of will. Up close, the smooth swells of her breasts beckoned him to feast. He hastily lifted his gaze to her face.

"I trust your day wasn't too distressing, Leopold."

He glanced at the footmen lining the walls, surreptitiously listening to every word Mercy spoke. He hoped she wouldn't set too many tongues wagging with her lack of formality in using his given name, because once Eamon Murphy learned every word they'd spoken tonight, the gossip would pass around quicker than lightning. He could feel his ears burning even now. "You have good workers, Your Grace. You should be well pleased."

"Oh, I am." Mercy set her hand to his sleeve, but then her fingers slid downward to squeeze his fingers. "I feel ill knowing I have continued my husband's habit of paying them so poorly. You must raise their wages at once."

Her bare fingers tightened on his and he caught a servant gawking. He twisted his hand free and stepped back, putting a greater distance between them. "I was intending to speak to you about that tomorrow in private. How did you know about the low wages already?"

Honestly, she should have raised them herself long ago if she'd known.

Mercy shook her head. "I hope you will spare me from confessing to an unsavory habit, something totally unfitting for a duchess to do."

Her odd smile had him thinking hard until he guessed that

she'd spent the afternoon secretly observing him. "You spied on me?"

She nodded ever so slightly. A pink blush spread up her cheeks.

Leopold couldn't imagine a duchess with her eye to a keyhole, which meant that there might just be hidden nooks within the walls of Romsey Abbey, the old duke's sanctuary, as his father had once claimed. At least that explained the odd sensations he'd experienced during the day. The hair on the back of his neck had stood up quite often. At the time, he'd imagined the old duke's shade had been breathing down his neck, warning him to leave the abbey.

Mercy smiled suddenly. "You need not bring every tedious matter to me. I trust you not to bankrupt the estate with every additional expense in order to make things run smoothly."

The waiting servant shuffled restlessly, no doubt curious about his response. "The estate belongs to the duke and, until he comes of age, his mother should make every last decision for him."

Her nose wrinkled and she gestured to the table. "I was afraid you'd say that."

Mercy sat and Leopold took a place at her side. Wilcox supervised a meal fit for royalty and throughout the many courses set before them, gradually Leopold relaxed. It helped that his glass was liberally refilled, as was Mercy's throughout the meal. They discussed all manner of harmless events, but most especially Mercy wanted to hear his remembrances of the district.

As her finger circled the top of her wineglass, making the half-full crystal sing, Leopold shifted in his chair and adjusted the napkin in his lap. Despite the setting, her actions aroused him. He fought to bring order to his mind and body but his gaze fell to her displayed *décolletage*. From the way the firm globes of her breasts pushed up, he assumed she wore a corset. He itched to replace the whalebone about her chest with his hands and test the softness of her skin to see if she was as enticing as he remembered. Leopold hastily strove to find the far wall fascinating.

"I understand that you drew a weapon on a debt collector a few days ago. Care to elaborate, Leopold?"

One of the footmen gasped in shock. Leopold scowled at him then glanced at Mercy quickly.

He wasn't surprised that she'd heard; only that she brought the matter up before the servants. He leaned back in his chair and wondered if he was about to be chastised. "The man had intended to force a boy into service to repay his mother's debt. The debt collector's stubborn nature required readjustment."

Mercy's rich laugh echoed through the room. "That is a fine way of saying you scared him witless."

"Did he have them to begin with?" Leopold threw his napkin on the table, thankful his body was once more in his control. "Either way the matter is settled, the debt is repaid, and Mrs. Turner will not be bothered by the scoundrel again."

She leaned toward him, resting her chin on her hand. "You are very loyal to your friends, Leopold. Mrs. Turner is a very lucky woman to have your support."

His skin heated at her praise, and with horror, he realized that Mercy had the power to make him blush. "It was nothing. Mrs. Turner is a widow and utterly defenseless against such threats."

"And very pretty by all accounts," she teased. She pressed her lips together in a rueful smile, and she threw a glance at her butler. Wilcox hurried to clear the room of dishes and servants. Once they were gone, Mercy smiled. "Do you find her attractive?"

Leopold frowned. "Turner's widow deserves my protection, not my pawing. Where do you get your intelligence from?"

"Same place as everyone."

Leopold rolled his eyes. "Eamon Murphy? What the devil has that idiot said now? He will ruin her good name by allowing such speculation to continue."

"The speculation was mine. Are you not tempted by her?"

"Good God, no. She is my friend's widow."

Mercy smiled suddenly, and then her fingers rose to her bodice. Leopold followed their movement as they trailed along the edge of fine white lace, wishing he could touch her instead of sitting still like a blasted saint. Her gown slipped, exposing the creamy, smooth apple of her shoulder. Her languorous gaze, better suited to the bedroom than the dining room, slipped from his and roamed over his upper body. "Eamon knows everything, including the fact that you left an exotic mistress behind in India. Do you miss her skills very badly?"

He bit his tongue to keep from confessing that he hadn't thought of another woman since the moment they'd met. Gods, she was unrelenting. She'd have made a grand inquisitor ashamed of his skill. "My personal life is not open for discussion, Your Grace. A man must have some privacy."

Her eyes lit up as if she sensed a challenge to be conquered. "Oh, I think you have secrets I'd like to hear. I'm very open to discovering all I can about you, Leopold. Your reticence intrigues me."

She was also attempting to seduce him, and he wasn't putting up much of a defense. His body had hardened to near painful levels as he'd watched her fingers at play on her skin.

Leopold stood, and the harsh grate of the chair over the parquetry snapped Mercy out of her slumberous seduction. She sat up quickly.

"If you will excuse me, Your Grace, I will leave you now. I have much to do over the coming days. Good night." Without waiting for her response, Leopold bolted for the safety of the hall and the fastest way out of the abbey before he acted on Mercy's invitation and made love to her on the dining room table.

Chapter Twelve

Mercy Evelyn Randall, fifth Duchess of Romsey, heaved a heavy sigh that her pleasant evening had ended far too soon. Leopold had gone up to bed, leaving Mercy afflicted by restlessness again. She leaned her head against the terrace door and looked out into the darkened garden.

Dinner had gone quite well at first. Leopold had been exceptional company yet again, telling her tales of India and his other adventures on the high seas. He'd even spoken of his childhood home, and he'd made her laugh until she had forgotten she was a duchess at all. She had been so caught up in the conversation that she hadn't noticed what she'd eaten—or that she was eating at all—until the last course was removed. She had been so enthralled by the sound of Leopold's deep voice that she had only noticed the servants when he had looked their way.

Having servants hovering had appeared to make him uncomfortable, so she had sent them away, assuming he would prefer greater privacy to continue their conversation. But without the presence of servants about them, Leopold had grown wary.

She did not want to be alone tonight. She wanted more conversation, more laughter, more Leopold. But if she were honest with herself, she feared he had run away from her and from the desire stirring between them. Had she read the signs wrong and made him uncomfortable?

Given he wasn't engaged in an affair with the widow Turner, or anyone else that she could determine, he was free to pursue one with Mercy. But he had held back, casting nervous glances around the room as if he were looking for the nearest doorway to make his escape.

The thought was very lowering.

A flash of white sped through the garden outside the window

and stopped several feet short of the pond. Mercy frowned as the patch of white moved from left to right. She couldn't tell what it was, but it didn't appear dangerous.

Very quietly, she eased the terrace door open and slipped outside.

The patch of white hovered six feet or so above the ground and paced the edge of the pond, stopping occasionally near the rose arbor. Was that Leopold out there in the dark instead of inside in his bedchamber? What on earth was he doing?

She gathered up her skirts and made her way directly to the rose arbor via the newly trimmed grass. Her feet made little noise, but the soft swish of her gown must have preceded her, because Leopold ceased pacing and turned in her direction.

When she drew close enough, she noticed his stiff stance but could not read his expression in the poor light. "Is something wrong?"

"You should return to the abbey, Your Grace."

She frowned. "I thought we had agreed you would call me by my given name when we are alone."

"Some requests are unwise."

Mercy couldn't remember the last time a man had fought so hard against spending time in her company. Even her husband, on his worst days, had never sent her away immediately when she joined him. Embarrassment flooded her skin with heat and she was grateful her companion could not see her discomfort.

"Please, Leopold, I do not like family to refer to me as duchess. I miss hearing my own name sometimes."

He sighed and raked his fingers through his hair. "You don't know what you're asking."

She wanted Leopold to consider her a friend, a good friend, and that meant always being there for him when he had need. Undeterred, she continued on to stand at the railing, putting Leopold at her back. After a few moments he joined her, setting his hands on the rail as they stood in silence listening to the night creatures murmur around them.

Mercy swayed until she rested against his shoulder. She'd never encountered someone who made both her pulse race and set her at ease. No matter how scandalously she appeared right now, Mercy understood that Leopold Randall drew her like a moth to a flame. She breathed his scent and turned her face into his coat. "Tell me what troubles you?"

"Everything," he whispered.

He shifted until she was snug in his arms, chin resting on the top of her head, his large hands tight around her waist. He didn't say any more, and Mercy was content to stand safe in his arms and listen to the rapid beating of his heart. His fingers skimmed her back, pressing warmth through her gown that was not quite suitable enough for the chill on the air tonight.

How long they stood like that, she didn't know. A few minutes, an hour, but when she raised her head to peer into Leopold's face, he set his lips to hers and kissed her gently.

Heat, possessive and sweet, washed over Mercy in waves.

Caught by surprise at his sudden action, she gasped but then angled her head to deepen the kiss, fearful that he would push her away again. He didn't. His fingers tightened on her body, dragging her flush against his warmth.

On a sigh, Mercy looped her arms around his shoulders and clung to him, letting him direct their passion as he saw fit. His desperate response amazed her. There was no restraint, no holding back as he had earlier in the day. He explored her body with his hands, kneading, stroking. He cupped her bottom and rocked her pelvis against his in an imitation of making love.

Mercy tugged at his cravat, eager to find the man hidden behind the proper clothing, and when she succeeded, she set her lips to his exposed throat. A masculine groan rumbled from him beneath her kisses and she nipped at his jawline before twisting to meet his gaze. In the poor light, she could not see his expression, but his eyes were black with hunger as he rubbed his erection against her core.

Mercy closed her eyes as her body rioted. She needed him. She was desperate for him to make love to her, for them to be connected at a deeper level. But the open garden was just a touch too exposed for her comfort. She stumbled back a step, and he followed.

Leopold tossed off his coat, threw it over a bench seat made for two, and drew her down to sit upon it. As she lay back on his coat, she tugged on the cravat still looped around his neck to bring him with her. Her encouragement settled Leopold over her, and she flung the dangling cravat across the space. She skimmed her hand through his hair and shifted her legs wider so he might be closer yet.

The heavy weight of him against her body curled her lips into a smile. She lifted her head to kiss him again before he changed his mind. Leopold cupped her head and face, fingers gently stroking her skin as if she were made of the finest porcelain. His breath huffed over her jawline, sending unending thrills down to her toes. The tender caress slowed the frantic race to connect enough that Mercy feared he would stop altogether.

But Mercy was not so fine that she could tolerate such gentleness for long. A wild surge of desire had taken hold moments before, and she wouldn't settle for anything less than Leopold's complete surrender to passion in her arms. She clenched her fingers in his hair, drawing him nearer, while her other hand slipped under his waistcoat to tug his shirt from his trousers. When her fingers found bare hot skin, she smoothed her palm over his lower back and kneaded the hard muscles.

Leopold shuddered, and his fingers left her face to cover her breast. Unfortunately, she could feel little beyond knowing he caressed her there because her corset strangled the sensations she craved most. She wanted his hands on her bare skin. She wanted his hands everywhere.

Frustrated, Mercy moved against him. She pressed up against Leopold's body with her own, feeling the length of him against her thigh. She wanted more. Mercy loosened her grip to tug up her gown. Her skirts were trapped between them, but Leopold lifted away slightly so she could draw the long lengths up her body to expose her legs.

Leopold fumbled with his clothes, and eventually pushed his trousers down to his knees. He settled against her, the burning length of his erection hot on her skin. Eager for more, Mercy clasped his face between her hands and kissed him, using her tongue in his mouth to wrest away any lingering resistance to making love.

Mercy curled her leg up around his thigh, opening her body to accept him, and flexed her hips upward to brush against his length. A low moan followed the contact, and then he was there, pushing inside her, filling her up until she cried out in pleasure. But the sensations didn't stop. Once he joined with her, Leopold began to thrust, fast, hard and without restraint.

Mercy curled both her legs high about his hips and clung to him as she was all but ravished.

She loved the way he loved her: so fierce, so complete, and so utterly devastating to her senses.

Eventually, before Mercy could catch her breath, Leopold's thrusts slowed, gentled, until he was barely moving. He was still hard within her. He hadn't found his release yet, but he had found his control.

Mercy loosened her grip around his neck as Leopold lifted his weight from her upper body. He levered up onto his hands and his slow, deep thrusts pushed the air from her lungs. Then he stopped. His breath churned in the darkness, the heavy weight and heat of his hips pressed against her groin. But what aroused Mercy the most was that he truly saw *her*, and not the prim duchess he'd expected to find.

She raised one hand and placed it against his cheek. The light stubble scraped her palm as he turned to press a kiss to her skin. Mercy couldn't help but sigh. He was a perfect lover. Exciting, demanding, and altogether too much fun to resist seducing into showing his wilder side.

Leopold's hips flexed, driving his cock in and out of her body. Mercy smoothed his hair back with her fingers as her body began to ache where they joined. She rasped her nails against Leopold's skull as he pushed deeper inside her. She shook as sensations rippled out from where they joined. Mercy arched her hips higher into him as her body stiffened and pulsed with a release she'd been dreaming of for years, but had never attained on her own.

She sobbed and pulled Leopold tightly against her, determined that he remain with her forever. But he resisted and, as her tremors subsided, he pulled from her body with a groan. Hot seed spilled over her thigh.

After a time, he pressed his head hard against her chest and then rocked it from side to side. "What have we done? Madness."

Mercy chuckled. "We've done quite well, don't you think?"

Leopold lifted off Mercy, found where she had tossed his cravat and quickly dressed himself. "This isn't a laughing matter." He wiped her thigh with his handkerchief until she was clean. He drew back when he'd finished and sat on the other end of the bench, as far away from her as he could get.

Mercy lay as he left her, feeling well loved, content, and wickedly smug about their tryst. No wonder Anna was always going on about taking a lover. She'd made the right choice to encourage Leopold.

When he didn't come closer again, she sat up unaided and put herself to rights. While she was dressing, Leopold paced the small space. He didn't seem as content as she'd expected him to be after such a wonderful interlude. Had he not enjoyed making love to her?

Mercy shook her head. He *had* enjoyed it while it was happening. Only now was he discontent.

When he passed close by, she caught the tails of his coat and tugged hard. He staggered toward her.

"Do not make a wonderful night of pleasure into something sordid. I enjoyed every moment in your arms and hope that you did in return. Do not make me feel bad for how happy you've made me feel tonight. Unless, of course, you prefer a paid Indian mistress to an honest English woman."

Chapter Thirteen

Not bloody likely. Making love to Mercy was the nearest thing to heaven. He had almost lost himself, and his precious control, in her arms tonight. He could not forget himself and get her with child. The scandal would ruin her good reputation, and he could not bear that. But he had almost failed to withdraw in time as his release had caught him by surprise. She had clutched him so tight against her that he'd had to fight his way to break free before he could spill across her skin. It had pained him, but he had done it for her sake. How could she suggest he had regrets about the rest?

A growl bubbled up inside him, and he pulled Mercy up from the bench and into his arms. "Making love to you outshines the paltry pleasures any paid companion could offer. They react to ensure the man's pleasure alone."

"So you were pleased?"

Leopold set his mouth to Mercy's neck and nipped lightly along her smooth skin. Her back arched, her fingers clawed at his shirtsleeves. *So damn responsive.*

That had been the problem between them from the first night, and why he would need to leave Romsey sooner rather than later. He might never get enough of her. "I was more than pleased. Mercy, you are more woman than a man like me deserves."

Her hands threaded into his hair, exactly the way he liked it. "Then it is a good thing I'm a charitable lady, because I plan to keep you all to myself for as long as I can."

Leopold drew back, stunned. "I cannot stay here indefinitely. I cannot keep doing this with you. There could be consequences if we are not careful." *More consequences.*

He hoped he held back the anguish that flooded him. He had missed her first pregnancy because he had not known he *might* have been the father. But if he got her with child now, the scandal would ruin her because he would stay close enough to ensure she was well looked after. But she was a duchess. She would not give up all of this to become merely Mrs. Leopold Randall. She would hardly marry to avoid scandal.

A child, one he was certain was of his making, would bind their lives together indefinitely. How could he stay away if he filled her belly again?

Mercy pushed him to the bench and settled over his thighs, dropped her head to his shoulder and curled her arms tightly around him. Her breath puffed against his jaw and he cuddled her closer, heart heavy that he must give her up.

She sighed heavily. "A pity. You make love to me so well. I suppose I will have to be grateful for any small crumbs you share with me."

Leopold rolled his eyes, astounded that she thought he was doing her a favor by making love to her. Any man would jump at the chance to take his place. "You must think of your reputation, and of Edwin."

"Edwin is *all* I think about." She rose from his lap suddenly and straightened her gown. "And you. I have no other life beyond these walls."

Leopold's heart pounded but he forced himself to remember that he had a mission to accomplish here at Romsey. Finding his siblings superseded any other desires. He forced himself to stand with his hands clasped behind his back and waited on Mercy's next startling declaration. She was about due to make another one.

She strolled closer, eyeing his bearing with a frown. "I require an escort back to the abbey, Mr. Randall, if you please."

Although Mercy's lapse into formality startled him, Leopold knew his duty to obey. He held out his arm for her to take and strolled up the lawn with her to the dark abbey. At the terrace door, he locked them in. When he turned, he spotted a lone candle burning on the table, which meant that Wilcox had spied Mercy outside with him. He picked up the candle, troubled by the ill that boded. Would the servants be gossiping already?

He held out the candle to Mercy, but she shook her head and would not take it. She settled her hand to his sleeve and guided him toward the stairs. Did she intend for him to walk her all the way to her bedchamber? She couldn't possibly suggest that.

She didn't suggest a thing. Said not one word, but she guided him through the dark abbey, leaving him in no doubt of her intention that he escort her upstairs, too. He wished he had the power to deny her. He wished one of them could do the responsible thing tonight.

When they reached the family wing, Mercy detained him at her son's bedchamber. She inched the door open, and Leopold held up the light so she might see her son clearly. Edwin slept on his side, tangled in lengths of linen. A footman dozed, propped up against the large bed. Leopold frowned, wondering why the boy needed a servant with him at night when she'd said he slept so deeply. But he was young enough to need protection, so he supposed Mercy was sweet to dote on him like this.

When Mercy turned, her face lifted to study his. The close inspection worried Leopold. Would she see the same resemblance he saw in her son? He dreaded the day she saw his guilt and guessed why. She would no longer look on him so kindly.

Her lips lifted in a soft smile and she turned away. "This way, Mr. Randall."

He followed along blindly and when they reached a door, he guessed it was her apartments. He hung back and allowed her to lead the way, but she stopped to wait for him. He closed the door quietly and studied the sitting room around him. Mess, chaos, and children's toys abounded. The space reminded him of his childhood home, his siblings perched at his mother's feet.

She hurried ahead into the next room, her figure illuminated by the firelight shining through the open doorway. Leopold gulped at the reminder of how wonderful her body was when he'd held her in his arms. He followed Mercy to her bedchamber, closing the door with a loud thump.

Illuminated by firelight, her room seemed startlingly feminine, and the familiar scent of her perfume robbed him of breath. He glanced around the chamber quickly, but saw no signs of a maid waiting to attend her.

"Put the candle down, Leopold, and blow it out. I will require your further assistance tonight."

There it was! There was the next shocking thing to pass through those wicked lips. He should not be here, he should ring the bell for her maid and walk away. But she was so very tempting. So lovely and soft that he was helpless to deny her.

He set the candle down on a nearby table and pinched the wick, leaving them with only the firelight playing over her body. She stood with her back to him, presenting the long line of buttons to him that he hadn't spared time to unfasten in the rose arbor. Each came free easily, and Mercy rushed to step out of her gown.

"My corset strings next."

Leopold gulped, staring down the length of her back and the teasing outline of her buttocks visible through the thin chemise. The corset strings almost defeated him. He seemed all thumbs to loosen them. But perhaps he was merely attempted to delay the inevitable. He certainly wanted to make love to her again. How his cock had hardened again, after being so well satisfied before, escaped him. He'd never wanted a woman the way he wanted Mercy. He wanted to hear her calling out her pleasure as he stroked inside her again and again.

At last he could fit his fingers beneath the loosened corset and tugged until she could step out of it. Firelight illuminated the outline of her trim figure…tiny waist, generous hips to wrap his hands about. She was the most desirable woman he had ever met and still he wanted more. Mercy stretched and swayed, rubbing her hands over her skin through the chemise. The sight stirred him beyond reason, and he stepped up behind her and slid his arms around her waist.

Although she leaned against his chest, Mercy's hands stilled his wandering fingers. "I thought you were done with me for the night, Leopold."

He'd certainly tried to give her that impression, but Leopold had given up on fighting his passions the moment he'd crossed her threshold. Tomorrow, he'd try to control them better.

He dropped his head and kissed her neck while he held back the words he was afraid to say. He feared he'd never be done with her. She stirred his desires too damn much for his sanity. But tonight he belonged to her. Tonight, he would love her until dawn lightened the horizon.

Leopold turned her head until their eyes met. "Not yet, my duchess. Not yet."

He kissed her and forgot all the reasons why sharing her bed again could not be in her best interests.

Mercy responded with no hint of hesitation, bending her body until she touched him from breast to thigh. A frown marred her forehead before she lifted her hands to tug at his clothes. She pushed his coat from his shoulders and then went to work on his waistcoat. "I want to see you. All of you."

The husky quality of her words washed over him like fire, and he shucked the rest of his clothes as fast as he could.

Mercy's chemise landed at his feet, and he looked up.

God's blood, she was beautiful in her nakedness, skin licked by firelight and shadow. Her breasts were full, nipples peaked with arousal, and the delicate thatch of curls between her legs made him want to fall to his knees.

But before he could do more than stare, Mercy stepped forward and stroked her fingers down his sides. His breath caught as she slowly slid her body forward to encompass him. Soft skin, heated and sweet, pressed against him as Mercy learned the planes of his chest and back. Her chin lifted, lips parted, so Leopold did what he'd wanted to since they'd first met. He scooped her into his arms and carried her to bed.

The cool linens curled around them, adding new sensations to their tryst. Mercy hummed to herself softly as her hands stroked his back and kneaded his skin. She rocked against him, pressing her curls to his aching length as she had before. He knew what she wanted, and he would see her satisfied as never before.

Slowly, he wriggled down her body and kissed her breast. He drew the hard peak into his mouth and teased her while she moaned. He shaped her other breast with his hand. Mercy writhed and shuddered, hands clenching and unclenching on his hair as he switched from one breast to the other.

She shuddered and pressed her pelvis against his stomach. The damp heat of her shifted him lower. He might shock her out of her skin in a moment, but he would taste her tonight and bring her to completion with his mouth.

Her belly was soft, and he kissed all around her navel, dipping his tongue inside and drawing wet circles on her skin. But he could smell her desire too keenly to ignore what he intended for long. He wriggled the short distance down the bed until his head rested on her thigh.

With her legs open, the firelight illuminated her folds perfectly. He stroked one finger through her curls, parting her completely to his gaze. Luscious, damp heat coated his finger as he played, listening to Mercy gasping his name as she thrashed her head from side to side.

He brought his face against her and inhaled deeply. His cock ached painfully to join with her again. But he couldn't do that. He could not risk impregnating her, so he kissed her lower lips…and kept on kissing.

Mercy bucked away from his mouth, a desperate wail echoing around the room. When she settled, he held firm to her hips and kissed her again, and then licked his tongue over the place that would bring her the greatest pleasure. She bucked again, but then her legs widened and her hands curled into his hair to keep him there.

He licked her nub slowly, feeling it rise toward his tongue. He drew on the nubbin as she repeated his name. She was close to finding her release but wasn't there yet. To make her come, he eased two fingers inside her body and twisted them.

Mercy tightened around his fingers as a desperate, feminine wail left her mouth. She called his name as she shuddered violently and rocked her hips against his face.

Leopold memorized it all—taste, smell, sound—because he knew he'd never find another woman who would respond to him like this anywhere. Despite the joy of making love to her, he'd made a mess of everything. He would never marry, never find a lover who could take her place.

The old duke must be happy in his corner of hell. He'd ensured Leopold would be miserable for the rest of his life.

Chapter Fourteen

The taper in Leopold's hands flared to life, brightening the dark bedchamber around him. He stood slowly, protecting the flame so it would not go out again before he could light his candle. He was doing everything he could not to wake Mercy. It was a long time until morning, and he still had to get back to his own chamber without being noticed. But most especially he did not want to wake Mercy because he simply did not know what to say. Saying *thank you for making my dreams come true* seemed paltry regards after such a frantic night of passion.

She had been everything he remembered and more.

He redressed quietly, but as a precaution, so he could move about the sleeping abbey undetected, he left off his boots and prowled toward the door barefoot. However, before he left her bedchamber, he took one last look at the sleeping woman; hair tossed about the pillow, a soft pale arm reaching toward the empty side of the bed. She was utterly captivating and lovely.

Why had her husband allowed her to be used in the old duke's plans all those years ago?

He shook his head and turned his back on his questions. There was no answer, of course. Not with her husband dead and the old duke long gone.

Leopold eased out into the hall. All was silent. Still. Carefully, he picked his way back to the blue suite and closed the door. He let out a heavy sigh, relieved to have returned undetected.

"Good morning, sir. May I take your boots?"

Leopold jumped out of his skin and turned around. "Damn you, Colby. What the devil are you doing here at this time of night?"

"Worrying about where you might be, sir. Wilcox said you'd

been detained on an urgent matter, but wouldn't say where or when you would be back."

"Well, I'm fine, or will be as soon as I reclaim the decade you just scared off my life," Leopold whispered.

Colby hurried forward and took his boots from his hands. "Sorry, sir. But you've been so tense and restless since we came here. I didn't know what to think when you didn't return, and I noticed you hadn't taken your pistol with you. I was just considering a search."

Unfortunately, Colby knew his habits too well. He'd dined with Nawabs in India, discreetly armed, many times before. He never liked to take chances. "A gentleman doesn't dine with a lady bearing arms, Colby," he lied. He had carried his pistol for the last several days in Mercy's presence. Only tonight had he felt at ease enough to let down his guard and pack the pistol away. Look at what that moment of foolishness had led to.

An odd smile crossed his valet's face. "Well, she is an unusual duchess."

Leopold raked his hands through his hair. Unusual was an understatement. Mercy was more dangerous than he'd realized. She made him want things best forgotten. "Well, the night was uneventful. You don't need to wait up for me again."

Colby's gaze flickered over him, lingering on the imperfect knot Leopold had tied in his cravat. His frown turned into a grin. Damnation, Colby had spotted the rushed job he'd made of dressing. Leopold could not have him spreading rumors about where he'd likely spent the night. With Mercy was an easy assumption for anyone to make, given they had dined together earlier. Leopold took a step forward. Better to cut off the damage now before any ill was done. "Not a word about my whereabouts tonight. To anyone, understood?"

The servant's eyes lit up with mischief. "I wouldn't dream of it, sir," he chuckled. "I'll say good night then." He tugged on his forelock, and left Leopold alone with his swirling thoughts.

Two servants, possibly, had an idea about his tryst with Mercy. How long before the rest of the household suspected?

Leopold paced his chamber, too anxious and restless now for sleep. He had to speed up his search of the abbey and remove himself before Mercy's reputation was utterly ruined by the attraction between them.

He stopped before the fire as a new plan formed in his mind. There was no reason he could not continue the search at night while everyone else rested. He was awake, he doubted he'd sleep a wink, and he did want to search Mercy's husband's bedchamber. The best time to do that was when no one was watching.

He found other footwear and prowled back the way he had come, turning into his cousin's bedchamber, which stood opposite Mercy's doorway. The door swung with a small grating of hinge and he squeezed through the gap and closed the door again. He held the candle high and surveyed the chamber. Dark timber, russet-red hangings, but stripped bare of personal effects on all the surfaces. He slowly circled the room, sliding open drawers and closing them again when he found nothing of interest.

It was as if the fifth Duke of Romsey hadn't existed. There was nothing left of Edwin Randall within this room; no book nor piece of clothing. No fob watch nor pipe. The only thing this room had in common with the other chambers of Romsey Abbey was that the walls were covered with paintings. Scenes of hunting lodges with dogs bounding around outside. Other stately homes Leopold didn't recognize hung here, too. But not one of these paintings seemed lovely to Leopold. There was a dark watchfulness about them that drew in the light and held it.

Leopold leaned closer to one of the paintings. There was something about the way the painter used color and light that repulsed him. Even the portrait of a ship on a storm-tossed sea was sinister. The way the artist had painted the scene hinted that all was lost for the vessel and its frantic crew.

He shuddered. If his cousin had chosen to surround himself with visions such as these, then his mind was of a far darker character than he had seemed on the surface. He tried to imagine Mercy married to his cousin and failed. Edwin, with his weakness and quieter watchful nature, would have dampened Mercy's fire, her joyous character, and her smiles. What had life been like for her after she'd conceived? Had his cousin known that Leopold had shared Mercy's bed? Had he treated her kindly after that night?

He shook his head. He might never know. He couldn't ask

without revealing more than he should, but wishing for answers might drive him mad. Mercy seemed to have suffered no lasting hurt from their past encounter. She'd gained a son that she loved, an heir for the duchy, and appeared happy enough with life. All he could be was a mild diversion from a life of order and duty to the boy. The life of a proper duchess held no room for him.

When he went away, she'd be just the same. He sighed. He had a lot to do before he could leave Romsey. He had an estate to bring to order. There was much to be done yet. Today he would see the upper dams breached and get on with the business of assessing the farms. Later, he would straighten the study and find out what else lay hidden here.

After a quick change of clothes, he headed down to the stables. The grooms appeared startled to see him about so early but quickly saddled his horse. "There you are, Mr. Randall. It's a fine horse you have there," the older groom observed.

"He's an energetic animal." Leopold squinted, trying to recall the fellow's name from yesterday's interviews. He looked familiar, but Leopold couldn't remember seeing him with the other servants. He guessed his age to be about ten years his senior. "Have we met?"

The older man smiled sadly. "Long time ago now. You've grown a fair bit since those days. Call me, Allen. Everyone does."

Leopold struck out his hand and they shook. Yet he couldn't remember an Allen from his past. He must have lived around here all those years ago and taken up duties on the estate. Eventually, Leopold would remember where he knew him from, but for now he had work to do.

Leopold patted his horse's nose. "I'll need a few men to meet me at the upper dam in half an hour."

Allen issued orders and the grooms scurried to obey. Horses were saddled and, to Leopold's surprise, Allen and two lanky young boys joined him. Allen waved them closer. "My sons, Jacob and David."

Leopold nodded, but he was curious about these two as well. Who the hell were they? He hadn't met them before, either.

Spine prickling with unease, Leopold set off for the high fields and the dams he needed to inspect, keeping one eye on his company. They rode well, very well for ordinary servants, but did not speak or offer up any conversation.

When they reached the dams, Leopold dismounted and surveyed the area. There were three holding dams staggered beside the watercourse, ready to divert water to where it was most wanted. Each was plentiful enough that they could feed the parched fields below. All he needed to do was deepen the spillway set into the side of the structure for a steady flow and let gravity do the rest. He chose the lowest dam but was disgusted with the growth of weeds and silt blocking the spillway. This would take all day to clear.

"No need to get your hands dirty, Mr. Randall. That's what I brought my boys for." Allen waved them forward. "Lads, open her up and let the water out at a slow rate. We don't want a rush."

Leopold stepped back as the two young men went at the weeds enthusiastically. Before long, they were covered in muck but had the spillway clear and were slowly digging out soil. Water rushed out in a murky wave, swirling around their feet and splashing their legs on its way down the hill.

"Careful there," Leopold called anxiously. He didn't want anyone accidentally swept away if the dam burst.

Allen barked a laugh. "They can swim like fishes, that pair. Unlike some Randall devils I could name."

A cold wave of recognition swept over Leopold, and he spun about. "You can't be *that* Allen."

Allen moved away, spoke to his sons in a low tone, and when they moved off, he turned back to Leopold. "No?" His eyebrow rose. "Who am I then, that the likes of you would know me?"

Whispers. Lies. Scandal.

Leopold tightened his hand on the reins, peering at the face before him, changing it, making the other man younger. His breath caught. This place was alive with the sins of the past. It was all there when he looked hard enough: the family resemblance.

"I remember now. You're the duke's other son. First son," he whispered. The one his parents had known about and spoken of in hushed tones. With everything that had happened in the last ten years, Leopold had forgotten this one small detail. What else had he forgotten?

Allen raised his finger. "Unacknowledged son, if you don't mind. Father could hardly look at me once he had his heir."

Despised illegitimate brother, if Leopold remembered correctly. Mercy's husband had hated him simply because he existed and had been born first—not that he could inherit.

"My father accepted you into his house when you came to call."

"More fool him. Befriending me did not do him any good in the end, now did it?" Allen mounted his horse with a groan. "My boys know nothing of that connection. I'd take it kindly if you don't speak of the matter again."

Leopold swung up into the saddle, too. "Then why are you here at Romsey, cousin?"

A sad smile crossed the older man's face as he looked back toward the abbey. "For all his faults, the duke kept a fine stable. Can't let the horses suffer under the duchess' ignorance of the beasts."

"Does she know?" Had she lied to him all along about her knowledge of the Randalls' whereabouts?

"Of course not. What would I say? If my father had done the decent thing and married my poor, penniless mother, then I'd be duke rather than her son." Allen snorted. "What good would that do? I've no wish to be despised. It is better she not know."

"The duchess might surprise you," Leopold warned. Hell, she surprised Leopold every day. What would she say about an illegitimate relation living on the estate? Leopold doubted very strongly she'd react in the expected way.

"Leave matters as they are. I'm content in the stables with the horses and my boys. Better you in the abbey, minding your p's and q's before the duchess' sister, than me. A sad, queer one, her sister. I don't envy any man the time spent in her presence."

He moved off, following after his sons, leaving Leopold gaping at the idea that another Randall, if not one so named or acknowledged, had come home to Romsey. Edwin had more family living at Romsey Abbey than he would ever realize. A shame Allen and his sons wouldn't be known for who they really were.

Perhaps, before he left Romsey, he could tell Mercy about Allen without giving his name at first. He would see how she took to the idea that the old duke had an illegitimate son living in the area. Perhaps he could smooth the way by mentioning he worked on the estate. It would be good to know that Edwin wasn't alone here when he left. It would be better if his cousin could care for the boy more than the horses.

***

Mercy opened her eyes. The room was quiet about her. Too quiet. Was she alone in her bed again?

She glanced left to the space beside her where Leopold had rested his head, but no sign of her midnight lover remained. He had slipped from her bed quietly sometime during the early morning, and she missed the reassurance of his presence.

She slapped her hand to her face as memories of last night surfaced. Leopold's bold demands for her surrender had inflamed her. She had unashamedly begged him for more. She'd thought he might consume her with his passions. He hadn't hidden how much he'd desired her and, even now, she wanted his hands on her skin, making her cry out, making her feel desirable and wanted once more.

Although the hour was still early, Mercy sat up, holding the sheet tightly across her bare chest. Her maid would be along in a little while but she had much to decide, now that her attraction to Leopold was out in the open between them. She had to determine how much to tell him about the threats plaguing her and Edwin. Would he want to help her sort out the mess, or would he turn tail and leave?

Well, she'd never know until she spoke to him, and to do that, she'd better be wearing more than nothing.

She flung off the bedding and reached for her nightgown. The soft silk caressed her skin, and Mercy blinked at how such a mundane action affected her. Would every touch of silk remind her of Leopold's caresses? If so, her day would be an unending torment of unfulfilled desire. She'd have to capture Leopold's attention somehow. She'd enjoy seducing him again if she could.

Feeling buoyed by her success last night, Mercy rang for her maid to come and dress her. But she was anxious to see Leopold and determined to kiss him again, too, if she could arrange it. What a talented mouth that man had. He had made her wanton with his very first smile.

While she completed her toilette, she ignored her maid's inspection of her unlaced corset flung to the far reaches of the room. The girl must be wondering how she'd set herself free last night, because they'd joked before about the inescapable garment. Leopold was correct; she had to take care to keep any affair between them hidden, even if she suspected the feat beyond her. She would not like Leopold to feel uncomfortable for wanting her. She couldn't have the servants gossiping.

As she sat at her writing table, sipping hot chocolate and eating corners of toast, she focused on the threatening letters.

The first had arrived during the summer, a bare month after her husband's death. That first day after the steward's hasty departure, trying to fathom the order of the ducal study, had worn her nerves to the quick. But she'd set herself the task of taking charge of the estate then, and that meant keeping abreast of the many invitations and letters of condolence sent to her each day.

She had dismissed the letter as a joke until she noticed another. The two letters, penned in the same hand and sharing the same threatening tone, had startled her.

Then, as she'd uncovered more unopened correspondence of the same ilk tucked behind the estate ledgers, her worries had compounded. Those earlier threats seemed real, but the taunting lacked urgency.

Of late, though, she sensed the writer of these awful notes coming closer, his mind resolved to punish Edwin for the affront of being the Duke of Romsey. But he was just a boy. He'd done no harm to anyone.

A knock sounded on the door, and Mercy acknowledged the knock immediately and invited whomever it was to come in.

But then she froze. Should she be so careless now?

Her breath whooshed from her lungs in relief as her son's night guard opened the door for Edwin. As he raced across the chamber to her, Mercy resolved to change her habits. She should not answer the doors unprepared anymore. She must exercise better care in the future.

Edwin climbed into her lap and kissed her cheek. "You're awake!"

Mercy tickled his belly until he giggled. "Of course I am. It's only you who sleeps the day away. Have you eaten yet?"

He nodded vigorously. "Cook made apple puffs. Does Mr. Randall like apple puffs?"

Mercy smoothed his dark hair back from his eyes. "I'm not sure. Perhaps we should go find him and ask. Would you like that?"

"Yes. But he's already gone out on his horse to ride the estate. Cook said so. He knows everything."

Mercy laughed. One day, Edwin would be the one to know everything, not Cook. "Ah, well, Mr. Randall is a busy man. He's going to help us with Romsey so we better not be too sad about it. Perhaps we could ask him later. I was hoping you might like to take a picnic this afternoon. Would you enjoy that?"

Edwin squealed with excitement. "Yes, yes! Could Cook make us chicken sandwiches and gingerbread? Can we play hide-and-seek, too? Can we invite Mr. Randall?"

Mercy laughed. "Yes, my love. We can do all of that. Now let us visit Cook and Wilcox to see what needs to be arranged."

As she caught up her son's hand, she decided to come clean to Leopold about everything today at the picnic, if he could be persuaded to come. She'd tell him about the letters and gruesome gifts left in her bedchamber. A picnic setting should be perfect for such a disclosure. Out in the open, where no one could hear her fears.

Chapter Fifteen

There was something to be said for the thrill of conducting an affair when you know it would only lead to ruin. But there was also the intense frustration of not being able to have what he wanted—when he wanted it—that tempted him to throw propriety out the window.

Leopold pushed a pile of old invitations aside and threw his quill away in disgust. He was acting like a green boy. But once tasted, he could not get the yearning for Mercy out of his mind. He shifted in his chair, adjusting his trousers to accommodate the sudden surge of desire that the thought of her passion aroused. She was quite simply a woman made for loving. Uninhibited. Free of any false artifice. Mercy's come-hither looks were driving him mad.

Even now, with a pile of work between them, she tempted him to whisk her away to somewhere more private and make her cry out in ecstasy. He'd used every trick he knew last night to keep her aroused and pleasured without his cock buried inside her too often. But there were limits to what a man could deny himself, and those limits could be breached.

Across the room, Mercy sat in carefree abandon, reading a document he'd thrust at her. The investment proposal had merit and should at least be given some serious consideration. However, all Leopold could think of at that moment was kissing away the frown lines on her forehead.

As if sensing his regard, her gaze rose. "This is utter gibberish to me. You decide." Mercy tossed the pages onto the chair between them and groaned.

Leopold snatched them up and straightened the sheets. "I cannot do that and you know it, Your Grace. If you would just read through the second page again, you can see the terms and expected return on your investment. However, I would suggest further investigation into the business affairs and principal operators before committing any funds to the project. If it is as good as it appears, the investment could be very lucrative."

Mercy stood, and so did Leopold. Another frown marred her forehead. "An investigation? Would my temporary advisor handle such matters for me personally?"

Leopold shook his head. "Not necessarily. Your London man of business can conduct the necessary interviews and hire a runner to ensure the business is legitimate. Then, if it is sound, the matter would need to be forwarded to your brother for his approval."

When she stopped a bare inch from his chest, Leopold's heart pounded. She had avoided all intimate contact with him since last night. She hadn't joined him until an hour ago, or attempted to kiss him when they'd first greeted each other, much to his disappointment. He had started to believe he'd imagined last evening altogether.

"Good. I should not like to have you depart from Romsey." Her fingers traced the pattern on his waistcoat. "Are you busy this afternoon?"

Leopold gulped as his body responded, cock throbbing for the woman to come closer. "I do have work to continue with here."

She licked her lips as she adjusted his cravat. "Edwin and I are taking a picnic this afternoon. We wondered if you might join us."

Leopold set his hand to her hip and she swayed closer. "I should not intrude on your time with the boy."

Mercy's face rose to meet his. Her gaze was sultry, her lips parted and damp. "We would not invite you if it were an imposition, Leopold. I want to spend the afternoon out of doors, and I think you would enjoy the fresh air, too. You have worked tirelessly all morning, and I am profoundly grateful for your diligence. But, if you must, bring some of those papers with you. No doubt Edwin will fall asleep at some point and you shall have leisure to peruse them."

Leopold cupped Mercy's bottom, dragging her flush against him. "You had everything planned out before you asked me to join you and Edwin, didn't you?"

Her lips lifted into a cheeky smile. "A woman, even a duchess, must tempt the man she desires to throw his reticence aside. I missed you when I woke this morning."

Mercy rose on her toes and set her lips to his. While Leopold struggled to hold back, Mercy twined her arms about his neck and plundered. She curled her arms tighter about him as the kiss continued, needy and desperate once again.

Leopold couldn't stop his reaction. He couldn't control the need to be inside her body. Slowly, he inched her gown up her legs, determined to touch her skin.

Mercy's soft *no* stilled him.

He drew back to look into her face. Had he got it wrong? Had she taken her fill of him already?

Her eyes were filled with regret. "Edwin is waiting."

Leopold stepped back, dropping her gown, surprised by his disappointment. "Ah. My apologies."

"Do not apologize for wanting me. I quite like how much you do." She leaned forward and pressed a kiss to his cheek. "Later. I promise. We should be ready to go in a moment."

As she swept from the room, Leopold considered how difficult the afternoon would be. At least the presence of the boy would temper his lust. But he doubted his heart would remain impervious to the time he spent in the boy's company. He already cared too much about Edwin for his comfort.

He snatched up a pile of unopened correspondence, hoping the contents would prove a reasonable distraction from his lustful thoughts, and followed Mercy into the hall.

A few steps from the main doors, the butler approached him. "Her Grace mentioned that you are joining the picnic, sir."

"Yes, Wilcox. Was there something you wanted me to attend to before we depart?"

"Just a small matter, sir." The butler drew Leopold aside, out of earshot of the lingering footmen. "Are you, by any chance, armed?"

Unsure of what to make of the question, but disturbed by it nonetheless, Leopold nodded. "Always."

The butler sagged with relief. "That is excellent news. Thank you."

Leopold waited for an explanation to follow the butler's pleasure at hearing he was armed, but Mercy and young Edwin arrived, followed by a maid. The little boy tugged on his mother's hand and, while she took his enthusiasm with great patience, Leopold rather thought she wished he would desist.

He stepped forward. "Good afternoon, Your Grace."

The little boy gaped up at him then clung to his mother's skirts. Leopold cursed under his breath. He hadn't meant to startle him into silence. He'd hoped to provide Mercy with a useful distraction. Perhaps he was out of practice with young children. It was probably for the best.

Mercy bent down to Edwin's level. "Sweetheart, say hello to Mr. Randall. You remember him, don't you?"

The little boy nodded, suddenly shy. Their eyes met. The boy looked just like his youngest brother when he was about to be scolded. Leopold smiled. "Shall we be on our way, Your Grace? It looks to be a fine day for your picnic."

On hearing the word picnic, the little boy untangled himself from his mother and rushed out the open front door and down the steps, heading for the waiting carriage at a run.

"Edwin, stop," Leopold ordered without thought.

The boy halted and spun about, shock clear on his face.

Had no one ever raised a voice to him before? He hadn't meant to frighten the child, and he slowly approached Edwin. He bent closer to the boy's height as Mercy had done and placed his hand on his trembling arm. "You must wait for your mother, lad. A lady must always be escorted."

Although the boy was very young, Leopold thought he understood, because he did wait for his mother to join him before clambering into the open coach door. But what if he hadn't stopped? Would Edwin have rushed straight under the horses' hooves or fallen beneath the carriage wheels if the horses had been startled into movement?

He glanced up at the driver's bench and met Allen's raised brow. His cousin seemed bemused by the outing, and Leopold's place in the procession. With a swift glance at the rear of the conveyance, he spotted Allen's two sons. It seemed the outing was to be a family affair. A pity Mercy didn't realize.

Leopold was unused to caring about the health of the Duke of Romsey. Yet he cared greatly about this boy, this child that could be his, one who should not be a duke at all. He couldn't bear the thought of him in peril of any kind.

Heart pounding, he climbed into the carriage and sat beside the maid.

The carriage lurched forward and Edwin squealed with delight over the outing to come. As Mercy fussed with straightening the boy's hair, Leopold tried to settle his anxiety. It was just a simple picnic outing. There was nothing strange about such an endeavor. There was no need to fret over the boy unnecessarily as he was doing now.

When the carriage turned onto a shaded lane a short distance from the abbey and stopped, Leopold exited and helped the maid and Mercy out. But when it was Edwin's turn, the boy didn't climb out. He launched himself into Leopold's arms with a giggle.

Shocked to be holding the child, Leopold put him down swiftly.

Mercy curled her arm around his and tugged him away. "I should have warned you. The grooms have made a game of getting him out of the carriage. Some days it takes three jumps before he's satisfied. Allen will keep an eye on him until he tires of the sport."

So she was acquainted with Allen and trusted him with Edwin. Perhaps the news they were related wouldn't come as too big a shock. He glanced back one last time as Jacob and David laughed with Edwin. They seemed happy in his company, and he with them.

Leopold scanned their surroundings and found the picnic spot set up under the shade of a large oak. Keeping one eye on the jumping boy and one on the uneven ground, Leopold escorted Mercy across the field to a low chair.

"I think that chair's for you, actually," she said, and then laughed as she settled to the picnic blanket in a puff of long skirts. She dug into the hamper. "If you wish to join Edwin in his games, I am content enough here."

Leopold dropped his correspondence onto the corner of the blanket and turned to watch the boy. Edwin had recruited all the servants into a game of tag, but the servants were letting him win by a wide margin and the laughter was enthusiastic. He was happy. "He has enough people dancing attendance on him for the moment. I'll step in should the servants become fatigued."

No sooner were the words out of his mouth than he wondered what the hell he could do for the boy that a thousand servants couldn't. Edwin didn't need him.

Leopold moved the chair out of the way then settled on the ground, discomfited by his realization. Where was his mind these days?

Mercy set a large jug before him on the blanket along with three glasses. "He will tire first, or become hungry and return here." She sat back on her heels and sighed. "I love this spot."

"The aspect is very pretty, Your Grace."

When Mercy turned to face him and captured his gaze, he couldn't look away. She licked her lips and the desire to lean across the cold fare to share a kiss gripped him. He wrenched his gaze from her and watched the boy's antics instead.

Mercy shifted restlessly, and then surprised him by moving to sit closer against his side. "Edwin loves it here, too."

"I can see that."

She sighed and leaned against his shoulder briefly. Leopold missed the contact as soon as she was gone. "It's not fair to him, I think. Not having other children his age to play with. Allen's boys do their best, but he needs other children about him that are closer in age. Jacob and David always do what he says. He'll never learn good manners if he can boss everyone around and get away with it."

No, he wouldn't learn good manners that way at all. But, as a duke, such behavior would be considered normal. "I've been meaning to ask you about Lady Venables, if I may. She is a widow, yes, and childless?"

Mercy resettled against him. "Yes. She had a boy once. But he passed away from a terrible illness, the same one that took her husband a few years ago. We both lost our husbands."

"I'm sorry. That must have been a terrible time for both of you." Leopold glanced at Mercy. "I noticed that Lady Venables has not come to call on you of late. Have you heard from her? Is she well?"

To his shock, Mercy set her head on his shoulder. "I haven't heard a word." She sighed. "I should have mentioned that we had a disagreement on her last visit. But I'm still somewhat in shock about it all and the things she said to me."

"Oh?"

"It seems my sister has taken a dislike to your presence at Romsey. She feels you could be a threat to my son."

Leopold took a deep breath and let it out slowly. "I'm not a threat to him. I would not hurt one hair on that boy's head." He climbed to his feet and began to pace. He did not want to come between the sisters. "I'll leave at dawn tomorrow."

"Oh, no, you won't," Mercy commanded. "Sit down before I injure my neck scowling up at you. I need family here with Edwin. Now more than ever."

Why now? Was it just because he'd returned?

Puzzled, Leopold sat and Mercy resumed her relaxed pose against his side. "The truth is, I've let my sister's grief go on for too long. She sees scandal in almost everything I do, and long before your arrival, I might add. I let her odd behavior pass because she'd lost her child and husband, but I will not stand for it any longer. She even accused me of other scandalous behavior. She went too far."

Leopold glanced at Mercy's sad face and realized there was more to the conversation than she'd let on. Although it wasn't his place to question her, he wanted to know what troubled her so badly. Perhaps he could help smooth things over with Lady Venables and reassure her he had no designs on the title. He twitched his shoulder under her head. "What else did she say?"

When she closed her eyes, his heart skipped a beat. "The truth. She saw how badly I am enamored with you, and chided me for behaving with such carelessness."

Mouth agape, stunned beyond words, Leopold struggled to decide how to respond. A certain way to smooth things over between them was for him to leave.

As he opened his mouth to offer to depart again, Mercy's finger sealed his lips. "Don't you dare mention leaving. We still need to find where the duke sent Oliver, Rosemary, and Tobias yet."

"You remember their names."

Mercy lifted her head from his shoulder. "Of course I do. They should be with you, and here with us. They're part of our family, too. I want to meet them."

Just then, Edwin headed for their tree at a run. Mercy used his shoulder as support to climb to her feet then skimmed her fingertips across the back of his neck. Shivers danced down his spine from the brief contact, but then she moved away to scoop her son up in a possessive hug before leading him back to the picnic blanket to begin their feast.

As Leopold watched, and then joined in the conversation about his favorite food, he realized that he was content for the first time in years. Despite the friction with Lady Venables, perhaps he could belong at Romsey one day.

"I have cousins," Edwin piped up in a sudden change of conversation.

"That you do, my darling. And they are coming soon, I promise." Mercy ruffled the boy's hair and smiled. "Edwin has Willow, Maisie, and Poppy; his uncle, Lord Grayling's children, are coming to visit with us this winter. And he has another aunt, Lady Cameron, but Patience wasn't so lucky in her marriage to have had children."

Leopold sorted through the information. "You never mentioned spouses."

Mercy's hands fluttered. "For all our wealth and position in society, we are a family of noble widows. Not one of us has retained their spouse or remarried."

"Not even Lord Grayling? I would have thought he'd marry again for the title's sake. He'll want a son to inherit."

Mercy's face scrunched up, but she didn't comment. She watched her son finish his beef pie and then waved him back to his games. When he was out of earshot, a rueful smile twisted her lips. "Constantine has no time for women, except those temporarily engaged to warm his bed. But I feel for those dear sweet little girls and try to persuade him to visit more often. Unfortunately, Constantine will not stay long, and he won't consent to the girls residing here with us. I wish he would. Edwin loves them so."

"Is his estate close?"

"Stanton Harold Hall, our family estate, is in Wiltshire. It's a drear place and I cannot believe he wishes the girls to grow up there. He hated the place when we were young."

Leopold smiled and drained his glass to hide his emotions. He had never belonged at Romsey before, but the sensation was slowly creeping up on him. "Opinions change as you age. How old are the girls?"

"Five, four, and two. So young to be motherless and raised by servants."

"It is the custom."

"Not in my family, it isn't," Mercy snapped. She took a deep breath, and then patted his knee. "Forgive me. My brother's attitude vexes me enormously. But he will be here soon, and I will endeavor to extend his stay beyond the meager two weeks he's agreed upon. I am hoping he will stay longer because you are here to provide much-needed male company. My sister, Patience, will be with us as well, but we ladies tend to babble too much for Constantine's comfort. You'll like Patience. She has a direct way about her."

Leopold hooked his arms around his knee and stared off into the distance. Hearing Mercy speak of her family gave him pain. Not pain that she was troubled by the push and pull of family relationships. His pain was that he was not similarly affected. Would his siblings be as he remembered?

Tobias had been a trusting lad, and Rosemary a veritable termagant. He and Oliver had been the closest of friends, but they had fought from time to time over the littlest of things—usually over Oliver's obsession with ridiculous calculations. He'd give anything to hear them now, however.

Hoping to banish his anxiety, Leopold reached for his correspondence. The foreign world of frivolous parties and pompous announcements would calm him.

A ragged letter caught his eye, standing out for its inferior stationary and careless penmanship against the expensive correspondence. Leopold opened the much folded paper and read.

. . .

My dearest,

You cannot imagine how I long to see you. To hold you between my hands and feel your breath quiver as you look into my eyes. Wait for me. I promise to make the occasion memorable for both of us.

Ever yours.

It read like a lover's note and they could only be writing to the duchess. Leopold quickly folded the paper and thrust it toward Mercy. "My apologies, your grace. I did not realize the personal nature of the missive."

As the paper slipped from his fingers, Leopold bounced to his feet and strode away.

How complete an idiot was he?

Mercy might have taken a string of lovers before he'd arrived. The discovery curled around his insides until he wanted to scream. To protect the innocent, he kept well clear of Edwin and the servants. But they all stopped their games and followed him with their eyes as he moved away.

The idea of Mercy welcoming other men to her bed clouded his vision in a red haze. He did not care where his steps took him. He forced himself to walk on, yet when Mercy hailed him, he stopped and let her catch up.

She rushed to his side, hands curling over his forearm and tugging insistently. "What am I to do?"

Leopold shook off her grip as the bitter stink of jealousy whipped him. "I imagine you'll be welcoming the chap with open arms when he arrives, Your Grace."

Mercy hugged her chest. "Why in heavens name would I do that? I don't know this madman!"

Leopold watched her closely. Her pale face and clutching fingers all spoke to him of great anxiety. Yet the wording of the letter hinted at intimacy between her and the writer. He didn't know whether to believe her. "Your beau seems anxious to see you again."

She bit her lip, a guilty gesture that sickened him. He turned away and watched where the boy played, innocent of his mother's capricious nature.

However, Mercy marched around him until they stood face-to-face. Her clenched fists landed on her hips. "He's not my beau, you obstinate man—he threatens to harm me and my son."

Chapter Sixteen

Mercy stared as the affable man she was familiar with transformed before her eyes. His posture stiffened, his gaze hardening to one of fury as it darted about the clearing in search of a hidden foe. In the blink of an eye, he had become someone who expected danger to leap upon them. A man who would give as good as he got when faced with a threat.

His fingers closed over her arm and drew her against him. In the next instant, he drew a weapon, a small pistol, from his coat pocket and held it at his side, muzzle pointing down at their feet. Leopold might have shown signs of jealousy a moment before when he'd thought a beau was writing to her, but those emotions had vanished as if they had never been.

If not for the danger they faced, Mercy might have been pleased that he liked her well enough to feel threatened by the madman writing to her. She might have even gently teased him with the idea that she had become dear to him. But the time for forgetting her troubles was over. The fears she had kept to herself were out in the open now.

That he believed her immediately was a comfort. That he would shoot first and ask questions later troubled her a great deal.

His grip tightened, and then he released her. "The picnic is over, Mercy. We'll collect Edwin and return to the abbey now."

Hearing the stern "no arguments" tone in his voice, Mercy picked up her skirts and turned toward where Edwin played. However, she hadn't taken more than two steps in his direction before Leopold cautioned her. "Do not rush about and frighten the boy. We do not want to draw unnecessary attention to our departure. Behave naturally."

Behave naturally? How exactly was that possible when his words and manner had sent her fear spinning out of control. They were exposed here, and she had not realized that very important fact when she had decided on the location. She had put Edwin in danger unnecessarily in order to partake of a romantic picnic with Leopold, blinded by her infatuation with the man. She must have lost her mind the minute she gazed upon his dimpled cheeks in the drawing room.

By the time Mercy had convinced Edwin that the day was too warm for a picnic, her nerves were in tatters. Leopold issued orders to the servants as she settled Edwin beside her in the carriage, fussing with his clothing because she had to do something with her hands or she'd scream.

When Leopold joined them inside, he dropped the blinds completely over the windows. "We need to change positions now," he said quietly as the carriage lurched forward.

It was a little awkward to do while the carriage was in motion, but they swapped sides so she and Edwin sat in the rear-facing seats. She met Leopold's gaze across the dim compartment and a shiver of fear raced up her spine. Leopold's firearm remained out of Edwin's sight and for that, Mercy was extremely grateful. But he offered her no reassurance. His smiles were all gone. He appeared furious, both with the situation and with her for involving him in her problems.

The short drive back to the abbey was conducted in tense silence. Leopold did not speak. Even Edwin seemed to realize that all was not right with his world. His gaze darted between them, and then he set his hand in Mercy's and gripped her tightly.

Leopold shifted the blind to peer out. "Almost there. I will step out first. Hold the boy and do not let him escape you until I give you leave. Understood?"

Mercy blinked. After years as a duchess, she was quite unused to being ordered about. However, given the circumstances, she would not make a fuss. She needed someone who knew what to do in this situation. She was completely out of her depth. Mercy draped her arm about her son's shoulders and held him against her side.

The carriage rolled to a stop and Wilcox hurried to open the door. Mercy sucked in a deep, calming breath as Leopold stepped out first, hand hidden beneath his coat to conceal the pistol. He stood in the doorway a long moment then turned and held out his hand for Edwin. "No jumping this time, Your Grace. Your mother has many things to do today."

Although his words were spoken calmly—for Edwin's benefit —his graze flittered restlessly about the surrounding gardens. He held on to Edwin's arm until Mercy joined them, and then released her son to her care.

Mercy proceeded up the stairs as pinpricks of discomfort raced along her limbs now. Leopold followed along, slightly behind them, until they passed over the threshold of Romsey Abbey.

When the front door closed, Leopold curled his hand around her upper arm in a tight grip. "To the study. Bring the boy."

Mercy stumbled down the hall, pulling Edwin with her as fast as his legs would carry him. Once ensconced in the chamber, Leopold checked the locks on the windows, drew the drapes, and even checked under his desk before he was satisfied that they were alone. "Take a seat."

Mercy's knees thanked her for sitting down. Her legs had become jelly in the face of Leopold's tension. He moved about the chamber, following Edwin as he clambered up on the desk chair and peeked into a drawer. Leopold moved his papers aside, placed a blank sheet of paper on the surface, and left Edwin to draw.

"Now," Leopold began as he approached. "I think you had better explain to me your understanding of that note."

Judging by his harsh, uncompromising expression, no evasions would be forgiven. "We've been receiving letters, infrequently, from a man I've come to fear. He speaks as if we are well acquainted, but I cannot imagine whom he might be. I cannot tell where the letters come from, and he never signs them with a name."

Mercy clutched her hands tightly together as Leopold sat on the cushion beside her.

"He speaks as if you are intimate acquaintances, Mercy. How long has this been going on?"

Mercy rubbed her hands along her thighs, startled by how long she'd lived under this cloud. "It's been a year since I read the first, but I have found older ones hidden in this room. My husband and father-in-law must have known about them, I think. But since my husband's death, the letters have become more frequent. The last was just two nights ago. The night before you agreed to move into the abbey."

Leopold's lips twisted as if he had tasted bitter fruit. "You invited me to live in the abbey only because of the threats against you and the boy, didn't you?"

Mercy caught his hand. "No. That is simply not true." She had invited him here because she had wanted to get to know him far better than she did. If he had stayed at the Vulture, they would never have made love last night. Even without the threats hanging over her life, she would have wanted him here.

He worked his hand free; his expression, when he turned his head, was bleak. Did he not believe her?

"I'll need to see the other letters if you still have them, Your Grace. Are they in this room?"

Mercy swallowed, hurt that he would speak formally with her again after they had been so close just last night. "No, I keep them upstairs in my bedchamber under lock and key. I didn't want the servants to stumble over them."

He nodded, and then tugged the bell to summon her butler. Mercy cast a quick glance at Edwin. Her son's dark head was bent over the page; he was oblivious to what happened around him for now. Leopold had chosen well to give him paper. The boy loved nothing better than to sketch whatever came to hand.

Mercy jumped as a knock sounded on the door.

"Come," Leopold called, withdrawing his weapon and tucking it against his thigh, out of sight but at the ready.

The door creaked ominously as Wilcox entered. "I'll have that seen to immediately, Your Grace. You called?"

"I called for you," Leopold corrected. "Don't fix the door, just close it behind you. The creak may come in handy later. Come in."

Wilcox hurried forward, but stopped when he noticed the weapon in Leopold's hand. His expression grew grim. "What has happened?"

Leopold put the pistol away slowly, eyeing the butler with suspicion. "You don't seem surprised to see me armed in the duke's presence, and you tried to warn me this morning by asking if I traveled with a weapon. I take it you are aware of Her Grace's admirer."

"It is a sick form of admiration to torment a woman and a child this way."

Leopold frowned and held up the letter. "This reads like a love letter, Wilcox."

The butler glanced at her guiltily, and she knew he would tell Leopold about the animal killings if she didn't. Mercy drew a deep breath but kept her gaze on her hands. "There has been more to the threats than just letters, I'm afraid."

"How much more?" Leopold demanded.

Wilcox cleared his throat to take over the telling. "The abbey has been penetrated. Gifts have been left in Her Grace's private quarters."

"What kind of gifts?"

"The most recent was the body of a rabbit, slaughtered on her bed and left to be found."

Leopold's gasp chilled Mercy. She risked a glance up at him— and wished she hadn't. His lips had drawn back from his teeth in a murderous snarl.

He turned away, stalked toward her son and, after a brief conversation, managed to wrest the pencil from Edwin's fingers. Then he picked Edwin up in his arms and tucked the boy against his chest. "Precautions must be taken. Come with me. Wilcox, there is a second pistol in that drawer behind you. Take it and remain close to Her Grace."

Mercy's heart raced as Edwin wrapped his arms tighter about Leopold's neck. Her boy must be scared if he would seek comfort from Leopold, a virtual stranger in his life. Mercy wished she might do the same. She stood, hoping her legs would hold and not buckle beneath her. "Where are we going?"

Leopold's head tilted to touch Edwin's, and he spoke quietly to her son. When Edwin relaxed, his gaze fixed on them. "Up. To your bedchamber first to retrieve those letters, and then we will secure you both in more defensible rooms, somewhere you won't be found so easily."

That sounded a sensible plan to Mercy, so she nodded and followed them to the door. Wilcox lightly gripped her arm and steered them in Leopold's wake. The fast trip up the stairs and to her chamber was conducted in tense silence.

When the door of her bedchamber closed behind their backs, Leopold searched the room to ensure they were alone. He placed Edwin on the center of the bed, ruffling his hair as he stepped back. "The letters?" He thrust his large hand palm up in her direction.

Mercy hurried for the writing desk and opened the drawer, fumbling with the correspondence in her haste. When Leopold's hand settled on her shoulder and rubbed, she took a deep breath, calming from his touch, and then handed them to him.

Leopold brushed her cheek with his fingertips. "You've been frightened for a long time, haven't you? That's why you were wary when we first met, and why the boy has a servant with him even when he sleeps. Go and rest with him while I read these. I'll be watching over you both."

"Thank you."

As she joined her son on the bed and began to play silly games with him, Wilcox crossed the room and spoke urgently with Leopold.

Edwin touched her face, and she turned to look into his sleepy eyes. She encouraged Edwin to lie down and rest and very soon he was asleep. But the men continued to talk, and she closed her eyes and her ears to the sound of their discussion. Wilcox knew enough of what went on here, and she trusted him to tell Leopold everything.

She woke abruptly as Leopold closed the bedroom door behind Wilcox. His expression was grim as he approached. Mercy sat up to face him and swung her legs over the side of the bed.

Leopold stopped a few feet away, just out of her reach. "I wish you had told me sooner."

She wriggled to the edge of the bed. "I wanted to. I didn't know you well enough, and I didn't want to scare you away by unburdening my fears on you. It is hardly a conversation to have upon a first meeting, is it?"

"You didn't trust me." He nodded. "That was the correct thing to do. We must protect the boy, and you, at all costs."

At last, Leopold closed the distance between them. He pulled her into his embrace, and she wrapped her arms about him. Safe. He smoothed his hands over her back, lulling her until her heart no longer beat with fear.

"Well, you have your wish, Your Grace. After this discovery, I'll not be leaving you and Edwin anytime soon."

Despite the reason, Mercy's heart soared, but she was wise enough to hide her smile in the folds of Leopold's waistcoat.

Leopold forced himself to be calm, despite the fury coursing through him at this unknown threat to Mercy and Edwin. As he had hoped, Wilcox agreed with him that serious steps must be taken to protect Mercy and the young duke from harm. Although Wilcox's suggestion that Mercy flee to London with Edwin had merit, they were safer here.

He glanced at the sleeping child and fury built anew. He would not stand for anyone harming the boy. Not while he drew breath. Mercy's fingers clutched at his waist, and he bent to press a kiss to the top of her head to reassure her that all would be well.

He wished Mercy had told him earlier.

He wished she hadn't let him care for her so much before she did.

He untangled himself from her grip and tipped her face up to his. "You must gather the few personal items you'll need for the night, things that won't be noticed as missing immediately, and be ready to move to another chamber after dining tonight. As far as the servants will know, you slept here. But you, Edwin, and I will spend the night elsewhere. Neither of you will be alone during the day or go on jaunts outside the abbey walls alone. Is that understood?"

The frown creasing Mercy's face would have been comical under any other circumstances. She had clearly grown used to being in charge and having everyone defer to her wishes. He wondered how difficult she would become when he told her to stay away from even the windows.

To his surprise, she nodded. "I won't need much. I'll need very little if you are with me."

He withdrew his hand from her face with regret. They couldn't be intimate again, not with danger stalking them.

Mercy captured his hands and pulled him into another embrace. "What I meant is that with you for company, I'll have you to speak with to occupy the quiet hours at night if I cannot sleep." She drew back and glanced up at him. "How long do you think we'll need to take precautions in our home? I should not like to hide forever."

Leopold cupped the side of her face, brushing his thumb along the soft skin of her cheek. "Until the danger has passed. But judging from the tone of those letters, and actions, we'll not have long to wait. His writing has a pattern of growing zeal. Whoever he is, he'll work himself up into a frenzy before striking at you direct."

"You think him mad?"

Leopold nodded. The letters on their own were disturbing enough without the brutal and callous killing of innocent creatures. Wilcox's description of the discoveries had chilled him. No sane person behaved in such a way. "You don't have to worry now. Whoever he is, we'll be ready."

When the madman came after Mercy and Edwin, Leopold would be squarely in the way. He stepped back.

Without prompting, she moved silently around the room, digging out a hairbrush and a handkerchief, along with a few other necessities and wrapped them in a shawl. She placed the bundle beneath her bed, out of sight, and turned to him. "Ready."

"Good. Now, I want you to behave as normally as possible. Wilcox will have taken the housekeeper's keys by now and will search and secure the unused parts of the abbey. Although we have interviewed all the staff since my return and approve of them all, only a few will be taken into our confidence about the threats against you and the boy. Tonight, I would like you to dine with Edwin, as I understand you often do, and send his nurse away early. I'll be listening from down the hall and will come for you both to take you somewhere safer for the night."

Mercy advanced on him and ran her hands up his waistcoat. "Why not dine with us? Edwin would like that, I think. Perhaps you could persuade him to use better table manners."

Leopold couldn't help the short burst of laughter that escaped him. He'd seen the boy's careless manners at the picnic and had already guessed he might be a tad messy. "If he is anything like my younger siblings, that feat will take some years to accomplish. Tobias, in particular, showed exceedingly messy tendencies. I cannot join you. I must keep watch."

Mercy's sad sigh touched his heart. "Let's hope Tobias has grown out of those poor habits by the time we bring him home, otherwise it might not be safe to introduce him to my sister. Blythe takes order to extremes and will likely cause friction."

"Tobias will sink or swim when it comes to your family. I have no idea what kind of life he has been living, but I hope the duke kept his word, and Tobias has enough gentlemanly qualities to appease Lady Venables and you."

"We will rub together well enough, I hope. If not, then Blythe could always offer your brother instruction in the social graces."

Egad! That sounded like a nightmare. "Few grown men like to be told what to do, Your Grace."

Mercy cuddled into him, "I was teasing you, Leopold. I'd never inflict my sister's standards onto any man. But let's worry about him when the time comes, shall we?"

Mercy was correct; there was more than enough trouble in their lives to worry about now without imagining problems to come in the future.

He moved to sit in a wing chair and pulled Mercy down onto his lap to simply hold her close. But as he pressed his lips to her brow, his future wavered and shifted, hinting at a future that terrified him utterly.

Chapter Seventeen

If anyone had told him a year ago that he would consider murdering anyone who dared threaten a duke or duchess of Romsey, he would have laughed in their faces and told them to go to the devil. But today he had felt such fury that it was clear he'd had an absolute change of heart. The boy was innocent and deserved his protection. Mercy was…

He couldn't decide what she was to him. But the thought of her in danger was torture to his soul. There was no need to feel so possessive about her, yet he was utterly powerless to turn his thoughts away from her for long.

She stirred from the bed, where she'd spent the last hour convincing Edwin to rest, and joined him at the window. "He's finally asleep," she whispered.

He had stood apart from them, alert for trouble, pistol loose in his hand. He glanced beyond her to the bed and relaxed marginally. "I thought he might be more difficult for you. This is not a particularly cheerful room."

In fact, this room was quite disgusting. Dusty—unused for perhaps a dozen or more years and smelling strongly of dampness —it was an insult to bring anyone here. But no one would expect the boy in this part of the abbey. No one would imagine a duchess would allow her only child near such neglect. Yet all Mercy had done was wrinkle her nose at the rising dust, and then focus her attention on the boy to keep him amused.

"I told you he has an agreeable temper," Mercy said. "When I informed him that we would never leave his side, he cheered up. He likes you. And he enjoyed the games you showed him earlier immensely."

A hollow ache started in Leopold's chest. Although he shouldn't, he liked the boy, too. He'd felt a profound connection to the child from the moment they'd met. Hiding how much could prove difficult.

He checked his weapon again, wishing heartily that he'd taken the time to collect a second from the duke's study before night had fallen. But he hadn't wanted to draw attention to what he was doing as yet. For now, all he had to defend them was one small pistol and a fury unlike anything he'd ever known.

Mercy rubbed her hands up and down her arms briskly to ward off the chill of the cold room. "What time do you think it is?"

"Nearing midnight." Or at least that hour was drawing close the last time he had checked his fob watch. That habit had grown far too often for his comfort during the course of the evening, so he had made a promise to himself not to check until dawn lightened the sky.

"Are you always armed, Leopold?"

He met her gaze. "Yes."

She flinched at his immediate answer and lowered herself to sit on the edge of the bed. "You must have had a terrible life to always be so prepared for danger."

What could he say to that? He'd learned his lessons early in life. There was no safe place for him. He had only himself to rely upon. He lifted the pistol and studied it. "I barely notice that I carry it anymore."

"You carried it the first day we met, didn't you? You carried it when you met my son?"

He nodded. It was best that she know the worst of him.

"Oh, Leopold. You have nothing to fear from us. The old duke is gone and so is my husband, if he ever harbored any ill toward you. There is no threat to you and your siblings here now. You never need to fear us."

"There is a threat to you and the child." He looked out the window to hide the panic he felt at saying it aloud. Who would want to hurt the child, or hurt Mercy? And to stalk them in such a heinous way made his blood run cold. He would protect them, or die trying.

When Mercy approached, he didn't turn. She spread her hands atop his shoulders and smoothed them over his back. One hand slid down his arm and settled on his fist where he clutched the weapon. "Put the pistol down, Leopold, and get some sleep. No one will find us tonight."

Although he shouldn't let his guard down by sleeping, he thought her correct that they were safe for the night. The surprise change of location would confuse her enemy for now, but later, he'd have to stay alert all night and day, perhaps. He should rest while he could.

He set the weapon on a table. Mercy tugged at his arm to lead him to the bed. She climbed up and then patted the empty space beside her. "There's plenty of room for all of us."

Leopold hesitated. Although there was ample room to sleep beside them, he really should not. Not with the boy present and likely to wake and find him beside his mother. What if he embraced Mercy while he slept? What would the boy think of that?

"I'll sleep in the chair."

Mercy tilted her head to one side then held out her hand palm up. She crooked her fingers to urge him closer and, like the fool he was, he joined her on the bed. She wriggled around to get comfortable then settled close against his side. Leopold glanced down at her curiously in the half-light spilling into the room.

She watched him. A frown marred her features.

Startled by her expression and scrutiny, Leopold lifted his gaze to the ceiling. The more time he spent alone with her in the dark, the more likely she was to recognize him. It surprised him that she hadn't already. They had been deeply intimate, and he'd never acted any differently with her than the first time they had lain together.

Maybe that first night had not been as memorable for her as it had been for him. Maybe she'd taken other lovers and the memory of him was dim.

His hands tightened into fists. Damn her. He wasn't used to caring so much for a woman. But Mercy had ruined all his plans to keep a polite and safe distance between them.

She curled onto her side, head pressing against his shoulder, and sighed. "This is how it should be. Just us."

Mercy didn't say another word, and Leopold couldn't help but be grateful because this thing between them, his growing possessiveness for the one woman he should not want, terrified him.

Her breathing evened out in sleep and he stared at the ceiling. He didn't want to need her like this. If it were possible to cure himself of his infatuation, he would.

Mercy raised her head from Leopold's chest as the room lightened with the approaching dawn. Despite the poor surroundings, she'd slept deeply, content to lie beside her lover and son. With Leopold here, Mercy didn't fear for her safety, or for Edwin's. He would never harm her child and she was proud she'd seen his character long before taking him into her confidence.

She eased down to the foot of the bed and climbed off carefully so as not to wake Edwin. While she drew on her wrapper, she glanced between her sleeping lover and son. She stifled a laugh. How could the pair sleep so completely perfect in arrangement, right down to the way their dark hair curled over their ears?

She stood at the foot of the bed to study their poses. One foot tucked against the other leg to form a triangle between, one hand pressed over stomach, the other open and relaxed on the bed. They could be twins, if two decades or more didn't separate their ages.

Or they could be father and son.

Mercy's breath caught in her throat as the idea caught hold.

Although she had originally dismissed the notion as a foolish fancy, her son did share more than a passing resemblance to Leopold Randall. Edwin might share her green eyes, but his hair color was dark, a shade closer to Leopold's.

Her gaze sharpened on her son's hands.

They were not similar to Mercy's long, slender fingers. The tips were blunt, the nails square. She had forgotten the precise shape of her husband's hands, but as she stared at Leopold Randall, she saw more similarities to worry her.

Had the old duke sent this man, a member of his own family, to her bed?

She stumbled into a chair. What was it Leopold had told her? He'd said he hadn't been here at the abbey for years. Not since the old duke threatened his family with harm unless he did him a service.

Leopold had not been comfortable, at first, in her presence, and he'd never fully explained what that service was.

She stared at him. Had she finally met the man who had shared that one long night of frantic bliss?

Perhaps she had.

Then there was the troubling matter of the sudden attraction between them that had caught her unprepared. She had never behaved like this before; pursuing a man who did his best to keep a respectful distance. She had attributed her fascination to Leopold's reticence. Mercy had always liked a challenge. She had wanted to learn everything about this man before the chance slipped away. Had she unconsciously recognized him when they had met again and feared losing him again?

Like Mercy, he must know what he'd done with her, and not said a word.

Mercy paced the room as bitterness and humiliation washed over her. They had been forced together once. Now she was pursuing him. Was everything a lie between them? What kind of man was he really?

She had fallen in love with the stranger in her bed. One night. One night of tender loving that had destroyed the fragile bond between her and her husband and brought about the ruin her marriage.

Her husband had not cared for her outrage at the old duke's plan. He had not cared that another man would bed her. When she'd confronted him before the deed had been done, he'd told her without an ounce of regret that she wouldn't enjoy the experience. Romsey needed an heir and that was all that mattered.

Mercy sat with a thump, ignoring the cloud of dust billowing up from the old cushion.

Edwin had been utterly wrong about that night.

The man sent to bed her had been sweet, and thorough, and more loving than her own husband had been on his best day. He had not done anything to her that she had objected to and when asked for more, he had tenderly swept her away. When her husband had come to her bed the following night, she had not wanted him to come again. Edwin had been cold, and determined to complete the deed without her participation.

She drew in a shuddering breath. No matter how gentle her stranger had been, he had been used and he was a liar. If it were true, she would not forgive Leopold for keeping his part in that night secret. How could she ever trust him?

"Mama?"

As was his habit, Edwin sat up straight away and threw himself sideways over Leopold.

Leopold started up suddenly, too, eyes wide on the small boy draped across his stomach. Edwin yawned sleepily and smiled up at him. Leopold stared at her child a long time, but then he must have registered her absence from the bed as his gaze searched for her quickly.

When their eyes met, Mercy couldn't force a smile to her lips. She didn't know what to say to him yet.

Leopold scrambled out from under Edwin, dropping her son to the bed in the process. Her son's widened eyes and hurt expression moved Mercy toward the bed to comfort him. She gathered Edwin in her arms, whispering a good morning against his ear. But she kept track of Leopold as he bent to replace his shoes and draw on his coat.

Her lover, the man who may very well have lied to her every moment since they had met, cleared his throat. "We can return to the family wing whenever you are ready."

"Of course." Although he was almost too big to manage, Mercy carried Edwin with her as she crossed the room to slide her feet into her slippers. One of them, of course, proved troublesome but she didn't want to release Edwin. She was afraid that if she did, she would blurt out her accusation at Leopold and, if he didn't deny it immediately, she'd start an argument while Edwin was near. Her fears could be groundless, after all. Mercy hated to be in the wrong.

Leopold crossed the room, bent to capture her ankle, and set her foot within the shoe properly. His hand stroked over her skin, another decadent, hungry touch that reminded Mercy all too painfully of what she'd allowed this man to do. She had pursued him and seduced him and begged him to make love to her.

When he rose, she couldn't meet his gaze directly. She stared at the roughly tied cravat and did her best not to want to fix it. "We are ready."

He nodded, crossed to the door, pistol already in his hand, and eased the door open a crack. After a few minutes, he widened it farther and stepped out into the hall. Mercy waited, pulse pounding when he disappeared from sight and returned again.

It may have been only a moment but that was all it took for Mercy to bury her concerns, at least for the present. They had other problems to face. The madman was still due to call.

"Can I help you by carrying him?" he asked.

Mercy pressed Edwin's head to her shoulder as he shifted subtly toward Leopold. "I can manage."

There must have been a touch of anger in her words because one of Leopold's eyebrows rose.

She hurried forward, along the hall toward the family wing, ignoring the man following in her wake. It would take a while to be comfortable with him again, but until that time, she would behave as a duchess should. She would keep Leopold Randall at arm's length and out of her bed.

She quickened her steps along the hall and slipped into her son's bedchamber. Then, because she was still very out of sorts, she set Edwin on his feet and slammed the door in Leopold's face.

Chapter Eighteen

As the door shut with a loud crash, Leopold blinked in surprise. He'd surmised Mercy had woken in a temper this morning, but he hadn't realized her dissatisfaction lie with him. What he had done between last night and this morning, he couldn't imagine. But her coldness today did remind him that he knew very little about the woman. Maybe she'd had enough of him. Maybe her actions were designed to put him firmly back in his place as her inferior.

Leopold retreated to the chamber across the hall, leaving the door ajar in case he was needed. Mercy had his thoughts spinning, none of them good, none of them satisfactory, and every one determined to drive him wild.

He grabbed a chair and straddled it, resting his arms across the back as he faced the door she had disappeared through. How had he come to be in this situation? How had he forgotten completely what he was here for? It seemed that the moment he'd learned of the threat to Mercy and the child, his whole world had changed direction, and all because he couldn't silence his unease.

Was that truly his cousin's son?

Or was Edwin his child?

A child's parentage mattered to society. Edwin was the legal heir, born within the marriage, and he had inherited the title of duke, the estate, and every responsibility when his father had passed away. But the boy reminded him of his two brothers when they were younger. Similarities he strove to ignore. For the devil's sake, he'd almost embraced the child this morning, and yesterday, when he'd carried the boy through the abbey, he'd thought his heart might burst with joy.

If Edwin was his offspring, he'd never be able to tell a soul, but neither could he turn his back on the boy if he were in any form of danger.

And the danger was coming to Romsey Abbey. He just didn't know from where.

Frustrated, he stood, checked the hall, and then prowled about the room. There was no telling where the danger might lie. Out in the open or already within the abbey walls? How could someone bring a live animal into a building, slaughter it, and no one notice? Wilcox had questioned every servant personally, but none had offered up any clues. Were some in league with this monster, a lover of words and grim offerings?

He didn't know who to trust in this place.

He stopped at the window and looked out. He trusted Wilcox and his valet, Colby—two people in a house full of dozens. And what about Allen and his boys? He claimed to want to live quietly out in the stables without Mercy knowing of his connection to the old duke. But he'd have the means of entering the abbey and leaving the grim gifts about the place. Hardly anyone would wonder what he did. He could very well be the source of the threat. Was he as cold-blooded as the old duke?

Leopold raked his fingers through his hair. Everyone had to be held in suspicion until he got to know them better. Even Mercy herself could not be overlooked. He set his hand to his chest as the memories of her in his arms, against his body, roused his desire. He couldn't even trust those moments with her to be anything more than mutual lust.

He did desire her. She gifted her body without hesitation. But her mind, motives, and her heart were a complete mystery to him. That she loved her son was in no doubt. But would she be happy if her son turned out to be his?

A movement in the distance caught his attention. A carriage rumbled down the drive. As he squinted to see the conveyance more clearly, he recognized it from his first visit to the estate. Mercy had company coming, and he should inform her so she might be ready in good time.

He turned on his heel—but then stopped.

Across the hall, Mercy stood in Edwin's doorway considering him. Her hand was on the door but she neither frowned nor smiled when he noticed her. She just stood there, as if she'd seen a ghost.

"There is a carriage coming up the drive," he said softly.

"Is there?"

Leopold nodded. "Yes. I remember the carriage from the other day. It is the same one that I passed as I came to see you the first time."

"The first time," Mercy said slowly, eyes traveling the length of his body and back.

The effect of her perusal, unfortunately, was immediate. His pulse raced and his arms ached to step forward and embrace her. Leopold quashed the notion as she folded her arms under her breasts. He swallowed. "Do you remember whom the carriage might belong to?"

Her head tilted to one side and she continued to stare at him without blinking. "Lady Barnet visited here a few days ago, along with her brother, Lord Shaw."

Leopold couldn't move. He was pinned in place by the coldness of her stare. For the first time since they had met, she resembled the woman in the drawing room painting downstairs. "Then it might be her carriage. It's not too far away," he warned.

She pursed her lips, called her son to her, and hurried toward her bedchamber.

Leopold hung back, confused by her behavior. He had upset her somehow, he was sure of it. But if she was upset, she was not going to give him any clues on how to make things right between them.

At her door, she stopped. "Are you going to inspect my chamber first or shall we both be slaughtered while you do nothing but stare?"

Puzzled by her hostility, Leopold stepped into her chamber first, checked beneath the wide bed, drapes and connecting chamber then gave her a nod. She flicked her hands at him impatiently and he hurried to the door. But at the threshold, he glanced over his shoulder and found her standing with her face buried in her hands.

Leopold couldn't bear it. He shut the door, ruffled Edwin's hair as he passed the boy, and pulled Mercy into his arms. "Don't fret, love. All will be well soon."

At first, she stood stiffly. It took a few moments before she softened, curling against him with a stifled sob. He stroked her back, comforting her as best he could. He wasn't surprised by her tension. Most people in her situation wouldn't have held up under the strain as well.

After a minute or two, she pushed him away. "I need to get ready for Anna's visit."

"Of course, I'll be waiting for you both outside."

Mercy drew in a shuddering breath. "You cannot stay with me while Anna is here. I should like to be alone with my friend."

If Leopold had felt like a dirty little secret before, he was drowning in muck today. So she did not want her friend to see him at all. He should have known his only use was in her bed. He spun on his heel. "I will await the moment for you to dismiss me then, Your Grace."

"Leopold," she called before his hand had touched the door-knob. "Will you keep Edwin with you during her visit? Anna has no interest in children."

He might not be wanted, but apparently he did have his uses. Minding the child would be no great hardship. He just hoped he didn't fret about Mercy's safety the entire time they were apart.

"Oh, my darling," Anna cried. "You do look under a dreadful strain. Is this Randall chap very vulgar and forward with you? Shaw tells me you couldn't send him away."

Mercy patted her friend's hand. "It's been an interesting week, Anna, but Mr. Randall has been very polite and agreeable."

"Yes, well. I do wish you had written me yourself. It is dreadfully sad when your brother knows more about a dearest friend than you. I must reconcile myself to that future pattern, no doubt. He said you had a cozy tête-à-tête yesterday. Are you coming to London with me next week?"

"Next week?"

Anna leaned against her side and winked. "The change of scenery will do you good. We can go to the theater, dancing, and my brother can court you as you deserve."

Mercy shuddered. She didn't want to be anywhere near Lord Shaw. But how could she tell her best friend that her brother's advances left her cold? There was no way to do it without offending the woman.

"Maybe another time. There is so much here to do just now that I could not possibly leave."

Anna drew back, a frown marring her features. "Are you afraid this Randall chap will take over the abbey in your absence?"

"Of course not. What a thing to suggest." She laughed, remembering she had done everything in her power to make him stay this long. The idea of Leopold wanting Edwin's inheritance was ludicrous, even more so if her suspicions had any truth to them.

Anna shrugged. "I have not slept easily since hearing of his return, and I've spent many an hour wondering what he is about. Why has he come at last?"

Mercy wasn't sure she should confide in Anna about Leopold's missing siblings. Leopold deserved a little loyalty, and certainly his privacy. "The news of his cousin's death did not reach him till recently and he's come to pay his respects. Since he'd traveled so far, I invited him to stay awhile. He is otherwise engaged at the moment, but it has been nice to have him here."

"Nice." Anna bristled. "Only you would call such a man nice. I should have liked to take a peek at him. A gentleman would have made himself known by now. It speaks poorly that he's skulking about here and has not been seen outside the abbey recently."

There were several good reasons why Mercy didn't want to have Leopold meet Anna today. The first, of course, was the threat to her son. Edwin needed protection more than she did. The second, she was still tremendously angry with Leopold. And third, sadly, she didn't know if she could hide how much she admired the blasted scoundrel. Even in her current temper, she found it hard to look away from him.

Anna would see her interest and could never be counted on to hold her tongue.

Her scrutiny would make Leopold uncomfortable— not that he didn't deserve a little discomfort today. He'd likely known he'd bedded the Duchess of Romsey five years ago. He must consider himself quite accomplished to fool her. And, knowing the current duke was likely his child, he'd still returned to the abbey and pretended they'd never met.

Well, maybe she could give him a small concession. She hadn't known her midnight lover's name, either. The room had been black as pitch, they'd not spoken above a whisper, and even then the most they had uttered were gasps and moans. She had never seen him clearly, and he may not have seen her either. She shuddered. Remembering. Feeling her emotions conflict inside her.

Damn him.

"Lady Venables," Wilcox intoned, standing aside so Blythe could join them in the drawing room.

Blythe's face was drawn and pale, so much so that Mercy leaped to her feet and caught up her sister's hands. "What has happened?"

"I'm sorry," she whispered. "I never should have—" The rest of her words died on her tongue as she spotted Anna across the room. "Forgive me. I didn't realize you had company already."

Mercy forced a bigger smile to her lips. "Anna came a while ago but I am very happy to see you. Will you stay and take luncheon with me? I've missed you."

When Mercy embraced Blythe, the hug was returned lightly. "Of course, Your Grace. I'd be happy to join you."

Mercy captured her sister's arm and steered her toward the settee opposite Anna. Anna looked a bit put out when Mercy didn't resume her spot at her side, but she ignored it all in favor of keeping hold of Blythe. She didn't look at all well. When Anna was gone, she would speak privately with her sister.

"And how do you get along, Lady Venables?" Anna asked with a touch of condescension tingeing her words.

"Very well, thank you," Blythe replied. "And you, Lady Barnet?"

Anna turned a bemused smile on Mercy. "I find Her Grace's situation vastly unsettling. Imagine the strain she is under by having that man reside here?"

Blythe frowned. "What man?"

Anna rolled her eyes. "Why, that presumptuous Randall fellow, of course. He is staying here, under this very roof, no doubt plotting to do the poor child in and steal the title for himself. We'll likely need to have Shaw come and remove him by force, I expect. What an outrage to find him encamped here."

Blythe's gaze flickered around the room. "Is that true? Is Randall here now?"

Mercy smiled, cursing Anna under her breath at the same time. "Of course he is here. He is family, after all. How else can one get to know new family without seeing them frequently?"

Blythe frowned. "I'd like to visit with Edwin, if I may."

Mercy patted her hand, but inside, she quaked. Blythe would be difficult about Leopold being here, and about him being alone with Edwin without her supervision. "Perhaps we could go together. Shall we?"

Mercy stood, and since Blythe did too, Anna had no choice but to follow them. When they reached the hall, Mercy could hear her son laughing at the top of his lungs.

Blythe's frown grew and her step quickened, dragging Mercy along with her.

Her sister didn't bother to knock on the door. She simply barged right into the playroom.

But if she hadn't, Mercy would never have seen the look on her son's face as he played with Leopold. The pair was across the room, Leopold lying flat on his back. But Edwin was perched atop his raised feet, arms spread wide as if he were flying. He was having a grand time with his new playmate, and Mercy's heart did little somersaults at the sight.

They looked to be having so much more fun than she was. They were becoming fast friends.

"Put the duke down now!" Blythe shouted.

Mercy restrained her sister. "It's all right, Blythe. He would never have dropped him."

At the request though, Leopold placed Edwin down carefully, and then rolled to his feet, tugging hard on his coat and waistcoat before turning to face them.

Edwin raced forward. "Aunty Bly, Aunty Bly! Did you see me? I was flying!"

Blythe bent over him and checked his arms, face and hands. "I saw you. But that is too dangerous for you, Edwin. You must remember you are a duke."

Edwin ignored her and crashed into Mercy. "I flew, Mama!"

Mercy brushed her fingers over his flushed cheeks. "Did you thank Mr. Randall for the pleasure?"

Edwin's face fell slightly. He turned slowly, and then flew back across the room into Leopold's legs. "Thank you!" It was like watching a whirlwind. Edwin was giddy with joy.

Leopold bent to whisper in Edwin's ear, and her son ran off to play with his toys.

Anna, ignored by Edwin so far, swept past Mercy toward Leopold. "Now I see why my friend was in no great hurry for us to become acquainted." She boldly held out her hand. "Lady Barnet."

Leopold's gaze flickered to Mercy then at the hand held out to him. He caught it briefly. "Leopold Randall, at your service."

When Anna eyed him appreciatively, Mercy ground her teeth. That was quite enough of that sort of thing. Mercy knew that look. It was the same one that crossed Anna's face when she saw something she intended to have. She wanted Leopold. *Her* Leopold.

The hot sting of jealousy burned through her breast. She drew Blythe forward. "You remember my sister, Mr. Randall, don't you?"

Leopold stepped away from Anna. "Of course. It's a pleasure to see you, Lady Venables. Her Grace has missed your company."

Blythe nodded, but didn't speak to him. However, she watched him just as carefully as Anna did, her gaze wary and full of distrust. Poor Leopold appeared decidedly uncomfortable.

Thank heavens this situation was so tense that he wasn't smiling. Because if he did smile, or laugh, Anna and Blythe might notice he and Edwin had matching dimples. She'd been a fool not to notice the likeness from the very beginning. Her son was undoubtedly of Leopold's making. But what could she do about it now?

"Well, then. I'll leave you ladies to spoil the lad." Leopold stopped beside her shoulder. "He's been asking after you. I've just sent the maid to the kitchen in search of a treat for him."

A quick smile eluded Mercy's control as she watched her son at play. "I'll see you at dinner, Mr. Randall. Enjoy your afternoon."

"Of course, Your Grace."

The tone he used, so reminiscent of their first meeting, made Mercy's heart skip a beat. She might be confused about his part in their past encounter, but she didn't want too great a distance to spring up between them. She flicked out her fingers and discreetly brushed them across the back of his hand. The touch sent a short spark of lightning along her nerves.

Mercy held herself rigidly in place as the desire to follow him, fling herself into his arms, grew. She couldn't do that while Anna and Blythe were here. But she had to sort through her emotions before she embraced him again.

The door shut with a soft click.

"Well, no wonder you will not come up to Town." Anna fanned herself with her hand. "What a lover he'd make."

Mercy did not like the sound of Anna's speculation. Although she wanted to stay mad with Leopold, she didn't want to share him either—which meant that she'd already forgiven him for not revealing his knowledge of their past association.

Wearily, Mercy turned for a chair and sat. She was very much attached to the dratted man, and it had only taken three nights in his arms, including their first night when she didn't know him at all. If she spent more time with him, would she ever let him go?

"You're not seriously suggesting that Mercy should pursue him," Blythe asked, shock evident in her tone. "He's an upstart."

Anna laughed. "Lady Venables, you are simply too naïve. A man with a presence such as that is perfect for a diverting, temporary dalliance. A grateful man is always the most willing to give a woman pleasure."

Mercy's heart revolted at her friend's words. How could she say such things about Leopold, or about any man? She'd have to stop this conversation or they might not remain friends. She cleared her throat. "You are speaking of my family, my son's family, Anna. I would appreciate it if you kept such thoughts to yourself."

Blythe gasped.

Anna smiled. "Of course, Your Grace. Forgive me for speaking out of turn. But you must admit, he truly is delicious to look at. If only he was a man you could trust, eh?"

Mercy licked her lips, suddenly afraid of Anna's quick apology. Had she guessed by her quick defense of him that she and Leopold were already lovers, and that Mercy had no intention of turning him away should the opportunity arise? She smoothed her skirts, suddenly self-conscious. "I think I shall have luncheon brought forward. Are you both hungry?"

"Not me," Anna replied quickly. "If you will excuse me, I have another call to make today."

"Of course, Anna." Mercy rose and kissed her friends cheeks. "Thank you for your visit. Do come again another day."

"I'll make a point of it, you can be certain of that." Anna swept out, and then it was just Mercy and Blythe alone, with Edwin playing quietly at their feet.

Blythe leaned forward. "Tell me you had no choice but to have him stay here?"

Mercy shook her head. "That wasn't how his invitation came about, Blythe, but I do need him here. There's been another letter since I saw you last. I've confided in Leopold, and he believes trouble is coming for Edwin. I must protect him, and Leopold is willing to help me do that."

Blythe scowled.

Mercy clasped her sister's hands and squeezed. She wanted peace between Blythe and Leopold more than anything. "You saw them together. Leopold is no danger to my son. There have been many instances where he could have harmed the boy, and he's done nothing more than play harmless games with him. Now that Leopold is aware of the threat, he has promised to do everything he can to protect Edwin. He is part of Edwin's family, after all."

"That may be so, but who will protect you from *him*?"

"Oh, Blythe, this is not the time to worry about propriety. I cannot do this alone anymore. You have no idea how often I have lain awake at night fretting over it all. Our brother scoffed at the first letters and will not come. I need a man I can trust. Leopold remains at Romsey Abbey."

Blythe rocked back a little. "Sister, I can see a disaster coming.

You know your own character. You will become besotted with him within a week, and then what will you do?"

Too late for that warning. Too late by five years. It had only taken one night for Mercy to crave Leopold Randall. Five years to know who he really was.

She would have to hide how she felt from Blythe better. She would have to make sure no one ever suspected Edwin was not her husband's true offspring. She would have to keep the secret of his conception forever locked away, even if it broke her heart to do so.

Chapter Nineteen

Leopold pushed off the low stone wall as Allen's two sons disappeared into the stables on an errand. The Romsey stables, a mammoth domed building of brick and glass, were quiet at this time of day. Only Allen labored at chores in the yard, rubbing down a gelding that had recently been exercised. His cousin worked with single-minded intensity, barely glancing up when Leopold joined him.

He had intended to wait until Allen was done with the task, but the man seemed in no hurry to engage in conversation. The old duke had done that in his day, too. He would pretend not to notice someone and make them wait or—heaven forbid—interrupt him so he had an excuse to be annoyed.

Just how much like the old duke was Allen? Although he searched his memory, Leopold couldn't remember what Allen had been like as a younger man.

He crossed the yard and approached Allen as he changed sides. The gelding fidgeted a bit, but Allen soothed the beast with firm strokes and soft words. "The building is still grand, isn't it?" Allen said without preamble.

Leopold looked up at the fanciful turrets that no one could enter and grimaced at the extravagance. "The old duke did love to house his horses in luxury."

Allen straightened, patting the horse. "Not that they care or notice. Like this fellow here, all he wants is a rub, food and water, and to gallop as often as he can. The stables need a bit of work done around the back. I hear you're the man to go to if something needs fixing."

"I am for the moment. The duchess will be hiring a new steward soon, but I will make a note of your concerns and see they are attended to."

"The walls could do with a lick of paint and a couple of panes of glass cracked last winter."

Leopold nodded. That wasn't too bad in the scheme of things. Some of the other outbuildings were in a sorrier state. "I'll see that it's taken care of."

"Much obliged. The horses don't care for the draft." Allen glanced at him sideways. "But that's not why you're here. What brings you to me, Mr. Randall?"

"Trouble."

Allen shrugged. "Nothing unusual there for a Randall."

"No," Leopold said quietly. "We were an unruly bunch in the past. However, in this instance, I have good reason to be concerned."

"Concerns your boy, then?"

Leopold ground his teeth, and then forced his jaw to work again. "It concerns the duke, yes."

Allen chuckled. "Don't get on the high ropes with me. You sounded just like your father when he was in a snit. Anyone with eyes and a good memory can tell that boy wasn't of the fifth Duke of Romsey's making. He's not a sickly child, is he? He looks like you."

Damnation! Was the resemblance that obvious?

Allen looked around, spotted his eldest child waiting in the stables' shadows, and then led the horse toward him. Once the beast had been passed over, and the youth had disappeared, Allen came back.

Leopold crossed his arms over his chest, determined to ignore the comment about Edwin's parentage. "Do you know what's been going on around here?"

Allen smacked his hands over his trousers. "Not much. Wilcox is watching everyone like a hawk, which does seem out of the ordinary. Usually, he's not such a stick in the mud. And he's become secretive when he comes out of the abbey. I don't know where he's going, but he looks like he's swallowed a turnip whole."

"He's had good reason for the secrecy."

"Such as?" Allen asked.

Tell the truth or leave him in the dark? If Allen was not involved, he could be useful. If he was involved, Leopold would be tipping his hat that he was aware of the danger posed to Edwin. Leopold did not want to believe that Allen could be a danger. "The duke has an enemy."

Allen snorted. "He's too young to have one yet. That takes years of scheming to arrange." He turned away, heading back toward the stables as if the matter was of no importance.

Leopold followed. "There have been letters sent to the abbey threatening him harm."

Allen slowed his steps. "Anyone can write nasty letters. What makes you think they are serious in their intent?"

"At first, I didn't. I thought they were love letters to the duchess."

"That must have got your hackles up. I've seen how you follow her about. She is lively, too kind by half for the likes of my sainted late brother. The only thing good about the marriage is that we have a bright spot of merriment most days when she's haring about."

Now that was interesting. If Allen were the one threatening Mercy and Edwin, he'd have had ample time to do the deed already. By his own admission, he had confessed to holding a soft spot for Mercy. "There have also been intruders in the abbey, or perhaps it's a servant doing work other than what the duchess pays them for."

Allen's eyes narrowed to slits. "What kind of work?"

"It's a grim business. Wilcox is finding and disposing of slaughtered animals. They have been left in the duchess' bedchamber, and in other well-used parts of the abbey, I'm told."

"Dear God! Why the hell wasn't I informed about this? Father would be spinning in his grave at the idea of strangers making free with his possessions. You know how he was about the abbey."

Leopold let out a sigh of relief. Allen wasn't involved. Not with that attitude. "Yes, I remember. But why would you be told specifically? It is my understanding that the duchess does not even know who you are."

"That bloody Wilcox does, however. Did the little turnip think that I might be responsible?" Allen's hands curled into fists. "I'll kill him for keeping me in the dark."

When Allen made to shoot past Leopold on his way to a side

entrance to the abbey, Leopold caught his arm and held him in place. "Wilcox said nothing about you, about any of it, actually, until I pressed for more information. I don't even know if the duchess would have confessed to it at all if I had not read that first letter."

Allen shook off his grip. "There have been more than enough secrets here to last a dozen lifetimes. Family should not hurt one another. Your side was the only part that was kind."

"So, we are in agreement then. The young duke and duchess must be protected at all costs."

Allen adjusted his sleeve and a small blade slid into the palm of his hand. "We have an accord. Wilcox is coming."

Leopold turned. "Put the knife away, cousin. We might just need to keep Wilcox a while yet."

Wilcox gestured wildly. "Come. Come!"

He fled back toward the abbey.

Leopold glanced at Allen, and then they both followed Wilcox at a run. The butler stopped at the side door, waited for them to catch up, and then led them both upstairs. At Mercy's bedchamber door, Leopold's heart raced. *What the devil has happened now?*

Without a word, Leopold stepped into the room first. And then wished he hadn't.

"Bugger me!" Allen exclaimed.

Leopold wished he could feel as surprised. Another small creature lay slain in the room, its blood splashed in a wide arc over Mercy's bed. The dead staring eyes sent a chill through him.

"You have to get them away from here," Allen said suddenly. "Somewhere safe. Maybe take her to the London townhouse and engage more staff to watch over them."

Wilcox sighed. "That has already been suggested many a time, but she simply won't leave. She is adamant that she will not be run off no matter what."

Now he was seeing this scene, one similar to those described to him before, it surprised Leopold that Mercy hadn't already fled the estate for the safety of friends or family. But she stayed, practically alone, ignoring this monster and caring for her son. Not for the first time did Leopold wonder why she hadn't done the expected thing and run away from the coming trouble.

Allen inspected the creature, and then stood back. "Whoever did this is good with a knife. I take back my earlier kind words. The duchess is a fool."

"Watch your mouth, cousin."

"What would you do if I don't? Shoot me?" A bitter laugh broke from Allen's mouth. "I've been threatened with that before, by my own brother no less, and you don't have the bollocks to do the deed."

Leopold raked his hands through his hair. "There is always a first time." He paced the room. "Lady Barnet and the duchess' sister were both here today. It could be someone attending them."

"It could be either lady as well," Allen said quickly.

"Nonsense," Wilcox scoffed. "Lady Barnet and Lady Venables may not like each other but they both love the duchess. They would never wish to hurt her."

"Are you defending that sanctimonious harridan? Didn't I hear Lady Venables tried to get you dismissed last month?"

"I may have deserved that." Wilcox smiled nervously at Leopold. "She does not care for me speaking my mind to the duchess, even when Her Grace seeks out my opinion. I should have waited until Lady Venables had moved out of earshot before speaking up."

Blythe did seem the kind to cling to proper decorum. Mercy's consideration of a servant's suggestion would likely set her teeth on edge. "I believe I understand your dilemma. What was the discussion about, by the way?"

"It was to do with the duke. Her Grace asked my opinion on providing him with a pet for company. Lady Venables believed him to be too young, but she says that about almost everything involving the duke."

A trifling matter, and not one that a servant should be dismissed over. "It is interesting that this latest development occurred on a day when Lady Venables was here."

Wilcox nodded. "She was here the day of the last one, too. Lady Barnet had been here earlier in the day, but had already departed before the discovery was made."

Leopold shook his head. He had a lead, two leads, but in both cases, the path to finding the culprit was unclear.

Perhaps the first thing he should do is become better acquainted with Mercy's sister. She was already here in the abbey and, according to the note he'd received, was expected to dine with them tonight. The next time Lady Barnet visited, he'd find out what made her tick, too.

As far as mistakes went, this fiasco was probably Mercy's finest. She had thought that, by inviting Leopold to dine with her and Blythe, her sister might have become better acquainted with him. Or at least become comfortable in his company.

Sadly, that was not to be the case. Blythe glared daggers at Leopold while he replied politely to her impetuous questions about his past, present, and future plans. It was a tense battle of wits that was bringing Mercy a megrim.

She should still be angry with Leopold. He had deceived her, manipulated her, and shared her bed without a word about their past. However, Blythe appeared annoyed enough for both of them at the present. She didn't want Leopold to think he wasn't wanted at Romsey, or that he could leave whenever he chose to go. He was not going anywhere until she had some answers that satisfied her. But at the rate this was going, he would be gone before sunrise.

She licked her lips nervously at the idea. "I saw you out by the stables earlier. Is anything amiss?"

He shook his head. "Simply admiring one of the horses and thinking it will be a good long while before the duke is old enough to ride them. Has he sat a pony yet?"

"The duke is too young," Blythe cut in.

Leopold regarded Blythe, a friendly smile on his face. "At what age would you suggest he be introduced to the saddle? It is my understanding that my cousin sat a horse from the age of two, or so he boasted. My parents were somewhat tardier than that. I had to wait for Oliver to be old enough to sit our pony, and then I had to share it with him."

Mercy liked the sound of Leopold's parents. They had been very practical-minded people. She cleared her throat. "We rode later, as well. Mother was terrified of horses and would not let us girls near them. My brother was already cantering about when we got our first chance at the experience. Constantine used to tease us that we were as slow as snails."

"That's what brother's do best. Tease." His gaze slewed back toward Blythe as he waited on her response.

Blythe shot him a defiant look. "Not before he turns five."

"Good. That gives us ample time to find a suitably quiet mount that will plod about, despite all the urgent kicks the boy is bound to inflict. There is not a horse like that out in the stable, unfortunately. My cousin has only excitable beasts, and they simply will not do for an inexperienced rider."

Oh, bravo, Leopold! With one answer, he had effectively foiled Blythe's fears, cited family tradition, and had taken her advice on the matter of Edwin learning to ride. Not many had handled Blythe so masterfully before. Usually, they tried to tell her she worried too much.

Blythe's lips pursed, and then she returned to her dinner without further comment.

Mercy glanced at Leopold. He offered a brief smile, flashed his dimples, and then he too returned to dining quietly at her side. How could she stay mad at him when he did everything else so well?

The problem vexed her. If he was not being honest with her about sharing her bed five years ago, should she necessarily distrust everything else he said and did?

Then there was his closer-than-expected relationship to Edwin that he never alluded to. He had never given her any hint that he wanted more to do with the boy than he should. If not for the problems facing them, he'd been determined to get his answers and leave immediately thereafter.

Mercy sat back in her chair to ponder her feelings. She was… disappointed. Angry. But when she thought about it, she wasn't even angry with Leopold. She was angry with her husband, and certainly furious with the old duke above all. They had known who was coming to her bed, and why he had been chosen for the task. For the continuation of the family bloodline. She simply could not imagine Leopold being a party to a seduction unless he was given no choice in the matter.

"Is something wrong, Your Grace?" Blythe asked.

Mercy forced a smile. "No, just thinking about the future."

Leopold pushed his plate away, and then motioned to Wilcox that the servants could be dismissed. Wilcox glanced at her and Mercy nodded in agreement.

When they were gone, Leopold addressed Blythe. "The duchess has been kind enough to take me into her confidence about the madman stalking her. I am greatly concerned and determined to protect my cousin from harm. He is too young for such strife in his life. But I am equally concerned about *your* welfare."

A frown line in Blythe's forehead appeared. "My welfare?"

Leopold sat forward. "I am concerned that this man may try to harm the duke through you. You live alone, just as Her Grace has these last years. You are vulnerable."

Blythe's spine stiffened. "I am not vulnerable. I can look after myself."

"I am sure you are safe in your own home, but the distance between the two properties worries me. Anything could happen to you, and we would not know until it was too late. Would you consent to stay here in the abbey? It would set my mind at ease, and the duchess' too, I'm sure, to have you safely under this roof."

Blythe shook her head violently. "I'm needed at home."

Mercy frowned at her words. There was no one waiting for Blythe at home anymore. Her husband and son had passed away. Walden Hall only waited for its mistress' return and would not miss Blythe for another night.

She set her hand on her sister's, and was startled by how cold Blythe's skin had become. "I would love for you to stay with us."

Blythe's gaze switched to stare at Leopold. "I will be perfectly fine on my own. You need have no concern for me."

Mercy rubbed her arm. "Please, Blythe. It is not just the danger. I would enjoy your company."

Blythe shook her head, and then stood. "I have a headache coming on. Do excuse me?"

She rushed for the door and, although Mercy followed and encouraged her to change her mind, she would not bend.

As the carriage rolled off, Leopold tugged Mercy away from

the open doorway. "I didn't mean to frighten her away like that. I had honestly hoped she would remain here with you and the boy."

Mercy's heart ached. "I know what you intended. Blythe is difficult at the best of times."

They walked to the library and Leopold shut the door behind them. "She's had good reason to be unhappy with her lot in life. She must get lonely."

"You would think that to be the case, but it is rare I can get her to visit with me for any longer than a day. It is as if she is waiting for her husband and son to return. I've tried to jolly her out of her mourning, but she resists. The only time she seems truly happy is when she is with Edwin."

"He is a wonderful boy," Leopold said quietly.

She met his gaze and held it. "He reminds me of his father."

At that, Leopold's expression grew grim, and he turned away. Mercy watched him pace the room. His posture had stiffened, his hands were clasped behind his back, and he did not look at her for a long time.

She sank into a chair as the possibility, no, the likelihood of Leopold being Edwin's father refused to go away. Did she mind that it could have been him? Did she care enough for it to make a difference between them? Would she change the past and undo Edwin's creation?

The answer to all three questions was no.

She stood again and placed herself in Leopold's path. He stopped suddenly, eyeing her warily. His uncertainty tugged at her heart. "I think we should go to bed now. It's already past Edwin's bedtime."

Chapter Twenty

In the space of a day, Leopold's usefulness to Mercy had gone from one extreme to another. This morning, Mercy had been cold, aloof, and dismissive of his attempts to help. By evening, her drowsy bedroom eyes had brought to mind a woman considering him for a night of pleasure. But then she'd asked him to carry her sleeping child to bed and that troubled him. Their procession up the grand staircase seemed horribly domestic.

He led Mercy along the hall, breathing in the scent of a certain sleepy small boy, and instead of turning down the hall to the family wing, he climbed to another level and stepped into a disused guest bedchamber. The room wasn't too bad for one night, but it was cold, and he was grateful he'd snuck up here earlier and stored some extra blankets. They might need them before the night was through.

Leopold, however, intended to stand watch all night and had no need for a bed.

Edwin grumbled as Leopold set him on yet another strange bed and rolled onto his side. Instinctively, Leopold covered him with the sheets, retrieved extra blankets and tucked them around his body as he had seen Mercy do last night.

When he turned, Mercy stood watching him. Yet this time her gaze had softened to one of pleasant warmth.

Leopold's pulse pounded in response, and he fussed with the bedclothes before withdrawing Mercy's satchel from under the bed. It held a nightgown, a comb, and a thick shawl. Thinking of those personal items helped to control his emotions. He was here to do a job—protect them—and not become emotionally attached to his charges. He couldn't guard them if he was constantly battling his growing feelings for the pair.

Mercy stilled his fussing with a gentle touch and drew him

away from the bed. She stood with moonlight spilling over her shoulders and fairly took his breath away. When she stepped into his arms, he didn't protest. She looked him right in the eye as she brought his head down within her reach. Her lips brushed softly, teasing a man pushed beyond endurance. Leopold tightened his grip for a deeper, more satisfying kiss.

A soft moan erupted from her mouth and the sound thrilled him. But the boy was too near for comfort. Leopold moved them away from the bed toward a connecting door. The room was empty, lit only by moonlight from the open drapes but secure enough to engage in a little temptation without leaving the boy unprotected.

Mercy went willingly, her hands on his clothing, tugging and pulling until she exposed his skin. What Leopold wanted was Mercy—her skin beneath his lips, her taste on his tongue. He settled her to a low chair and dropped to his knees.

Mercy's sigh was loud as he ran his hands up her legs, beneath her gown. He teased the material higher until the soft white of her thighs was exposed above her stockings. Her legs trembled under his hands, and he dropped his head to press his lips against her warm skin. She sighed again as Leopold kissed higher. He tugged until her bottom rested on the edge of the chair, and then settled comfortably at her feet. He urged her legs apart.

Moonlight illuminated the dark patch of hair at the apex of her thighs. He gently combed his fingers through the strands until he touched dampness. He rested his head against her inner thigh while he probed deeper. She was wet, warm, and open for their pleasure. But he would only give *her* pleasure tonight. His could wait. He'd waited for years to pleasure a woman of her passion, but they did not have long tonight.

Leopold pressed his lips to her skin again and licked a path toward his fingers. Mercy shuddered when he reached her opening and he tasted her desire on his tongue. All his—just for this brief space of time allowed. Leopold lifted one of her legs over his shoulder as he kissed her. The soft moan above his head, the fingers tightening on his scalp, made his cock swell for release from confinement.

He pushed into Mercy with one finger, feeling her depths grip him as he set his mouth to her tender skin. Mercy hissed and wriggled as he lapped at her nub. But she was open, pinned in place by his mouth and hands, and didn't fight him too hard for release. He curled his tongue over the hard bud and sucked gently while his finger moved in and out of her body. He loved her taste, loved the power of giving her pleasure, and the way she couldn't hide how aroused she was.

All because of him.

He lifted his mouth when her moans grew too loud, startled that her release appeared imminent. He wouldn't grant her mercy so soon. Not at least until he wished it. Leopold added another finger inside her as he looked up along her body. Her careless abandon, bedroom eyes, and parted lips inflamed him. He widened her legs farther and carefully added another finger to her depths. The fit was tight, constricting. He loved that she would allow him this.

He dropped his head, painfully aroused by her responsiveness, and lapped at her nub again. She breathed in rough pants as he moved his fingers, as he drew upon the tight nub to increase her pleasure. All of a sudden she stiffened, body clamping on his fingers, and sobbed. Leopold swiftly covered her mouth with his free hand, smiling that she'd made so much noise.

He stilled his fingers when she twitched away and slowly withdrew them from her body. He pressed a quick kiss to her folds and then sat up.

Mercy's leg slid from his shoulder with an inelegant thump. Her breath churned in and out.

Leopold, despite having blue balls, was quite proud of himself.

He rolled to his feet, ignoring his own unfulfilled desires, and left Mercy to check that their activities had not disturbed the boy. Edwin still slept, so he pushed the door closed again and returned to Mercy.

Mercy tossed her head from side to side. "You astound me, Leopold."

He grinned and tugged her gown over her knees. "How so, sweetheart?"

Mercy's face broke into a huge grin at his endearment. "I have been led to believe that most men would take what they want first.

You prove them all wrong. Why have you stopped, Leopold? Do you not want to feel as good as you made me feel?"

"Of course I do." Most men would hardly find themselves in this situation. He had to take particular care not to leave Mercy with her belly full. He would have to abstain to save her future embarrassment. "It's just too great a risk."

"Do you mean the danger coming to Romsey, or the danger of wanting to stay here with me?"

He smiled at her and slid a lock of dark hair behind her ear. "Both. I cannot protect you like this. I will be more vigilant after tonight, I promise."

Mercy stood and Leopold backed up two paces. She was delightfully disheveled, with her flushed cheeks and rumpled skirts. "You will protect us. I am sure of it. But remember that I am here for you, too. I may be a duchess, but I am not so selfish as to deny you pleasure. If you think it too dangerous tonight to continue, so be it. But I warn you that I will find a way to repay for every pleasure you bestow on me."

Leopold shook his head.

Mercy settled her finger over his lips. "Shh, Leopold. Not tonight. But later, you and I will have a long and very necessary chat. Now, I think I should retire so that you may be easy again." She lifted onto the balls of her feet and pressed a kiss to his cheek. "Goodnight, my dear sir."

Mercy stepped back, turned, and disappeared from the room. His cock ached again from that simple affectionate kiss, and he wished he could call her back. But the night was passing, and he had family to protect.

He eased open the door to the hall and listened for any sound. When none greeted him, he closed the door and slipped into the other room. Mercy had already changed into her nightgown and was just settling in next to her son, so he pulled the blankets higher up her chest, and pressed a kiss to her hair.

She snuggled down for sleep without a word and Leopold was profoundly grateful. He didn't want to preempt the discussion she felt they needed because he feared she would ask him to stay with her forever. To his vexation, he didn't know how he might answer anymore. Always in the past, his answer was certain: he would leave Romsey behind like a bad memory. Unfortunately, the good was now outweighing the bad.

He crossed to the window, stood concealed behind the drapes and peeked outside. Romsey Abbey's grounds were lit as bright as day by the moonlight, and Leopold was pleased. He could see the north drive and eastern fields as if it were early morning. If he moved to the next chamber, he would have an even greater view. But he was hesitant to move so far away from Mercy and Edwin.

There was a chance they might call for him during the night. Another foolish thought. They hardly needed him as it was.

Leopold straightened as a shadow moved across the grounds.

The figure was human, dressed in a flapping coat and trousers, but without a hat covering their longish hair. His heart raced as the person avoided the main door and approached the abbey's lower windows.

The stranger tried window after window, and Leopold strained to see them when they disappeared out of sight. Whoever it was seemed very determined to get inside the Abbey. It couldn't be a servant; they'd have gone around to the servants' entrance immediately and knocked.

After a few tense moments, the shape came back into view, but this time the stranger scanned the upper floors where Leopold hid.

Leopold ducked out of sight, fearing the moonlight might illuminate his location. He did not want the stranger to know they were observed.

But Leopold couldn't hide forever, not when someone prowled the exterior of the building. He eased the drape back an inch, peering out on the grounds again.

The stranger was gone. No trace of them remained anywhere on the grounds, and although Leopold kept watch until the early morning sun lightened the horizon, he gained no further sightings. All he had gathered as to the stranger's identity was that the person was fully grown and determined. But at this distance, he couldn't tell for certain whether the stranger was male or female.

Mercy roused herself from the worst sleep of her life. She had heard every movement, every soft breath that Leopold had taken during the night, or so it seemed. She rubbed at her eyes wearily and turned for her son. But Edwin was gone from the bed.

Alarmed, she looked around wildly. The room was empty, but then voices drifted in from the connecting chamber. Leopold's deep rumbling tones and Edwin's piping queries. She drew her knees up under her chin to listen.

Edwin asked a lot of questions. Leopold never sounded like his next answer would be his last. He had much more patience than Mercy did at this hour of the morning. There was nothing harder than to give a satisfactory answer when you were half asleep in bed. If she had been lucky to have been blessed with more children, Edwin would not be as alone as he was now. She had only conceived once during her marriage. Edwin was destined to be an only child.

Perhaps if Leopold could be convinced to stay here at the abbey, and he managed to find Oliver, Rosemary, and Tobias, Edwin might have the benefit of cousins to play with one day. It wouldn't be as good as having real siblings at his side though. She had always wanted him to have the kind of childhood she'd had.

As little Mercy Hunt, eldest girl in a family of four, life had been very sweet and uncomplicated. It was only when she had grown older and married that she'd discovered life did not always go according to plan.

Like discovering that your new lover was really an old one.

No matter how she tried to turn aside the idea, it had taken a firm hold in her mind. Leopold had deceived her, had shared her bed since arriving and never said a word. Yet he had not attempted to impose on her either. That had been all Mercy's doing. His obvious restraint, as Mercy had teased him, was the only impediment to their relationship progressing. Could he not want more from her than pleasure?

She wanted him very, very badly for so much more than that. So much more that she shocked herself with her sudden decision.

She could marry him, and give Edwin brothers and sisters to play with as soon as it could be done.

Edwin giggled.

Mercy lifted her head as he dropped into her lap.

Edwin bowled her over and planted wet kisses on her lips. "Mama, I woke up so early!"

"Did you now? And what did you do while I was sleeping?"

His gaze shot to Leopold. "We played I spy." Edwin burrowed under the covers completely, playing under the sheets.

"Good morning, Your Grace." Leopold's smile was as warm as the deep chocolate of his eyes. "We didn't want to disturb your rest too soon. I hope you don't mind that I kept him occupied in the other room."

Impulsively, she reached for his cravat and pulled him down until their faces were close. His eyes were red-rimmed. "Good morning, Leopold. Did you get any sleep at all?"

His gaze darted to where Edwin hid beside her. "Some."

Mercy shook her head. "I think you are a terrible liar, Leopold."

"Of course, Your Grace." He winked and tried to rise but Mercy kept hold.

She tugged until their lips connected and kissed him soundly.

He pulled back quickly. "Don't."

Edwin emerged from the bedding with a wide grin on his face. Leopold stared at him, but Edwin had not noticed the kiss. He was oblivious to anything but his games. Mercy ruffled Edwin's hair as she climbed out of bed. Leopold backed away.

"He will have to grow used to such things, Leopold. My parents kissed each other in front of their children quite often. I could tell the mood of their marriage by the way they kissed. My parents never hid their affection, and I shall do the same before Edwin."

Leopold stepped back farther. "We are not married, nor shall we ever be. All you will teach him is wickedness."

Mercy pressed her lips together over a laugh. Poor Leopold really had no idea that she intended to keep him for the rest of his life. Strong emotions were impossible to contain, and Mercy had no intention of trying anymore. She would avoid scandal if at all possible, but she would have Leopold at her side for the rest of her life or die trying.

Mercy prowled after him. "Is that how you think of me, as a

wicked woman of low morals? I think the pair of us knows the truth of that."

He shook his head. "You don't know the first thing about me. I should never have come home." He glanced at Edwin. "I will leave the minute the danger has passed."

"You will not." Mercy gathered up her robe, slipped it on, and belted it around her waist before she spoke again. "You still have to find your family. We both know your best chance of success is remaining here. With us. We are family too, or had you forgotten."

Leopold swallowed. "I have not forgotten."

But he still did not say directly that he had a closer acquaintance to Edwin than he was supposed to have. Would he never admit his part in that night?

Vexed, Mercy moved away from him to the window and stared out. Why would he not want to claim her son even privately as his own? Edwin was a good boy, healthy and sturdy, and so unlike her husband's disposition that she felt incredibly stupid not to have realized that her midnight lover could have been Leopold.

She turned slowly, catching Leopold watching her son. His expression was open and the raw look he directed at the playing child made her heart clench. Perhaps he did want to claim her son, but was hesitant to do so. Under the circumstances, he might expect her to be angry about the deception.

She had been. Yesterday.

Today, she wanted to build a bridge and create a new life. With Leopold smack dab in the middle of it. Filling her belly again and making this place come alive with the sound of many voices. With more Randalls.

She crossed the room and slipped her hand into his.

His fingers tightened about hers. Strong, steady, sure. "Are you ready to depart, Your Grace?"

"Yes, Leopold." She leaned against his shoulder. "We are ready to go whenever you wish it."

His thumb caressed her knuckles. "May I carry Edwin? I'd like to move swiftly through the halls in case danger lurks."

She squeezed his hand as a lump formed in her throat. "You never need ask that again."

He released her hand and stepped up beside the bed. "Come along, Your Grace. You have a busy day ahead of you."

Edwin rolled toward the end of the bed. "Will you take me riding today like you promised?"

Leopold lifted Edwin to his knees. "Not today, but I think I could convince Cook to whip up some pastries. Would you like to help him dust them?"

Edwin nodded briskly. "I should like that very much."

He allowed Leopold to pick him up and carry him back to his room. A servant was waiting outside.

"All is quiet, Mr. Randall."

Leopold nodded, and then shifted Edwin in his arms. "Your Grace, may I present my valet to you. This is Colby. He will be keeping you company for a short time, if your mother is agreeable. If you grow bored later, ask Colby to sing. He has a very fine voice."

The valet scowled at his employer, but then smiled quickly for her son. Edwin threw himself at the valet and they disappeared inside her son's chamber.

Leopold caught her elbow. "We need to talk."

Hope soared in her breast. Had he been waiting until they could be alone before he would confess to their past encounter?

He harried her along to her bedchamber, but once inside, he released her arm and rang the bell three times. Mercy sat on a chair with a thump. She didn't need the butler to hear this confession. She only wanted truth spoken between them, and then she would let the matter rest. "Well?"

"I'd rather say this only once. We will wait for Wilcox to arrive."

Mercy frowned at him, but Leopold merely paced the chamber.

When the door finally opened, Leopold stalked toward Wilcox. "He was here last night, in the grounds, outside the windows of the abbey."

Wilcox looked about them wildly. "Are you sure?"

"As sure as I can be without leaving the duchess' side." Leopold raked his fingers through his hair. "There one minute and gone the next. They could be hiding any bloody where. I'd hoped to catch a glimpse of a direction when they left but they were too quick."

Wilcox wrung his hands. "What can we do?"

"We need to change places. Tonight, I want you at the duchess' side. My valet will also be with you to help guard the boy."

Mercy stood. She didn't like the sound of this. "Where will you be?"

"I'm going hunting."

Leopold dropped his hand to his coat pocket where Mercy knew a small weapon resided. She shook her head. "No. I won't allow it. You put yourself in danger unnecessarily."

"I will not sit quietly while he roams the grounds at will. I will not allow him to come any closer to you or Edwin. I will stop him tonight, and that will be the end of it."

Mercy covered her face with her hands. What he suggested was terrifyingly dangerous. He could be hurt himself. Left to die out on the grounds, and she would never know until it was too late.

Warm hands guided her into a chair and settled on her head.

"It is the only way to keep you both safe. Remain here with Wilcox and let me deal with the problem. I have my uses."

Mercy lifted her head and stared at him through blurry eyes. "I need you."

His fingertips caressed her jaw. "I'm sorry."

She leaned into his touch and kissed his palm. "I will not sleep a wink while you are gone and will expect to see you first thing in the morning to prove you are safe."

"As you wish, Your Grace."

A door clicked closed.

Leopold sighed. "Now Wilcox knows for certain that we are involved."

"I do not care, and you know it."

Leopold sighed again, dug into his pocket, and held out his small pistol. "Keep this with you at all times. Fire only should it become absolutely necessary." He moved toward the door. "Go about your day as usual, but stay within the abbey. We will all be watching over you and Edwin."

When he hurried away, Mercy let her tears fall down her

cheeks. Now she would worry about him the whole of the day, if he intended to keep a distance.

She scrubbed at her cheeks and drew in a deep breath. She had to get through today, get through tonight, and then she would tie Leopold Randall to a chair if necessary and demand he fall in love with her before it was too late.

There simply was no other acceptable way to go on.

Chapter Twenty-One

Leopold finished stacking the table with firearms and looked at them grimly. To think his life had turned so far around that he might be required to defend the Duke of Romsey with his own life. The old bastard had known his character well when he'd sent him to Mercy's bed. He'd never harm his own child and never turn his back if he were in danger. He was soft where family was concerned, and the old bastard had counted on it.

He cursed under his breath and wiped at his stinging eyes. Weariness tugged at his senses but he couldn't sleep. He had to finish this task, check on Wilcox minding Mercy, and then he could catch a few hours' rest before night fell.

Methodically, he cleaned each weapon and readied them for firing, thinking about where he could place them around the abbey; several to the drawing room and library, one behind the potted plant on the staircase, another within the suit of armor at the top. All logical choices, all places a servant might stumble upon and start asking questions. He'd have to get more creative than this.

He needed more men. He needed people he trusted at his side to guard Mercy and the boy. He wracked his brain for someone in the district with unquestioned loyalty to him and to Mercy.

Eamon Murphy sprang to mind immediately. The man might be the biggest gossip known to mankind, but he was loyal, and that made him perfect for Leopold's needs. He jotted a note to him, summoning him to the abbey as quickly as he could come, and stepped out into the hall to see it delivered. He did not want to draw the other servants' attention to the arsenal of weapons he was preparing in case they tipped off the madman.

When the messenger had departed, Leopold locked the study door, and then crept down the hall to check on Mercy and Edwin.

Wilcox nodded all was well inside and moved away. Their voices carried through the closed door of the playroom, and he eased it open. Mercy and Edwin were romping on the floor again, absorbed in the toys around them. His heart tripped over at the happy pair they made. He wished he could join them and play with Edwin's toy armies again. Leopold found Edwin's delight fascinating to watch and very hard to stay away from.

He leaned closer to the gap to listen to them talk.

Edwin knocked his armies flying. "Where is Mr. Randall, Mama?"

A sad smile crossed Mercy's face. "He had some business to take care of for the estate. I'm sure he will come and visit with you later."

Edwin moved his toys around. "I like him," he said suddenly.

Leopold closed his eyes.

"I am very sure he likes you too, Edwin," Mercy said.

His heart couldn't take much more of this.

"Can we go see him soon?" Edwin asked. "I want to show him my general."

Leopold opened his eyes to see Mercy ruffle her son's hair. "I'm sure he would enjoy that."

More than she realized. His son made him so proud, not that he could safely acknowledge those feelings. He had to bury them deep before he blurted out the truth.

He closed the door quietly and hurried away. He was here to do a job, not to get too personally involved with Edwin. He had to maintain a distance to keep his sanity.

He had just finished hiding the last of the weapons about the abbey when Eamon arrived. The poor fellow looked so discomfited by the opulence of the entrance hall that Leopold ushered him quickly into the study, a simply decorated, masculine room, and closed the door behind them.

Eamon's shoulders eased. "You wanted to see me, Mr. Randall?"

"I did, Eamon." It was a huge risk bringing Eamon into his confidence like this since he tended toward gossip. "Have you noticed any strangers in the district?"

Eamon shook his head. "Just you and that valet of yours."

"No peddlers that anyone mentioned gave them a bad feeling? No travelers lingering where they ought not to be? There is always someone on the road. It's important."

Eamon screwed his face up as he thought. "Now, there was someone who mentioned seeing a figure hugging the trees." He held his finger up. "Someone over by your old family's place. In the woods behind, if I remember correctly."

Leopold had not ventured in that direction since his return. The thought of standing in his mother's parlor again had been too much to bear. He would rather remember his childhood home as it was, well-tended and full of life, than empty.

He sat on the edge of the desk. "Can you describe the fellow?"

Eamon scowled. "The widow Turner is a fanciful creature."

"Regardless, what did she say about him." Leopold crossed his arms over his chest and waited.

"That he was trouble, whatever that means. She calls half the lads around here trouble, me included."

Despite the seriousness of the conversation, Leopold grinned. "You *are* trouble, Eamon. She is correct about that."

Eamon laughed. "Too right, too right. She said he frightened her near to death. Terrible visage."

"So, not a handsome man? A brute?"

"She didn't say he was big or nothing." Eamon scratched his jaw. "An ape. That was her exact words."

Leopold frowned. This lead could amount to nothing, and it didn't fit with the man he had seen on the grounds last night. Although at something of a distance, he'd not describe the intruder as ape-like. "Anything else?"

"Nope." Eamon looked about him curiously. His gaze skimmed over the table, where three weapons lay concealed beneath a cloth. He took in the rest of the chamber, and then settled his gaze again on the concealed weapons. "What's under there?"

As a younger man, Eamon had been a fairly good shot. With those weapons, the duke's finest, he had a decent chance of hitting any target he chose to aim for. Leopold moved toward the table and set his fingertips on the cloth. "Do you remember playing spies as a boy? You always wanted to defend the king, if I remember correctly."

Eamon laughed. "Toby always got his way, and I had no choice but to be a villain."

"Well, Tobias isn't here, and I control the game now." Leopold uncovered the guns. "How would feel about defending a duke instead of a king?"

Eamon gaped.

Leopold handed over a weapon. "The boy's life is in danger, and he has only us to protect him. Are you willing?"

Eamon took the weapon from him and tested the weight. "Thought you'd never ask."

It was now Leopold's turn to gape. "What exactly do you know?"

"That the duchess is terrified. The whole village knows of her situation and, despite the danger, are ever so glad you're back. Can't understand why she's still here but we'll catch the bastard. You just wait and see." Eamon winked. "I moved some friends onto the grounds when I got your note. I took that as your permission. They'll advance on the abbey as night falls and take up positions around the place wherever I tell them. We'll keep you safe and snug here."

Leopold frowned. "I'll be outside with you on the grounds."

Eamon shook his head. "Oh, I don't think that's such a good idea. After all, you're next in line for the title. You'll need our protection, too."

Patience had never been Mercy's strong suit. She paced the chamber while her son napped and couldn't control her anxiety, counting her steps as she crossed the room. Twenty-three wide, sixteen across. She frowned and turned around. Counting again, she retraced her steps.

Where was Leopold, and what perils was he facing?

Worry gnawed her insides. Her troubles had placed him in danger. The whole duchy's future was in jeopardy if Leopold and Edwin fell victim to this unknown madman. She shivered and rubbed her arms. The estate would fall to the crown, and she would be cast out unless the king allowed an unprecedented change to the succession. She doubted that would happen.

She stopped at a sudden thought. If Leopold's siblings were found, there was still a chance for the estate to remain with the Randalls. She may only have married into the family, but she was uncommonly fond of the ones she knew. Strange Randalls would be better than seeing the great family fall.

"What are you plotting now, Your Grace?"

She looked up at the interruption. "Blythe, thank goodness you came back! I was beginning to worry about you."

"I told Mr. Randall last night I was perfectly safe." A frown grew across Blythe's brow. "But I do appreciate his concern for you and the duke. As such, I packed a few things and will stay here until the danger has passed."

Mercy embraced her sister tightly. That Blythe had changed her mind and would remain here relieved Mercy beyond belief. Now she had only one soul to worry about outside the abbey walls.

Blythe's embrace grew stronger, and then her arms fell away. "You look tired."

"It's been a stressful morning. Can you stay with Edwin for awhile?"

"Of course. But what is going on? Your butler was behaving very strangely. He questioned me about the servants I brought to the abbey. He even demanded their names."

Mercy clutched her sister's hands. "Leopold saw a stranger outside the abbey last night. He is convinced it is the person threatening us."

Blythe cried out softly. "You are not thinking of going outside, are you? You must stay close to Edwin."

"No. I will stay inside the abbey, but the waiting is driving me to the brink of madness. To distract myself, I want to continue searching for clues about Leopold's siblings. If the worst comes to pass, the estate may very well need them."

"Surely it won't come to that. But I understand your thinking. If not for my husband having a son from his first marriage, that estate would have fallen to the worst side of that family." Blythe nodded slowly, her gaze fixed on Edwin where he slept. "I will guard him with my last breath."

Blythe was always a touch too dramatic. Mercy threw her arms around her sister. "I'm sure it won't come to that but thank you."

She turned around and approached the wall containing the only entrance to the duke's other study—a narrow space connected to three main chambers: drawing room, dining room, and study. The one place she had not searched already but the place she probably should have checked first when Leopold had told her of his lost siblings.

Mercy slid her fingers over the rose carvings and set her fingertips apart on the wood. She pushed each petal evenly until the wall issued a clicking noise.

The house had so many bolt holes like this. She should have led Leopold to this chamber from the start, but he'd fixed on starting in the study and she'd thought they'd have plenty of time. The chamber was not marked on any architectural plan for the abbey that she had ever seen, and she had no idea how long ago it was constructed. It was very likely that Leopold had no knowledge of the chamber. She would tell him when the time was right.

Blythe handed her a lit candle. "I do not like it much in there."

Mercy pushed the candle away. "I don't particularly care for the confines either, but it is our best chance for success. I'll return as soon as I discover something. If you need me, knock on the wall. The sound will travel to me easily enough and I will return to you."

Blythe nodded as Mercy closed the door softly. She turned as her eyes adjusted to the muted light and then moved into the room, keeping her steps slow and her breathing shallow against the dust that rose up to fill her nose. She only came here when she absolutely had to, and it was only by accident that she had spied the old duke disappearing into the space at all. When he and her husband had passed away, Mercy and Blythe had explored the chamber. Blythe was always anxious to leave the tiny, windowless space, preferring to wait at the door to ensure they could always get out.

Mercy moved to the left wall and to the peephole that looked into the study. She stretched up onto her toes and peered inside.

Leopold stood with his back to her, bent over a large map. The estate map? She couldn't tell from this distance, and she shifted slightly to look beyond him when she saw another shape.

What was Eamon Murphy doing here with Leopold?

She ducked from view as both men lifted their heads suddenly and looked around.

Spying was an unsavory habit. But for the time being it was best not to distract Leopold with thoughts of his other concerns. If she found the answers he needed, then she would tell him as soon as the danger passed. She just hoped he would not disappear immediately after that.

Most of the light illuminating the chamber drifted in from diamond-shaped holes cut behind three mirrors in the adjoining rooms. Those large and heavy mirrors had never been taken down and could only be cleaned in situ. A cunning design, indeed. Not one servant to her knowledge, not even Wilcox, had ever mentioned the irregularity or the odd dimensions of the adjoining chambers.

She sat down on a leather-upholstered chair. In his day, the old duke had dabbled in many things—investments, successions in other duchies, and matters likely addressed in parliament. But there had been nothing she had read so far that hinted at the whereabouts of any Randall relations. But then, she reasoned, their disappearance had been many years ago.

She scanned the spines on the bookshelves above her head. There were dozens of volumes, some marked with numbers on the spine. She took down the first one and opened it to a random page. The handwriting was bold, strong, and undoubtedly belonged to her late father-in-law. But the writing was not in exact English.

Why ever had he written them in an addled code?

She grabbed another and flicked through the pages, squinting in the hopes of making sense from the squiggles. She spied a date that seemed familiar, and as she followed the lines of characters down the page, she thought she saw a pattern. The dates advanced at odd intervals, matched with more indecipherable squiggles.

She flipped the pages. There were pages of notations, all leading up to a year ago when her husband had died.

The final line—September, 1812—"Gone to God" was written in a different hand.

She looked at the date again and her hands shook. Her father-in-law had been dead six months when Edwin had died and could not have possibly recorded it.

She glanced around nervously, half expecting someone to emerge from the shadows to catch her snooping in here. Someone aside from herself and Blythe knew about the room and its contents.

Although her heart hammered, she slid her finger over the page until she found Edwin's date of birth, the date the stranger came to her bed, and the date of her marriage. However, there were so many notations in between that she wondered what on earth her husband had been doing with his days that the duke felt the need to mark them down.

Her husband had been an unexcitable man, or so she'd thought. This couldn't be all about him.

She pulled down the next journal, marked with the number three, and on a whim, flicked the pages until she reached the end.

The last entry had been made yesterday in the same unfamiliar handwriting as found in the first book. It simply said: home.

Was this book about Leopold?

After a quick glance through the pages, it seemed very likely. The book contained many notations of money and foreign-sounding names that twisted her tongue. Heart in her throat, she rechecked the dates carefully. There were four around the time her stranger had come to share her bed, evenly spaced around that heavenly night.

What to do? She had only her suspicions, but she was certain these journals could contain important keys to finding what Leopold sought. She couldn't resist digging further, but puzzles were not her specialty. However, Blythe was good with puzzles and games.

But could Mercy risk exposing her suspicions to a sister who thought her on the brink of scandal every other minute? She might discover she was right if she cracked the code and uncovered Edwin's parentage.

Mercy pressed her head into her hand. She was so tired of

keeping the secret from her sister. She would take the risk of showing her the journals, and if she uncovered the secret herself, she would confess to the possibility. If she did not, Mercy would tell Blythe herself once the danger had passed.

Mind made up, she closed the journal, gathered the first three in her arms and returned to the drawing room.

Chapter Twenty-Two

Darkness cloaked Romsey Abbey in sinister shadows, reminding Leopold of all the nightmares he'd endured while away from England. Visions where Rosemary pressed against the glass of an upper bedchamber window, calling for him to come save her from the old duke's clutches, teased at his mind. During the dream, he'd not been able to storm the abbey and save his sister. He'd been trapped outside and alone while the old duke hovered, watching like a specter.

Leopold had thought that dreams of his sister in danger were the worst his imagination could conjure up on a wind-tossed night. Not so, however. His mind now imagined the worst terrors for his son. Edwin, too young and even more defenseless than Rosemary had ever been, faced an unknown threat that Leopold wasn't sure he could protect him from. In the past, he'd been assured that his siblings were safe from harm, so long as he obeyed. The duke had given his word, and a Randall never went back on that.

This threat coming toward Edwin made no sense. Who the devil would want to harm a child or Mercy? The threat must be from some trouble of the old duke's making. And he had made sure Leopold would stick around to clean up the mess should he ever come here again.

Leopold ground his teeth as anger ripped through him. God, what a mistake he had made five years ago.

He'd given the old man control of his life even from his grave.

Leopold eased closer to the rough timber door and peered out at the kitchen garden. All was quiet and still, and from his vantage point, hidden in a garden shed out of sight, he gazed longingly at the windows where Mercy and Edwin should be resting for the night. He'd love to return to them and take them in his arms. He'd stand between them and danger until his last breath left him.

Why couldn't the Randalls live peaceably for once in his life? Why must there always be contention and strife? He delighted at watching Edwin play his games. He'd like to have the chance to grow old watching them.

His thoughts about Mercy were less comfortable. Being with her reminded him of all that was missing from his life. Laughter, easy conversation, and a sense of belonging in a place he'd never imagined would feel like home.

But there was no future here with her. A duchess would only have a man like him for a lover. Anything more permanent was completely out of the question. He could never ask for more from her. What little he'd been granted was more than enough. As it was, they were running the risk of discovery. When this was over, he'd move north—far, far away from Mercy so he would never be tempted again. He'd still worry about Edwin, but if he faded from his life, it would avoid awkward questions about the similarities in their appearance when the boy was fully grown.

He shook his head. Better to deal with the here and now than worry about the future. Somewhere out there was a killer.

He leaned a little closer to the door and looked to where the next man hid. Brown, from the Vulture Inn, had come, too, like many men of the village. But Brown had claimed a spot closest to Leopold, despite Leopold's assertion that he did not need protection. Eamon had surprised him by overriding his objections very firmly. So he was stuck with Brown as his shadow and guardian, something he'd never had before.

Brown's head came into view, slowly emerging from the shadows when he should have remained hidden.

Leopold frowned. Perhaps he'd been wrong to let the other man hover so close. He'd give away their positions too quickly like this.

The whole of Brown was now visible. He stared at the abbey with fixed attention, shifting slightly as he looked up at the walls.

Leopold looked too—and gaped.

A dark shape, a man, clung to the abbey walls…and was slowly ascending toward Mercy and Edwin's floor. All windows on that floor were locked and many had even been blocked by tall furniture as night had fallen. Leopold was confident that, short of smashing a window, the man could not enter.

Leopold stepped from the shed's safety, stunned by the intruder's audacity and astounding ability. Good God, the man possessed skills more akin to an ape than a gentleman. How could he hang there without any apparent effort? He scaled the abbey walls slowly, clinging to the stone work as if he was simply climbing steps.

Although Leopold's first thought was to fire at the intruder, he skirted the abbey via the shadows to get a closer look.

The man wore no harness or apparatus that he could see. He was completely vulnerable clinging to the walls the way he did. If they shot at him and scored a good hit, he'd fall from the wall and be dashed to pieces on the flagstone path below for sure when he landed. Leopold could shoot him easily enough, but he wanted to question the stranger first before any punishment was handed out. But how the devil was he to catch a fellow who climbed like that?

Leopold jumped out of his skin as a shot rang out.

Brown had fired, but had luckily missed his target. The intruder clung to the stonework a moment, glanced over his shoulder to where Leopold stood, and then, quicker than he could blink, scuttled sideways and disappeared out of sight, around the corner of the building.

"Damn it. He's getting away!"

Leopold hurried after him at a run. He collided with Brown, who'd had the same idea, and then took up the chase in earnest. But by then, the intruder was down and off the abbey walls, fleeing across the grassy lawns quicker than Leopold could believe possible. The man was also hooting with laughter, as if what he was doing was a great game to him.

It wouldn't be a lark once Leopold got his hands on him. He'd rip him to bloody shreds for threatening his son.

The wind blew hard against Leopold as he ran through the long grass, hampering his progress. But he clearly heard the intruder's taunting float back to him on the wind. "Run, run, Randall, before there's a scandal. Don't let Papa catch you with your hand on your candle!"

More laughter whipped past on the wind before the stranger left the path and disappeared into the tree line without looking back.

Damn it!

Leopold stopped, gasping for breath, as more shots rang out. Bark splintered and rained down on the path ahead where the intruder had vanished moments before. Too little, too late, unfortunately. Whoever it was who had come to Romsey was quick, efficient, and far wilier than Leopold had considered. Given the rate of his disappearance, he knew the grounds and paths around the estate very well to have gotten this close without being noticed. He'd be a mile away from them by now or hiding up one of those blasted trees, out of sight in the darkness.

Who the hell was this man?

Eamon Murphy puffed up the rise and joined him. "How the devil did he get around us like that? We had three men near the paths from the trees."

How indeed? Leopold scanned the darkness around him, and then shook his head as he remembered something from his childhood. He pointed. "He came up through the dry stream, keeping low and out of sight of the watchers. Damn it. He knows the duchess has reinforcements now; we've lost the advantage of surprise. Bring everyone in. We'll need a new plan, and we need it now."

When Eamon scurried off to do his bidding, Leopold scanned the tree line. How the hell had anyone else recognized that the low gully was the perfect approach to the abbey on a dark night? Only someone born and bred on the estate might notice the possibility, and take advantage of it to get a closer look at the abbey. How could he protect them from a man who knew the abbey as well as he once had?

***

Mercy sobbed into her fist to muffle the sound from Edwin. He slept the sleep of an innocent, while Leopold might very well be dying. Despite his earlier warning, Mercy crept to the window and peered out. Below, a large group of men had gathered on the grounds. She scanned them quickly, looking for Leopold among their number. It was hard to tell who was who from this distance, and her heart hammered painfully when she could not make him out in the crowd.

It was still too dark, the weather too wild, and she had little patience tonight.

Suddenly, a dark shape turned and looked up. *Leopold.* Thank God. He raised a hand in greeting and turned back to the other fellows. Mercy sagged onto the nearest chair and buried her face in her hands. He was alive and well enough to move about with ease. He had survived the danger, despite the shots she'd heard.

Blythe came closer. "Is it over?"

"I don't know. They are all milling about on the grass below."

Blythe peered out the window. "They will tell us what we need to know. In the meantime, I think you should plan to leave this place at first light. We must get Edwin to safety."

"Go where?" Mercy demanded. "If one is not safe in one's home then we'd have little chance upon the road."

Blythe sighed heavily. "I suppose you are right, but I do not like to leave all the decisions about Edwin's safety to this Mr. Randall. He has taken control of the duke's life far too easily."

"His own life is in danger, too," Mercy reminded her. "He is a Randall, and my son's heir. Who knows what that deranged fellow wants with Edwin, but he could very well turn his attention on Leopold. I could not bear it if he should be hurt in the defense of us. His family has suffered enough."

"Must you speak so informally of Mr. Randall?" Blythe fussed with her peach silk wrapper. "You encourage him to overstep his bounds at every turn."

What would Blythe say if she confessed she'd thought of little else but Leopold for the whole day? What would Blythe do if Mercy confessed she was considering marriage to him? "Family cannot overstep, Blythe."

A scowl crossed Blythe's face. "Well, since all seems in order now, perhaps you should get some sleep while you can. If the intruder hasn't been run off, then you should be safe for the rest of the night."

Mercy slewed around to stare at her sister. "Are you not afraid?"

Blythe blinked. "Of course I am afraid. But there is no sense in getting hysterical over something I cannot control. I learned that lesson years ago. You should do better to control your anxiety from those around you, especially around Edwin. You will make him prone to fret."

Mercy gaped. Even in the midst of danger, Blythe thought to give her a lesson in raising her child. Damn it all if that didn't make her see red. She might be correct that she should hide her emotions better in front of her son, but when this was over, the pair of them were going to sit down and thrash out their differences. She would not tolerate this any longer.

When Blythe lay down on the bed next to Edwin, curling her arm over him protectively as he slept, Mercy's heart gave a thump. She was so very good with Edwin that if anything ever happened to Mercy, she could be assured Edwin would have her love and support in the years to come. It was the only thing keeping her sane.

That, and the journals. Together, she and Blythe had begun work on the code, finding surprising translations for names. Using the dates, and Blythe's idea of using the family bible for reference, they had determined that the duke referred to women as flowers. Mercy had been dubbed Poppy. Her mother-in-law he called Ivy. And someone, Mercy couldn't determine who yet, was called Blackberry and mentioned extensively in Edwin's book. Not a nice way to think of a woman. She must be an utter termagant and someone the duke disliked immensely.

Males were named a little differently. The old duke had had a very religious view on them. He referred to his son as a fallen angel by the end of his life; the stranger in her bed he termed Lucifer, the devil. None of it was proof absolute that Leopold had been that man. But the dates matched what little Mercy knew of his birth year. It was a fairly obvious conclusion to her that he was the one. Did she care now?

No.

Mercy pressed the heel of her hands to her eyes. She wanted

this ordeal to be over so she could get on with her life, find Leopold's brothers and sister, and be happy once more.

She was so tired of being afraid. She dropped her hands, crossed to the bed, and lay down beside her son. Tomorrow, she would speak to Blythe and Leopold about the past. With luck, her life would begin to move forward from then.

Chapter Twenty-Three

Leopold staggered as a small pair of arms wrapped around his legs and prevented him from moving forward. He'd had a long and frustrating night and hadn't noticed Edwin barreling across the room toward him. He glanced down at the boy and his heart skipped a beat. He could not get used to such greetings, but he did enjoy Edwin's enthusiastic displays of affection.

Reluctantly, he pried Edwin's arms from his legs. "Good morning, Your Grace. How are you this morning?"

"Good," he replied excitedly. "I want to show you my generals." Edwin grabbed his hand and drew him farther into his playroom. Leopold looked around, spied Mercy smiling and Lady Venables scowling, and let go of the boy's hand before they reached their destination.

"Good morning, Your Grace. Lady Venables," he said quickly.

Mercy approached. "What happened last night? I've been worried sick."

Leopold checked that the boy was far enough away to not overhear them. "The bastard climbed the walls of the abbey. I'd like to say we almost caught him but I'd be lying. He's a phantom."

Mercy wilted against him, while her sister gasped. Thankfully, Lady Venables turned her attention to her nephew and fussed with him as Leopold carefully embraced Mercy to calm her down. "It will be all right. We know now what he is capable of, and just how determined he is to reach you both."

Mercy burrowed her face against his chest. "I was so scared for you all alone out there."

He held her closer, keeping one eye on Lady Venables and Edwin. "For me? Why? I was hardly alone. The whole damn village was out there."

"You know why," Mercy whispered. "Don't make me say it where my sister can hear. She will screech the building down and likely say something very cutting."

Leopold's heart raced at Mercy's protectiveness. He had done nothing to deserve it. Reluctantly, he stepped away from her. "I don't know what you're talking about."

"Don't you?" Mercy wiped at her eyes, and he was astounded that she'd been worried enough for tears. "Do you really have no idea what you've become to me?"

He held up his hands in supplication. "Stop. It's just the stress you've been under. When the danger has passed, you will see you were mistaken and will regret your words."

Mercy crossed her arms over her chest. "I know my own heart. I know what I want for my life."

"So do I." He wanted Mercy and Edwin in his life. "Wishing for the best has never made it happen."

She shook her head. "This time can be different. Will be different, if I have my way."

Mercy's jaw had clenched stubbornly, and he marveled at her determination. They were all wrong for each other, despite the attraction.

He shook off the sadness that gripped him. There were more important things to talk about right now. "In light of the danger this man poses, I want you to remain in one part of the abbey only during the day. It is far easier to guard you that way. I have organized a rejuvenation of the gardens on the east side of the abbey. We will have servants in the grounds on that side and no one will get past them during the day."

"What about inside the abbey? It's a vast space."

Leopold smiled and caught up her hand. "Taken care of already. Come with me."

He led her toward the door of an adjoining chamber and opened it wide. Wilcox and the housekeeper were in the next room, polishing the already perfect silver contained within.

Leopold nodded to them and closed the door again. He drew her to the other door next and opened it wide. Allen and his boys were stationed inside the next smaller room, talking quietly to each other as the boys bent their heads over books.

Allen glanced up. "Everything all right, Mr. Randall?"

"Everything is fine."

Allen gave a tight smile, and then ignored them.

Satisfied with the arrangements, Leopold closed the door again and turned to Mercy. She was frowning. "What bothers you?"

She tipped her head to draw him away from the door. Leopold followed.

She clenched her hands together. "What do you know of Allen?"

"What do you mean?"

Mercy scowled. "You are being evasive again. Don't do that."

"Beg your pardon, Your Grace?"

"Don't do that again, either."

Leopold sighed. He was too tired to fence with Mercy today. "I see I cannot win today."

Mercy's eyebrow rose. "Are we engaged in a battle?"

"Since the day we met. You would know everything that I am? I am not used to sharing my thoughts so freely."

"Then you will need to change." She shook her head. "Tell me what you know about Allen."

Leopold hid a grin. She was the most determined woman he had ever met, and he loved her for it. "Allen is good with horses."

Her glance turned sullen. "Then why would you bring him into the abbey?"

"Because I trust him."

"Why?"

"I knew him when I was a boy. He and my father were on friendly terms."

Mercy's frown grew. "Then he lived in the district before? He never mentioned that he was from the district when he interviewed with Wilcox."

Had Allen lived close to the abbey before? Leopold couldn't remember precisely where he might have lived, and he doubted that Wilcox had actually interviewed Allen. The man wasn't on the estate books to be paid each quarter day. It seemed he'd just moved in and made himself at home in the stables. Leopold would have to see if he could change that when this was over.

He stroked his hand down Mercy's arm to reassure her. "I

remember him visiting with us infrequently. He was on good terms with my mother, too."

Mercy set her hands to her hips. "I still find it odd that a groom should be stationed so close to us. There are other servants in the abbey that have served the family for far longer than Allen."

But none that Leopold could trust to be completely loyal and place themselves between the duke and danger. He was uncertain how to phrase that without revealing the facts around Allen's illegitimate birth.

"Don't even think of lying to me again. I simply won't stand for it, Leopold."

Leopold ground his teeth. Damn this was awkward. "I trust Allen because he has good reason to help me and your son. That will have to be enough to satisfy you, Your Grace."

Mercy stepped close, her hand landing on his chest, fingers spread wide. Leopold quaked as she pushed at him. "Just be aware that every time you lie to me, or withhold your confidences from me, that you give me pain."

Leopold licked his lips. "Some secrets cannot be shared without causing pain."

"I'm stronger than you think, Leopold. There is nothing you cannot tell me that I do not want to hear from your lips. When will you believe that I am not your enemy?"

But she was. She was the embodiment of everything he had wanted and lost. She roused in him such feelings of possessiveness that he struggled to hide how he felt. She had come to mean the world to him, and he could never tell her the truth. She would hate him for his part in Edwin's making, and he was not prepared for that day to come just yet.

Her hands slid around his chest, under his coat. "Let go of your fears and tell me."

Leopold swallowed. "There is nothing to tell."

"Liar." Mercy drew back.

What could he say to that? Every word he'd spoken to her was calculated to spare her discomfort, pain, and embarrassment. He couldn't admit to the truth.

"I'm not done with you, Leopold Randall. I shall never be."

She turned away toward her son and Leopold was profoundly

grateful. If she'd pushed much harder against his resolve, he would have ruined what little happiness he had. He'd been moments away from confessing everything.

He wiped his hands over his face as weariness tugged at his senses. He stumbled, fell into a nearby chair and set his head to the plush back. He hadn't slept properly in days and couldn't afford to now. Not with the danger circling them. He watched Edwin at play, sure that the boy's noise would keep his attention.

Edwin was a very lucky boy.

He was loved unconditionally.

"I'll be right back," Mercy whispered to Blythe as she eased Edwin's head down onto the blanket.

Blythe stirred from her doze. "Where are you going?"

"I need to speak to Leopold."

She glanced toward the playroom door. "Do you think he's awake already?"

Mercy pushed a strand of hair behind her sister's ear and smiled gently at her sleepy state. "I don't know. He's been so quiet. But I wanted to check on him, too."

Although Blythe frowned, she didn't prevent Mercy from leaving. Mercy quietly crossed the room and slipped into the playroom, where Leopold had fallen asleep earlier. He lay exactly as she had left him, sprawled across the narrow settee that was far too small for his large body. She'd been half afraid he'd tumble off while he slept.

She smiled at how still he was. Just like Edwin. He didn't twitch when she passed him to sit on a nearby chair. He didn't snore at all. But Mercy was aware of every breath he took, the rise and fall of his wide chest, the look of peace about him as exhaustion held him in a tight grip. How long had it been since he'd slept a full night?

Part of his exhaustion was her fault and, although she smiled at the memory of sharing a bed with him, she did feel a little guilty. He needed someone to look after him as much as she needed the same. She would do better by him as soon as he agreed to their marriage.

She leaned back in her comfortable chair, prepared to wait for him to wake. Edwin would sleep a while yet, but Mercy had not liked to leave Leopold alone as if he was of no importance. He was in just as much danger as they. She should never have allowed Blythe to move them to the next chamber when Leopold had fallen asleep so suddenly two hours ago. They should have remained together while the two most important men in her life slept.

Leopold's chest rose suddenly as he drew in a larger breath and his eyes opened. He sat up and looked around wildly. When his gaze settled on her, his breath hitched and he relaxed. "Is everything all right? Where is Edwin?"

She loved that his first thought was of their son. "Edwin is in the next room. We didn't want him to wake you."

He scowled and threw his legs over the side of the chaise to sit properly. "You should have woken me."

"You needed the rest. How long has it been since you allowed someone to take care of you?"

"I have a valet for that."

"Has there not been someone else? A mistress, perhaps?"

He wiped his hand over his face suddenly. "You should return to the boy. I'll join you as soon as I'm awake enough."

Mercy allowed him to avoid her question, although his habit of trying to spare her discomfort was unnecessary. She wasn't a fool. He'd had other lovers before her. Luckily, she got the benefit of his extensive experience now and would keep it if she could. Hiding a smile, she played with the folds of her gown. "There is no rush."

He rubbed at his face again, and then speared her with a hard glance. "Are you avoiding your sister?"

"No. It's just when she is around, I have to behave like a proper duchess. I cannot be myself with you as I'd like."

Leopold sat back in his seat. "Please don't say such things. I will be leaving the abbey when the danger to the boy has passed. I will likely need to travel to retrieve my siblings."

Mercy's chest tightened at the idea of him leaving them

behind. "I like to travel, and Edwin has never left the estate. He will enjoy the adventure with you."

He shook his head violently. "I don't know where I'm going and the boy is safer here."

Mercy fell to her knees and crawled awkwardly across the floor until she knelt at Leopold's feet. "I won't let you toss us aside so easily."

Leopold's mouth opened, to deny her no doubt, but she pulled his head forward and sealed her lips to his before he could deny her feelings again. For a moment he resisted, but then his lips firmed and his tongue tangled with hers.

Mercy wrapped her arms around his shoulders and clung. He couldn't leave her. Not when he made her feel like this—cherished, desired, loved.

He lifted her onto his lap suddenly so that she straddled his thighs. Mercy quaked at the sensation of being so close to him again. She wanted him like this every time they met, regardless of the circumstances.

His hand stroked her thigh under the gown, and then closed over her bare bottom. Mercy moaned at the sensation and shuffled forward until she sat over his erection. They could make love like this if they were quick, if they were quiet, and swept away by the moment.

A door opened, and then crashed shut again.

Leopold threw Mercy off him as he slewed around to stare at the doors. She landed on the end of the chaise, rumbled, aroused, and utterly embarrassed. Blythe could have caught her and finally have a reason to call her scandalous. She covered her flaming cheeks. "Which door was that?"

"Allen's."

A servant had found them. "Oh, dear."

"Don't worry. Despite his assertion I'm not aggressive enough, I'll kill Allen if he breathes a word of what he just saw to anyone."

"You can't do that. Let me speak to him."

Leopold's skin mottled a dark red. "If you so much as mention this catastrophe to my cousin, I will put you across my knee and spank your arse until it's as pink as your cheeks are now."

Mercy flushed at the harsh words and at the threat of being

spanked. And then her mind caught up with what Leopold had just said. "Cousin?"

"Damnation. I'm too tired for this."

"Cousin," she repeated as she righted her clothing and rose to face Leopold.

He nodded.

Leopold didn't have any cousins that she knew of, according to her copy of Debrett's. "On which side of the family?"

"The worst side." He sighed. "You won't find a record of the connection or his place in the family. He's an illegitimate son."

Mercy stared at the door Allen had burst through. "Whose child was he?"

"Maybe we'll kill each other." Leopold tugged his fingers through his hair one more time. He looked up at her with a bleak expression. "Rejoice, Your Grace, Edwin has had more family about him than you ever realized. Allen is theoretically, but not legally, Edwin's uncle. The old duke's firstborn son, Charles Allen. His mother was a chambermaid here."

Mercy's brain caught up with Leopold's words, and then she sat down with a thump. The old duke's son had been shoveling horse excrement in her stables for the past year. Why didn't anyone in this dratted family tell her the truth without having to be tortured first?

Chapter Twenty-Four

All in all, Mercy took the news of the enlarged Randall family rather well. She didn't demand more details. She didn't raise a fuss. She merely gave him a look that spoke volumes of displeasure at him keeping secrets and headed for the door leading toward her son.

He marveled at her unpredictability. She truly was cast from a very unique mold.

However would he forget her when the time came to go? She had wormed her way into his life and destroyed every trace of contentment he'd thought he'd have when he left Romsey for the last time. Being with her filled the void of loneliness he'd carried with him this last decade. The years to come would be barren and filled with yearning for what might have been if the circumstances of their first meeting had been different.

Would he have met her if she'd not become the duchess? Would he have found his way to her side at a ball and never walked away again? He liked to think they would have had a fair chance of happiness, if his cousin hadn't married her first. He liked to think he could have courted her properly, taken her driving, and danced with her in a crowded ballroom. He also thought he'd have stolen her away for a kiss. There was no denying he would have wanted that if life had given them free choice.

Walking away from her would kill him.

At the threshold to the next room, she turned back. "Well, are you coming?" Her gaze dropped to his groin, her lips turned up in an impish grin at the double meaning to her words. He shook his head to dispel his gloomy thoughts. Wicked wench. Maybe he should paddle her bare backside just once to see how she liked the experience of being teased without mercy. He crossed to her, but she didn't open the door.

Instead, she straightened his cravat, smoothed his hair back from his eyes, and then rose on her toes to kiss his cheek. "There now, perfect once more."

He rubbed his thumb across her smooth cheek. "What am I going to do with you, sweetheart?"

He lowered his head to brush her lips with his. She tasted sweet, like the sweetest treat at the market…and he loved her with all his heart.

He, who had never wanted anyone so badly in his life, was destined for misery without her.

Her smile grew dreamy. "Hold that thought until later. I'm sure we can come up with something."

Lord help him, but he would likely be thinking about what he could do to her until his dying breath. With a simple touch, and one chaste kiss, he'd renewed his desire for her once more. To rid himself of the uncomfortable arousal, he thought of the one thing sure to cool his desire. He thought of what the old Duke of Romsey had done to them both.

He drew the anger deep into him and gave it free rein. They had all been hurt by the old duke in one way or another. It was just that Mercy didn't know how much. He would have to tell her eventually. But when the danger had passed was soon enough. Then he could leave when she demanded he go and not worry about any danger to Edwin. Allen would be here. He could ask his cousin to send word if trouble ever darkened their door again.

Lady Venables sat up straighter when they joined her and Edwin. The boy appeared sleepy, draped across his aunt's lap, quiet and watchful for a change. Blythe seemed so unhappy to see him that he decided he would only stay a short while and then leave. There were many things he could still be doing. Watching out for trouble was imperative.

"I see you are awake again," she commented, her voice dripping with disdain.

"Forgive me, an inexcusable lapse on my part. It won't happen again."

Her gaze raked him from head to toe. Not a nice sensation, at all. He sat at a distance from her, listening to Edwin prattle to his mother. When the boy had enough of his mother, Edwin picked up his toys and approached.

Leopold smiled. "What have you there, Your Grace?"

Edwin leaned against his legs. "This is Captain Winston, he's the best sailor there is."

Leopold admired the piece and set it on his knee. "I'm sure he is."

"This one is an infidel." Edwin shoved the piece in his face. "Mama says my papa gave me that one."

Leopold's chest tightened as he took the small figure from his son's fingers. The piece was supposed to be an Indian prince. Leopold had found it in the marketplace in Surat and impulsively sent it home to Romsey as a birth present to the boy, along with a whole regiment.

He had never imagined that something so small had the power to move him to tears. His eyes stung. His son had something of his that he had given freely, without coercion or threats involved. He glanced at Mercy, watched her eyes widen, and then quickly looked away. It hurt that his cousin had the credit of giving the boy something Edwin clearly cherished. It hurt very much indeed.

Edwin placed the little prince figure in his pocket and gave Leopold another to admire.

"Mr. Randall?" Blythe asked suddenly. "Where was it you said you were while in India?"

"Surat."

"Do they have such toys in Surat?"

"Yes, I believe they do. They are common enough in the marketplaces."

"And you have sent gifts home to the family for years now. Tell me, when was the last time exactly that you were here at Romsey."

Although Leopold's heart raced, he dared not look up immediately. He was afraid the truth was there for all to see; five years and a few weeks ago. The dates he had last come to Romsey were imprinted on his soul. "Years ago now. I've forgotten exactly when," he lied, and then looked up.

Lady Venables' gaze fixed on Edwin. Her lips had a pinched look about them, as if she'd tasted sour lemons. "And one more question. When are you leaving again?"

"Blythe!" Mercy cried. "Don't speak like that to Leopold."

Lady Venables stared at her sister. "And when exactly did you first meet Mr. Randall, Your Grace?"

Mercy's eyes met and held Leopold's for a mere second before a blush crept up her cheeks. She turned away and answered the question after a long pause. "Six days ago. You were here that day if you remember."

The delay in answering caught Leopold by surprise. Mercy had had to think about her answer. Which meant, God in heaven, Mercy had just lied to her sister about their first meeting. Did she already know, or suspect, he could be Edwin's father? His palms slicked and he clenched them to control his emotions.

Blythe's eyes narrowed on them both. "I don't believe you."

"Of course, we've only just met." Mercy sat with her chin up, defiant but far from offended by Blythe's disbelief. "Why ever would you think otherwise?"

"Because we're sisters and I know you better than anyone."

Mercy held her ground. Saying nothing to try to convince her sister she was wrong.

A single tear slipped down Blythe's cheek, and she hastily wiped it away. She stood abruptly. "I've always known when you lie, sister. I put up with it before but no more. Excuse me. I need to take a turn about the garden, and then I will return to Walden Hall where I belong."

Edwin, unnoticed by all, suddenly climbed into Leopold's lap and wrapped his arms about his neck. Leopold didn't know what to do. Should he push away the anxious boy, or let him seek comfort from him just this once? Neither Mercy nor Blythe had noticed the boy's anxiety yet. They were too focused on each other.

"I have had enough of this!" Mercy followed Blythe to the terrace door. "You are not going to walk away again from another discussion. You have no right to be rude to Leopold, and certainly not while he puts his own life at risk to protect us. I've tried to be patient with you. I've tried to understand why you constantly criticize, but it is time to put your mourning aside. It's been years since Raphael and Adam died. You cannot mourn them forever."

Edwin shook, and Leopold cuddled him close. The two women clearly had a lot of unresolved tension between them. It would be better for them to get it out now and be done with the matter. Then, hopefully, they would come to their senses, embrace each other and take the boy off his hands. Of course, it had been a long time since he had argued with a sibling.

Blythe turned on her heel. "Who are you to lecture me? I loved *my* husband. I'm not happy that he is gone, like you."

Mercy shook her head. "I am not happy to be a widow, and you know it. But, given my husband had a weak heart, there was always a possibility he would die before me. His death didn't end my life, too, and I have many things left to enjoy. He left me a son to raise, an estate to manage. I have my family. I have you. There are many things left to smile about. Not everything has to be drear or scandalous."

"There is nothing left to smile about when everything you love is ripped away from you!" Blythe glanced around and, when her gaze fell on Edwin snuggling in Leopold's arms, her expression hardened. "*Everything.*"

She slammed the door behind her and quickly disappeared outside. Mercy remained at the doorway, one hand on the glass, shoulders heaving. She pressed her head against the pane and a strangled sob escaped her. "Oh, she's impossible!"

Edwin raised his head long enough to peek at his mother and then buried his face again in Leopold's cravat. Although he knew he shouldn't, Leopold pressed his lips to the boy's head. "It's all right, my boy. Your mother and aunt are fine now. Just a little to do between them. Nothing for you to worry about." He set his chin to Edwin's head, breathing the scent of small boy deep into his lungs. To hold his son like this was foolish in the extreme. It would only make parting that much more painful.

Mercy straightened abruptly and turned around, wiping at her eyes. When her gaze fell upon Edwin curled up in his arms, a tender smile broke out across her face.

She did know the truth about their past. She didn't appear to resent him for it.

He took a deep breath to steady his emotions. He'd been so afraid she would hate him.

She drifted across the chamber toward him, and then sat at his side. "Thank you for taking care of Edwin." She rested her head on his shoulder, and then brushed her hand over Edwin's hair. "I'm sorry for raising my voice to Aunty Blythe, little one. It won't happen again."

Edwin merely cuddled closer against him.

Leopold turned to Mercy. "Are you all right, sweetheart?"

"I will be eventually."

Leopold pressed a kiss to her head, too. "I'll speak to her and set things right before I go."

"You're not going anywhere, my love. And if you do, I will follow you this time."

Leopold's heart broke. "You cannot do that. You and the boy belong here. I never have." Very gently, he lifted Edwin from his arms and placed him in his mother's lap.

Mercy grabbed his arm. "Where are you going?"

"If all goes well, you'll find out in due course."

He pushed up from the chair and headed to the doorway without looking back.

It took a while to find Lady Venables. She had stormed from the abbey in a rage and had disappeared into the gardens as if a demon chased her. Now that he had found her, perched on a bench beneath a tree, he wondered what it would take for her to forgive her sister. What she would demand of him. None of the situation was Mercy's fault.

She looked up when a twig broke under his boot. "What do you want? Come to destroy another woman's reputation?"

"I've come to confess if that will help."

Lady Venables blinked. "Confess to what? That you're the boy's father?"

Being accused was no easier to bear the second time around. "There is the possibility of that, yes. However, the boy was born well before my cousin died. He is the duke in every legal sense, and I have no intention of protesting otherwise."

Her gaze hardened to flint. "You slept with my sister and cuckolded your cousin."

"I never knew who it was, and Mercy was likely given no choice in the matter."

"But *you* surely had one?"

Had he? When it came to his family, the only choice he had was to protect them. "I had a choice, yes. I chose to submit to blackmail."

Her eyebrows shot up. "Blackmail? Don't you lie to me, too."

Leopold seated himself beside the fuming woman and took a deep breath. "If I hadn't bedded the woman when told to five years ago, there would have been worse consequences for both of us. I know now that the old duke was determined to get an heir at any price. My cousin, for reasons I cannot fathom, handed over his wife to a man he hated. Me. He and the old duke loathed my family, and my very existence. But they loved Romsey and the family's good standing in society.

"From what I have been able to determine, the old duke wanted to ensure that his line continued unbroken for posterity. He didn't care how he managed it. He never wanted my side of the family to inherit what was his. That is why he sent me, and not another to her. He ensured I would never be a threat to the boy. He could have sent just about anyone to her bed; someone who could have been cruel. He chose someone of his own blood, his own son's heir."

Blythe shifted on the bench. "Why would you agree to such a bargain? You could have pretended to go through with the deed."

"He had hidden my sister somewhere. If I had not done as he had demanded, he promised her a life of hardship and degradation. He had more disreputable contacts than I care to think about, and I was terrified for Rosemary. She was just a girl when he took her away. I had to protect her, and all of them, in any way I could."

He glanced at the abbey and shuddered. "Besides, the woman I bedded was to be examined afterward if there was the slightest doubt about what we had done that night. I couldn't bear to put the lady through yet another indignity, on top of sharing a bed with me."

"She loves that boy," Blythe said suddenly.

"Then she is a better duchess than the last. My cousin was

raised by a never-ending parade of servants. He was not a happy child. But Edwin is lucky to have a loving family in his life. I hope you will not hold his origins against him. It is clear to me he loves you very much."

When Blythe turned her face away, Leopold prayed he had done the right thing in confessing so much. There was no defense he could offer to excuse his part in that night, but at least Mercy's sister had as many facts as he knew in her possession. He hoped she would forgive Mercy because she was utterly innocent of any wrongdoing.

"You and my sister are lovers still?"

Oh hell, that was a further complication to all this. He was so tired of lying, and he didn't want to anymore. He took a deep breath. "Yes."

"When were you going to leave her?"

Leopold turned to gaze at the abbey, his heart a heavy weight inside him. "When the danger has passed, and I am assured Edwin is safe once more. I had always intended to move away once I found the information about my siblings. But I can leave before I find them if you demand it. Mercy loves and needs you. And you need her as well. I would like to hire a steward for the estate first, though. She and Edwin will need good help to manage Romsey in the years to come. A place like this cannot be left neglected for long."

Lady Venables nodded slowly. Her gaze swept over the surrounding countryside, and then landed on him. "I fear my sister has grown unduly attached to you."

Leopold bowed his head. "I am sorry for that. It was never my intention to get involved in her life, or the boy's. I don't belong here. I reminded her of that just this morning in fact."

"I'm sure that went over well. My sister is impetuous. She never thinks beyond the moment to what will lie ahead."

Leopold laughed. "Duchess or not, she just cannot have what she wants all the time."

His companion raised a brow, either to his laugh or assertion, but didn't comment. Leopold had the distinct feeling that Mercy wanted him to remain her lover for a long time. Unfortunately, they didn't have that long together.

Lady Venables raised her hand to shield her eyes. "Is that a carriage approaching the abbey?"

Leopold stood and squinted in the direction she indicated. "It is, damn it." He turned to her. "Will you return with me, my lady? Despite the servants lingering about the grounds, I am still concerned for your safety out here alone."

After a long moment of hesitation, Blythe stood and joined him as he walked toward the abbey. "Who do you think it is that comes?"

"I am unsure at this distance, but I believe it is Lady Barnet come to call again."

Blythe stopped. "Lady Barnet," she snarled.

"You don't like many people, do you?"

"There are plenty of good reasons not to wish to spend time with that scandalous viper." Her nose wrinkled with disgust, and then her gaze raked him from head to toe. "I don't see you winning over people easily, either."

Leopold smiled tightly. "That is because I do not care to be any different than I am. I want nothing from the people I meet. They can take me as I am or go to the devil."

"A man with a singularly brave attitude. Interesting."

Blythe's expression was speculative as they returned to the abbey, and Leopold couldn't decide if her last comment had been a compliment or an insult. It was only after they had sat down again with Mercy to await the arrival of Lady Barnet that he wondered what exactly she thought of the situation they were in now. Her expression had blanked of emotion. The lady appeared as regal and as cold as stone.

"Lady Barnet and Lord Shaw, Your Grace," Wilcox announced.

Leopold stood to greet Mercy's guests. Lady Barnet barely acknowledged Blythe, Lord Shaw offered a little flattery, and then focused on Mercy.

"We came as soon as we could this morning to tell you our trip is delayed," Lady Barnet gushed. "Mama is ill and taken to bed, so you will have ample time to come up to London with us when we go now. No more excuses."

Chapter Twenty-Five

Mercy gently removed her hands from Anna's surprisingly firm grip. "Oh, dear. I do hope your mama is not too ill. Whatever is the matter? Have you summoned the physician?"

Since Anna's mother was often taken to bed, Mercy wasn't unduly alarmed. But the zeal with which Anna had clutched at her was slightly unnerving.

Anna waved away Mercy's fears. "Oh, no. I'll not let them at Mama with the leeches just yet. I thought perhaps you might consent to visit with her. She simply adores your company."

Unfortunately, stepping out for a social call was likely impossible just now. She glanced quickly at Leopold and saw a subtle shake of his head to confirm her suspicions. "I do wish your mother a speedy recovery, but it is unlikely I shall leave the estate in the near future. But do please send for Dr. Heyburn immediately. He told me only recently that he's having better luck with scented waters than with leeches."

Lord Shaw stepped forward to claim her hand. As it was raised to his lips, she saw a happy smirk cross Anna's face. Leopold's lips pressed together as if he didn't like what he was seeing. Lord Shaw's lips dragged across her skin, and she repressed a shudder before tugging her hand back.

"It has been too long, my dear duchess, since I have had the pleasure," Shaw said. "You do know how to keep a gentleman waiting."

Oh dear. She had hoped he would have taken her word she'd had enough of his flirtations. Given the way he looked at her, he still thought he had a fair chance. But there was only Leopold she wanted, and only Leopold she would have, or none other. "I have been much involved in the estate at present. I'm sure you made do without my company."

Lord Shaw's smile repulsed her. "Made do but never could replace. You shall have to take mercy upon me."

Since Leopold's hands had curled into fists, and Blythe looked about to erupt into flame, Mercy swiftly set Edwin on her knees to keep Lord Shaw at a distance. Neither Anna nor Lord Shaw cared for Edwin's company on their visits, unlike Blythe and Leopold. Although he never said one word on the subject, she was starting to suspect that her lover had grown fond of her boy.

His boy. Their son.

She suppressed a smile.

When everyone had settled in comfortably, Anna leaned forward. "Now, since our trip was delayed, I am determined that you should come to London with us. I so want your company for a short while. It has been an age since we have done anything fun together." Her glance shifted to Blythe and back again. "There is this splendid new modiste on Bond Street who makes the most delicious gowns. We simply must see for ourselves before she becomes all the rage. When everyone engages her services, the bloom will be gone from her style. I do hate it when that happens."

Blythe snorted. "You mean another scandalous dress that will damage Mercy's reputation as a proper lady. The last modiste you took her to put her husband in a snit for a week."

Oh dear. Blythe had hated Anna's influence on her wardrobe during that season, and she was correct that Edwin had been in a snit about those gowns. Given she and her sister had not spoken directly since Blythe's return with Leopold, she hoped Anna being here wouldn't make things worse between them.

Anna stoked her gold bracelet and smiled at Blythe with such condescension that Mercy considered throwing up her hands in defeat. "His Grace was right to be jealous of the attention Mercy received. She *was* very lovely in her youth."

Although alarmed that Anna thought her less lovely now she was a few years older than the green girl she had been, Mercy strove to ignore the comment and control the flush of embarrassment heating her skin. Did she really look so different?

"Actually, I think the room is filled with naturally beautiful women," Leopold said suddenly, his gaze dipping to where Anna still fiddled with her jewelry. "I cannot help feeling particularly lucky to be introduced to such remarkable women."

A hot flush of pleasure raced across Mercy's skin. Leopold had never given her a compliment before except in private. To hear him do so in public endeared him to her more. She wanted everyone to know how great his heart was. But her heart also swelled in wonder that he included Blythe in his comment. He would not be Blythe's favorite person at the moment, yet he considered her remarkable, too.

Her sister scowled at him, and then glanced away, a blush coloring her cheeks.

"Yes, yes," Lord Shaw chimed in. "I cannot imagine a better place to be than at Romsey Abbey."

"I quite agree," Leopold said immediately.

His glance landed and stayed fixed on Lord Shaw. They sized each other up as if they were combatants. Thank heavens they were supposed to be on their best behavior during social calls, or she feared Leopold would take umbrage at the heated looks Lord Shaw kept throwing her way. It was nice he was unsettled, but it was also quite unnecessary.

Mercy turned to Anna, hoping to distract the men. "Anna, you looked equally exquisite that year. The embroidery was so remarkable that I always thought I could reach out and prick my finger on the thorns. The ladies were all agog for the design, and Edwin told me you cut quite a swathe through the gentlemen's hearts."

"They were blackberry vines; His Grace's favorite fruit." Anna preened a little, and then turned her gaze on Leopold. "I see you are still enjoying the delights of Romsey Abbey."

"Yes, it is very good to be at home again. I quite understand why Her Grace is hesitant to leave. The abbey is as I remember it from years ago."

"But leave she must," Anna interjected with a quick glance at her brother. "A woman must have greater society than this if she is to be admired as she deserves. The Duchess of Romsey must grace London's ballrooms. She cannot allow herself to become a recluse."

Leopold scowled. "I would have thought that what the duchess chooses to do with her time is nobody's business but her own. She has her own mind, and is as stubborn as her predecessors. My cousin chose well for his wife. She does the family proud."

Color leeched from Anna's face, her hands curling into fists. "You did not know your cousin well, I'm told. He never mentioned you to me."

One of Leopold's eyebrows shot up at her last words. "I imagine he didn't mention my existence to anyone. We were not on the best of terms. But I am curious as to why he would mention me to *you*, in particular. Have you enjoyed a close acquaintance to the Randalls for some time?"

Anna shifted in her chair. "For a good while, yes." She wouldn't meet Mercy's gaze.

"Ah," he murmured. Leopold's gaze fell, his lips pursed. What was he thinking now? Was he as surprised as Mercy was by Anna's comment? She'd had no idea Anna had an acquaintance with her husband before she married him. She'd thought Anna had been her friend first.

Edwin squirmed off her lap, distracting them all with the movement.

"He's likely hungry," Blythe murmured. "I'll take him and see that he eats."

Mercy smiled at her sister in appreciation. At least she harbored Edwin no ill will so far. "Thank you. Cook was to make him apple puffs again. He has become rather fond of them."

When Blythe hurried Edwin out of the room, Leopold frowned at their disappearance. Was he as conflicted as she was about Edwin leaving her sight? If Edwin were not with Blythe, she would be greatly uneasy. But Blythe loved him. She would never let him come to harm.

Leopold caught her eye. "How long since you've been up to London?"

"Going on five years, I believe."

"Yes, yes," Anna agreed. "Much too long a time spent here."

His frown grew. "Why so long?"

She smiled. "There wasn't anything in London that I couldn't find here. Besides, the country air is good for Edwin, and Blythe was nearby and needed me."

"That woman needs a life of her own," Anna muttered.

"Anna, you are speaking of my dear sister. If I were ever to go to London then I would surely invite Blythe to come and stay with me at the mansion."

A quick grin crossed Leopold's face then disappeared.

Anna, however, looked offended by her plan to invite Blythe to London, too.

"Well, then," Anna said. "If I cannot convince you yet again to see sense, I shall bid you good day. Send a note round if you should change your mind. You know where to find superior company."

Since Anna still played with her gold bracelet, Mercy closed the distance between them and lifted her arm for a better view of the piece. Blackberry vines were engraved into the soft metal.

Mercy's mouth grew dry. She swallowed the lump forming in her throat and met Anna's gaze. "I've always admired your jewelry. You must love the piece to wear it every day."

Anna's smile turned a little bitter. "It was a gift."

She didn't say who from but Mercy was starting to wonder if the woman the duke had written about had been her friend, Anna. Blythe had not deciphered much of the text, but the word blackberry had featured heavily in the duke's remarks.

Had Anna been engaged in an affair with her husband behind her back? Was that why he was always too tired to visit her bedchamber?

Mercy stared at her friend.

Anna tugged her arm back. "Good day, Your Grace."

"Lady Barnet," Mercy replied.

Anna turned for the door. Lord Shaw moved somewhat slower, bid her a good day in his usual lecherous way, eyes fixed on her bodice, and then followed his sister out.

The silence after their departure was deafening. The clock chimed the hour, startling Mercy enough to jump.

"I believe I shall see your guests out, Your Grace. I know you like them, but I'm afraid they both make me uneasy. Do excuse me for a moment while I ensure that they have gone. I'll check on Edwin before I return to you."

Mercy nodded, thinking of Anna's remarks about how long she had known the Randalls. And the bracelet, and her assertion that blackberries were her husbands favorite fruit. Mercy could not remember that about him. Just how intimate a friendship had Anna and her husband shared?

She put her head into her hands as a door clicked shut. Why would Anna claim her husband would have confided in her about Leopold? Edwin had always discouraged Mercy's invitations to Anna, which was why Mercy had gleefully resumed a close friendship after her husband had passed away. Yet Anna was not comfortable at Romsey Abbey for any length of time. She was not at all comfortable with her son, and was always trying to get Mercy to leave the estate for one reason or another.

A hand settled on her shoulder and squeezed.

Mercy sighed heavily. "I'm so sorry Anna was rude to you, my love. If she cannot be at least civil to you, I will ask her not to call again."

Cold pressed against her temple. "You'll not have to worry about that for long," an unfamiliar voice whispered in her ear. "Now get to your feet, don't you dare say another word, and come with me. I'll not hesitate to put a hole in that pretty head of yours, Duchess."

Mercy lifted her gaze and caught her reflection in a mirror. She gasped. A large pistol barrel rested at her temple, a wild-looking stranger stood at her back. "What do you want?"

He winked at her slowly, curled his arm about her waist, and hefted her and the chair backward. "Everything that was taken from me. We're going to sit quietly and wait for the duke to come back. And then, my dear duchess, Romsey will fall to those who deserve it."

Once the carriage had gone and Wilcox had reported that all of Lady Barnet's servants had been accounted for, Leopold went to check on Edwin and Lady Venables before returning to Mercy's side. No matter how things went, her friends and family would dislike him. Once they all spotted the resemblance, Mercy would undoubtedly be slighted. He might have wealth enough to make him acceptable to some, but without a title, he was far beneath her social circle.

He eased the door to the morning room open and caught sight of Edwin sitting at a small round table with his aunt. Edwin's face was covered in sticky cream, and Lady Venables was dabbing at it ineffectually. The sight made him smile. "Do you mind if I join you for a moment, my lady?"

"Could I stop you?"

"Perhaps, but I wanted a word with you. It's about Lady Barnet."

"What about her?"

Leopold eased into a chair. "Did you know that the lady was acquainted so well with my cousin?"

A frown spread over her face. "I did not. She befriended Mercy shortly after her marriage, and I must confess I did not like her from the start."

"Did you think her attachment insincere?"

Lady Venables' expression grew grim. "She was always trying to get Mercy alone. She would offer her advice on how to deal with the duke and none of it was to his liking. She even lived here for a time, toward the end of Mercy's pregnancy, but once the boy was born, she wanted nothing at all to do with him. I thought she was more interested in Mercy's husband, especially when his health began to decline. She was here on the day he died."

Leopold didn't like the sound of that one bit. Had his cousin and Lady Barnet been lovers up until his death? If so, then his cousin had had rocks for brains to dabble anywhere but beneath his own wife's skirts. "Lady Barnet has a husband somewhere, correct?"

His companion scowled fiercely. "If you could call it a marriage, then yes, she is married. But Lord Barnet spends his time in London and, when not in Parliament, is a great patron of the theater. I cannot remember the last time he returned to the country with his wife. I cannot remember the last time I saw them together."

A nasty image was starting to form in Leopold's mind. Had the attachment been so strong that Lady Barnet sought to drive

Mercy from the abbey by frightening her into leaving? But to what end? There was no reason to do so when her lover had died.

It wasn't beyond the realms of possibility for Lady Barnet to feign poor penmanship and send threatening notes if she'd come to resent Mercy being his cousin's wife. But to destroy animals so callously, so cruelly, and leave them on Mercy's bed. He wasn't sure a woman could be capable of such atrocities. He wasn't sure he wanted to meet them.

In all honesty, Leopold had not taken a liking to Lady Barnet, especially when she suggested that Mercy was not the most ravishing woman in the room. Mercy took his breath away with every smile. It was not particularly nice to criticize a friend before others.

He glanced at Lady Venables. "Well, she is gone for the day with no trouble caused."

"She has gone, but will be back as surely as the sun rises in the morning."

"Let's hope we have a longer absence than that." He glanced at Edwin, saw a streak of cream remaining on his cheek and grabbed a napkin to wipe it away. "Well, at least she took that scoundrel Shaw with her."

Lady Venables' eyebrow rose. "If you are leaving, sir, I think it vastly unkind to fuss about the boy in this way. He will become attached to you."

"Would you rather have the cream smeared over his face attached to your gown instead?"

A rare smile crossed the woman's face as she looked upon Edwin. "That is the way of boys. They are messy and unpredictable."

Leopold grinned. "That we are. Shall we rejoin the duchess? I do not wish us to be separated for long."

Her smile vanished. She nodded primly, held her hand out to Edwin, and headed for the door. Leopold followed, bemused by Mercy's younger sister. She was as changeable as the weather. One moment hostile; the next almost on good terms with him. It seemed to him that she couldn't work out precisely whether she liked him or not. At least, she didn't view him as her enemy for the moment. However, it would not pay to relax around her. He could easily offend her without trying.

He glanced up when she stopped suddenly, blocking his way forward.

He looked over her shoulder to see Mercy, sitting regally in a high-backed chair far across the room. She smiled. Yet tears rolled down her cheeks.

His heart ached. The poor woman. She had so much strife in her life that he wondered if his staying at Romsey might be better. Could he make her life easier to bear?

"Please do take a seat." She indicated to the chairs opposite.

He frowned. Why was she behaving as primly as her sister? Why had she moved the chair so far away from its usual placement?

Leopold moved ahead of Lady Venables into the room. Mercy didn't so much as twitch at his approach. When he got closer, her eyes slid downward and to the side. He followed where her gaze drifted and saw a pistol digging into her ribs.

"Don't come any closer. Give me the boy."

The harsh male request shocked Leopold, and then his anger destroyed the shock. While he'd been gone, Mercy had been set upon. If she was harmed, he'd tear strips off the intruder. He couldn't place the unrefined accent, but a common thug held Mercy at gunpoint.

Behind him, Blythe gasped, and he heard sounds of struggle. Leopold flung his hand backward, moving to step between the stranger and Edwin, to stop them advancing farther into the room. "Hold him. Keep him safe."

Leopold approached Mercy. "Show yourself, coward."

"Oh, I'm no coward," a deep voice rumbled. "Just prudent. Rumor has it you travel armed. Put it down on the floor, if you please."

Leopold put his hand in his pocket, and then remembered he didn't have the piece on him anymore. He'd given it to Mercy for her protection, but it appeared she'd not had time to use it. Was it hidden in her gown?

He withdrew his hand, and spread them wide, palms out from his sides. "I am unarmed."

A wild mane of tangled blond hair appeared around Mercy's shoulder then disappeared again. The man, some years younger than himself, was dressed no better than a common sailor.

"Are you all right, love?"

Mercy nodded, then winced as the pistol was dug deeper into her ribs.

"Get on your knees," the stranger ordered.

Leopold closed his eyes briefly, his mind sifting through possibilities and strategies. In that position, he'd never stand a chance of getting Mercy away to safety. The stranger would win. He shifted a little to try to get a better glimpse of the man behind Mercy. Although he was mostly hidden behind the chair, Leopold judged him to be of average height and build. If Mercy was out of the way, Leopold would be a match for him in a fair or dirty fight. Except for the scoundrel's speed when he moved. If he ran, Leopold would never catch him. Leopold wouldn't make that mistake again.

"Who are you? What do you want here?"

The stranger laughed. "Nothing from *you*. Nothing you've got to give would ever change things. Only their deaths can make me whole again. Bring me the boy."

Not a chance in hell. Leopold shifted his weight subtly from foot to foot. There was no way he would allow Mercy to suffer any more of this when he had the strength to protect her. He met her terrified gaze, let all the love he felt for her show in his eyes, and silently said goodbye.

The only way to stop this was a frontal assault and the hope that Mercy could flee to safety. There was no other way that he could see. He took a deep breath. "Over my dead body."

He charged.

Chapter Twenty-Six

Mercy shrieked as Leopold rushed forward, murder in his eyes.

"You," he growled as he reached her, but then pushed Mercy from her chair as he passed, shoving her to the floor and out of danger. "You bloody stupid beggar!"

"No, don't!" the stranger cried out as they crashed to the floor. "You'll ruin everything!"

A gunshot rang out, making her ears ring, and the sounds around her became muted. Mercy covered her head, but then couldn't bear not knowing what was going on. She turned around and lifted her head.

Leopold had her attacker flat on his back, fists wrapped around his throat.

Mercy glanced around wildly and saw that her son and sister were safe on the far side of the room, huddled behind a large chair, eyes wide with terror. She relaxed for a moment, but then Blythe dragged Edwin into her arms and fled with him, crashing through the door as if demons chased her.

"Mama!" Edwin screamed, crying out as Blythe took him away from danger.

But Mercy couldn't follow him. She couldn't take her eyes off the men longer than a second; Leopold was choking the stranger beneath him, and his frantic attempts to gain his freedom worried her. What if the villain fought free?

"I should wipe the floor with you," Leopold growled, drawing her attention to him again.

"You haven't got the bollocks for it," the man beneath him croaked. "They deserve to die. Slowly and painfully for all the evil they have done!"

Leopold leaned closer until their faces were inches apart. "I'll kill you if you harm the boy. I'll make the old duke proud of the pain I'll inflict on you."

"Leopold, no!" Mercy cried out. This was getting out of hand.

"No, King Leopold, don't kill me," the man on the floor mocked. His head lifted. "You couldn't kill me. You couldn't kill your own brother."

Brother? Mercy gaped at the stranger. Brother? Who was this? She put her hands on the floor to support herself.

"Oh, I could do that in a minute if you so much as twitch toward the boy."

The doors burst open, and Allen and Wilcox raced toward Leopold. They caught the stranger's arms and legs and pinned him to the floor. That it took three men to hold him still alarmed Mercy. What would have happened to Edwin if Leopold had not come home before his brother?

Allen leaned down to stare at the stranger. "Bugger me, but that looks like…"

A look of disgust crossed Leopold's face as he stood. "It is," Leopold growled. "I'll get something to tie him up with. Once he's secure, I'll decide what to do with him."

Leopold destroyed the drapes getting the ties, but Mercy was beyond caring. While they wrestled the squirming brother into a chair and bound him to it, Mercy tried to make sense of it all. The stranger wasn't really a stranger. He had called Leopold brother, which made this man either Oliver or Tobias Randall. Leopold's long-lost family.

Mercy curled over in despair. All this time, and the danger had come from within their own family.

After much swearing, Leopold left his captive and lifted her from the floor. He held her in his arms, squeezed gently, and then guided her to a chair set at a distance from the struggling man.

Leopold's skin was ashen. His dark eyes dim. Desolate. "I am so sorry. I will deal with him, and then you will never have to see us again. I promise."

Mercy caught his hand as his words sunk in. "Who is he?"

He glanced over his shoulder. "This is Tobias Randall, my soon to be dearly departed younger brother."

Mercy clung to him. "You cannot harm him. Not after you've

finally found him! Or he's found you, in this case. Please, don't do anything rash."

"I'd like to know why the hell I can't kill him. Think of what he's done to you. He's shamed us all with his actions. I cannot expose the boy to the likes of him. I cannot take a risk with Edwin's life even for the sake of my brother. We'll be gone at first light."

"He doesn't know the truth." Her eyes filled and tears fell down her cheeks, beyond her power to stop. "Tell him."

He brushed them away with his thumb. "Life will be better for you soon, sweetheart. I promise you that."

Mercy shook her head. "It won't be."

"I don't have any other choice." Leopold left her, dragged a chair toward his brother and settled into it, sitting backward as he faced his errant brother. "What the hell do you think you're doing here?"

A chilling smile curled Tobias' lips. "Getting revenge for us. The duchy must fall to better hands."

"Fool. The duchy is already in better hands. They are gone."

"The boy is the last," Tobias growled.

Mercy trembled at the hatred in his voice.

Leopold shook his head. "The boy is innocent of everything."

"That will change. The evil is in their blood!"

A harsh bark of laughter left Leopold's throat. "Not a possibility, although with this stunt, you leave me with doubts about our *own* purity. What gives you the right to terrify a woman?"

"Rosemary's tender feelings weren't spared. They dragged her away screaming blue murder! I never saw her again."

"I didn't know that." Leopold's head dropped low. "Tell me what happened that day."

Mercy wanted to go to him and give him what comfort she could, but she was a little afraid of Tobias Randall. She didn't want to get too close just yet. "Please," she asked. "He's been so worried about you and the others. He came to Romsey to begin a proper search for you all."

The pain that crossed Tobias' face broke Mercy's heart. Any animation that had been there before, even anger, had vanished behind a violent mask of desolation. He drew in a shuddering breath and met his brother's gaze without flinching. "The carriage wheels broke, two of them at once, and we were pitched to the gutter. Rosemary and I scrambled out first, but Mama was hurt and couldn't be moved. The grooms were dead on the ground. Papa sent Rosemary and I back to the last village we had passed to get help for our mother. He wasn't strong enough to lift her out without causing her great pain. When we came back with the blacksmith, there were many horses surrounding the carriage, two men standing on top of it."

Tobias closed his eyes. "They shot into the carriage where our parents lay trapped. They didn't make another sound. The blacksmith we'd brought with us to help disappeared into the trees."

When Tobias opened his eyes, they were as cold as a midwinter blizzard. "Rosemary ran at them, shrieking like a fiend. One of them, a groom from Romsey, caught her and tossed her up onto his horse, slung over his thighs like a common trollop. He took her away, screaming at the top of her lungs."

Leopold's hands had curled into fists on the chair. "And you?"

"Impressed." Tobias' jaw clenched tight on the word, and Mercy had the distinct feeling that so much more had happened to the young man than he was prepared to admit. Her heart ached for the grim picture his single word evoked. A life lived onboard ship was cruel if you were not well connected. Men who were impressed didn't often survive. According to Leopold, Tobias had been only thirteen at the time he disappeared. It didn't surprise her that Tobias Randall had grown into a bitter man. Not after seeing his parents murdered, his sister taken by force.

And Rosemary had never been seen again. The old duke had truly been an evil man to have done this to his own family.

The difficulty she faced was deciding how deeply Tobias' resentment, his need for revenge, was planted.

Leopold's head bowed, and then he tossed it from side to side, as if he was trying to dispel the image Tobias' words painted. Mercy wished him luck. She doubted she would ever sleep well until Rosemary was found, whole and sound. Returned safe here to them.

"When did you return to Romsey?"

"Last new moon."

A heavy frown marred Leopold's face when he raised it. "You've been prowling the estate for weeks? Why not just knock on the door and make good your threats? Why behave so sickeningly?"

Tobias lifted his chin defiantly. "Wanted to make sure who was who around here. You were dead, too, or so I was led to believe. Never expected to see you dancing to their tune." Tobias sneered in Mercy's direction, and she shrank away from him. "Or is it *her* tune you're dancing to now? The rose arbor is a lovely, quiet spot for a quick tumble, not that you were quick or quiet. Voices carry well across water."

Mercy winced as Leopold cuffed Tobias across the jaw. "Speak ill of the duchess again and I'll drown you."

Tobias tossed his head to shake off the pain. "Won't drown. I know how to swim better than you now."

"Well, that's a relief," Allen snorted. "Last time I had to fish you out by your boots and pump the water from your insides."

Mercy stared at them. Now the Randalls were together in one place, there was a definite resemblance between every single one. It still astonished her that Allen, the old duke's illegitimate son, was here at all. But since he had been no trouble for her, she had no good reason to turn him away. Others might look down their noses at a duke's bastard but he was still family. And Allen did a good job working with the horses. There was no reason to make a fuss about him.

Tobias threw Allen a dirty look. "Who the hell are you?"

"Our cousin, Charles Allen. Remember him? He saved your life. Isn't having the family all together positively grand?" Leopold muttered sarcastically. He looked over his shoulder at Mercy. "Your Grace, I am confident this is your stalker. Our problem, if you will. Would you mind giving us some privacy? I'd like a few moments alone with my youngest brother. He needs to learn his proper place again before it is too late for us."

Mercy could understand Leopold wanting some privacy with his brother. He had been searching for him a long time. But she did wonder at Leopold's eagerness to get her out of the room. What was he going to do when she had gone? "I'll check on

Edwin, and then return. I'd like your assurance that you will both be here, and he will be breathing when I get back."

Leopold shook his head. "I cannot make a promise about the latter."

"Then I am not going to leave," Mercy replied sweetly. She sat back in her chair and clasped her hands in her lap. She hoped she was giving him the impression that she was not going away anytime soon. He could not harm his brother. He'd never forgive himself.

"All right, all right. I won't harm him as much as I would like."

Mercy squinted at him. That was at least a fair concession. "Good. I've no desire to face questions should a body be found in the woods. We will keep this matter within the family and, since I am the nominal head of the family until Edwin comes of age, I say he lives. There are many more ways to punish him. A haircut and bath would be a very good start."

Leopold smiled, his dimples as deep as ever Mercy had seen them.

Although she was attempting to make light of the danger that was Tobias Randall, Mercy climbed unsteadily to her feet and left them alone, her thoughts churning. To think Leopold's own brother, a man he had been desperate to find, had been at fault all along. What would Leopold have done if he'd had his pistol in his pocket? Would he have shot first and asked questions later? Mercy had read his intent in his eyes the moment before he had leaped forward. He had meant her to escape, leaving him alone with the stranger.

But he surely would not have been at peace with the guilt of killing his own brother. Perhaps Tobias could be persuaded the threat from the old duke's line was gone from the earth. Well, except for Mr. Allen and his sons. Since it seemed Leopold trusted Allen, Tobias might do the same given enough time.

What would it take to make Edwin safe around Tobias Randall?

There had to be a way to salvage this rather than rip the family apart any further. Perhaps he needed to hear and see the truth about Edwin. But that would require Edwin's presence and two sets of dimples on display. If Tobias could be convinced of the truth about Edwin's parentage, then she might feel more comfortable around his brother.

"Do you know where my sister went, Wilcox?"

"I'm afraid not, Your Grace. She sped past us with the boy in her arms and fled upstairs. I was distracted by Tobias Randall's arrival. Now that you mention it, it has been very quiet up there. Shall I fetch her for you?"

"No, I can manage. I shall find them myself." She glanced into the room she had just left. "Perhaps, it would be better if you were to stay close to the discussions taking place in there. Leopold is in somewhat of a temper with his younger brother. I should not like anything unfortunate to occur in my absence."

A slow smile spread across her butler's face. "I will ensure no lasting damage is done. It will depend on whether the lad will be reasonable."

Mercy shook her head. Men. Why were they so eager to do things the hard way? She'd never understand them. She doubted she should try. The only two males she had to worry about were Edwin and Leopold. They were more than enough of a challenge for now.

Mercy hurried upstairs and along to the family wing. She slipped inside Edwin's room, expecting to hear his greeting, but was met with utter silence. Although she searched every room in the family wing—including her husband's and Leopold's bedchambers—she found no trace of them.

She headed downstairs to the kitchens, wondering if Blythe had taken Edwin there for something more to eat. It was out of the ordinary for Blythe to visit the kitchen, but it had been that sort of a day. Her heart pounded, however, when she saw no sign of Edwin or Blythe at the end of the long table in the cavernous kitchens.

Cook wiped his flour-covered hands on a cloth and came forward. "Can I help you, Your Grace?"

Mercy swallowed the lump in her throat. "I'm looking for the duke and Lady Venables. Have you seen them?"

"No, I've not."

Mercy turned around in a circle to peer into each doorway, hoping they were approaching from another direction. Blythe knew the danger was caught and captured upstairs. There was no need to hide now. But they had vanished as if they were still in danger. They couldn't be gone. They just couldn't disappear.

Mercy took a step backward. There was no other reason for Blythe to be so hard to find. Not now. But panic suddenly gripped her. Could Tobias have an accomplice in the abbey?

She'd never thought of that until now.

Chapter Twenty-Seven

Leopold paced the drawing room, glancing occasionally at his youngest brother with competing feelings of alarm and joy. He wanted to embrace him, welcome him home properly but it was unsafe to loosen his bindings. He would hurt Edwin if he was released.

And then Leopold would kill him.

"I cannot believe you told the duchess about me," Allen growled.

"You try keeping secrets from her," Leopold muttered. "She's a force of nature."

Allen scowled. "Will you be needing me much longer? I've got duties out in the stables that need attendance."

"No." Leopold held up his pistol—he'd taken it from Mercy's pocket as he'd helped her to a chair—and turned it this way and that. "I can manage him if he becomes difficult."

Allen's frown grew. "You're not cold-blooded enough. Neither is he, by the way. I don't think he wouldn't have really gone through with it."

"How can you be so sure?" Leopold asked.

"He's been full of piss and wind since he was a boy. He and my sainted brother, Edwin, had that in common. Some things never change, but this one always took after your father."

Tobias looked as safe as a pirate standing before an open chest of gold bullion. His hair was long and unkempt, skin deeply tanned. Clothing aged and untended with a definite seaman's aroma. Leopold's nose twitched. But did those things make him dangerous? His eyes were the same ones he remembered, golden brown in a tanned and scarred face. Once he had been trusting, if slightly mischievous. Life had not been kind to Tobias, and Leopold's heart ached for what appeared lost.

Allen left and they were alone.

Tobias tried his bonds one more time. "Untie me and we can end this. You deserve to be duke."

"I deserve nothing of the sort, you idiot. I never wanted the title," he growled. "I cannot untie you. You cannot be allowed free inside the abbey. I don't trust you."

Tobias scowled. "But you trust *them*. She might look like Christmas morning, but for all you know she could be bringing reinforcements."

"Mercy wouldn't harm you. And she's had other punishments for me and plenty of time for it."

Tobias rolled his eyes. "She got you hooked all right, but wasn't talking about the duchess. It's the other one I'd be watching."

"Other one? Lady Venables?"

Tobias shrugged. "If that's her name. I've seen her about. Always talking to herself and the dead. Roams the forest leaving carrots in her wake for little bunnies to feast upon. Mad as a hatter, she is. If I was sleeping here, I'd do it with one eye open."

"Gray rabbits?" A feeling of dread crushed Leopold's chest. He yanked his brother's chin up and held his gaze. "When did you spy on Lady Venables? When, damn it?"

"Here now," Tobias protested, "don't you be getting rough with me. If you're bedding them both, you're a lot braver than I gave you credit for."

Leopold squeezed Tobias' jaw between his fingers. "I swear to God I will kill you if you do not answer my question."

"Last week. Perhaps Thursday morning. As the sun rose."

Blythe could have had ample time to capture the rabbits, secret them into the abbey, and leave the dead creatures to be found. The woman had free rein inside the abbey and grounds. Mercy would never suspect her sister.

He shook his brother. He had to know the truth. "Did you or did you not slaughter animals and leave them inside the abbey to frighten the duchess? Your answer will decide the fate of your miserable life."

Tobias' eyes widened. "I'm not mad."

"But you could threaten a *boy*."

"I was threatening our slimy cousin to begin with. I did not know he was dead until I returned to England and came back to Romsey. There's not much news to be heard in the places I've been sent to. It's not like anyone ever wrote back to me. When I found him gone, I settled on giving the duchess a good fright and taking a look at the boy so I knew who'd be coming for me later."

Leopold slumped and did a quick calculation. The first dead animals had been left well before Tobias had returned to England, if he could be believed. Would he lie about it?

Leopold wasn't sure, but if Tobias hadn't been the culprit then there had been two threats to the boy all along—the letters from Tobias, and the other grim business from someone infinitely more cold-blooded.

The door burst open and Mercy raced across the room. "What have you done?" she shrieked at Tobias.

Tobias recoiled. "Nothing!"

Leopold caught Mercy and held her back as her fingers stretched to claw at Tobias' face. Mercy struggled toward his brother. "Where are they?"

"Who are you talking about?" Tobias squeaked. "I've been tied up here for the past quarter hour."

"Then who is working for you? Who has taken our son and my sister?"

Leopold spun Mercy around to face him and gripped her tightly. "Is Edwin missing?"

Tears fell down her cheeks. "I cannot find him or Blythe anywhere they should be. But I bet Tobias knows what's been done with them!"

Panic gripped Leopold. He turned and wrapped his hand about Tobias' throat. "Where is the duke?"

Tobias fought against his grip. "I swear on our mother's grave, if I knew where she was buried, that I have done nothing to the duke and the mad one!"

"Mad one?"

Leopold released Tobias. Of all his siblings, Tobias had been the closest to their mother. He would never swear false on her memory. He wasn't involved in Edwin's disappearance. There was someone else working against Mercy.

His best guess was Lady Venables, her own sister. "He speaks of Blythe, Mercy."

"Blythe…but why?"

"I cannot be certain, but she may be involved in your troubles. All along, we have assumed that Tobias here was your problem, but what if two threats existed? He has admitted to sending the letters, but not to killing the rabbits you've found. What if someone else has been stalking you? What if it has been your sister all along? You mentioned that she has not been herself since her son died. Could Blythe be unhinged?"

"That's impossible," Mercy argued. "She would never harm Edwin. She loves him."

"Enough to want him for herself?" Leopold wiped away the tears streaming down Mercy's cheeks. "She is a changeable, complex woman. I never considered her a threat, but after hearing what Tobias has observed of her when you are not around, I'm uneasy. Could she be trying to drive you away from Romsey and leave Edwin to her care? She dotes on him like a mother does her son. When was Blythe last seen?"

Mercy wiped her tears from her face, but more fell to replace them. "When she fled this room, she went upstairs and disappeared. No one has seen them since."

Leopold drew her into his arms. "We'll search for them. My concerns may be for nothing. She is likely only hiding from the ugly scene she witnessed. No doubt my fool brother has scared her witless."

"She's very protective of Edwin, but she would never do what you suspect." Mercy pushed at his chest to gain her freedom and turned to face Tobias. "How important is family to you, Mr. Randall?"

Tobias glared at her. "*Everything.*"

Mercy smiled. "Untie him. He can be useful to us."

Leopold grabbed her by the shoulders and shook her. "That wouldn't be wise. He is still a threat to Edwin."

"Nonsense. He'd never hurt his nephew, would he?"

Tobias gasped. "Nephew?"

Mercy leaned close to Tobias. "If you harm your own flesh and blood, Tobias Randall, I will do worse to you than your brother can dream. Do we understand each other?"

"Nephew..." Tobias repeated rather stupidly again as Mercy drew back.

Did Leopold have to draw him a picture?

Mercy scowled. "Leopold, you never said your brother lacked for wits. I had assumed him to be rather more intelligent than this."

"It has been many years since I've been in his company. Oliver is the clever one. Perhaps Tobias has used up what little wits he had."

Mercy's lips lifted in a sad smile. "Untie him so we can recover Edwin, my love. Bring him with you so he cannot disappear again."

She swept out in a rush and began issuing orders to Wilcox and the housekeeper where they waited in the next room. Leopold glanced at his brother and saw bewilderment on his face.

"You and she and...the boy?"

Leopold rushed to untie his brother. "Now is not the time for this conversation."

"Now is exactly the time," Tobias protested. "Is the boy of your making or not?"

"Possibly," Leopold hedged.

"I will have the truth, King Leopold. Did you cuckold our cousin?"

"It seems I did. And don't call me King Leopold. We are far too old for those childish games to continue."

"You never did have much of a sense of humor." As the ropes fell away, Tobias surged to his feet, swung around and tackled him in a tight embrace. "You bloody brilliant bastard. What a way to get back at them. That changes everything!"

Leopold embraced his brother in return, but he didn't like misleading Tobias as to Edwin's conception. "I didn't do it by choice, you idiot. I haven't had control of my own life since our parents died. Let's go."

Although a frown crossed Tobias' face, he couldn't wait around to answer more questions. His boy was missing. He had to find out where Blythe had taken him before it was too late.

———

"Are you certain they are in there?" Mercy asked for the hundredth time.

Leopold nodded. "Edwin tried to answer me when I called out. Maybe he's fallen asleep in the interim."

Leopold didn't say what else was on his mind. Had Blythe hurt Edwin to prevent him from calling out?

He squeezed his eyes closed. His boy lived. He was sure of it. But for the moment, Edwin was beyond Leopold's reach. Blythe had taken him to a chamber and locked them in. She refused all entreaties to open the door. She did not believe Edwin was safe.

He ran his hands over the heavy door a second time. The hinges were on the inside and unfortunately he didn't know how to pick a lock. "Lady Venables, please, won't you let Mercy see her son. She is desperate to hold him, too."

"Please, Blythe, I need my boy!" Mercy called.

"You cannot protect him. Not with a devil in the house."

Leopold drew Mercy from the door before she could respond. "It's a good sign she didn't flee the abbey with him. She's trying to protect him, but that door is inches thick. We'd have to use an axe to get through which is not my first choice. We need to make her feel it's safe to come out of her own accord."

Once released, Mercy leaned against the door. "Tobias Randall is very sorry to have frightened us with his letters. He thought he was writing to my husband. He has apologized and sought forgiveness from me. After hearing what was done to him, I understand why he was angry. But not at us. It is safe to come out, dearest."

"Nowhere is safe. I'll not lose Edwin, too."

Fear clutched at Leopold. Just how odd was Blythe? She had seemed sane, if a little more reserved than the usual lady he met. Were her mind and her heart completely broken?

He cocked his head at Tobias, and they moved down the hall, away from the door while Mercy continued to plead for her son. Wilcox rushed up the staircase to join them.

"We need to get in there," Leopold said without preamble. "Now."

"The door is inches thick," Wilcox warned. "The only thing you'll break is your shoulder. I've sent for an axe."

Leopold raked his hands through his hair. "What about a second key?"

"I didn't know there was a first one. Maybe she could be coaxed out with a cup of tea and biscuit," Wilcox muttered.

"She's not a simpleton, man," Tobias muttered. "What we need is a distraction." He looked up and down the corridor. "We could set a fire and smoke her out."

Leopold rolled his eyes. "For God's sake, we are not setting fire to the abbey. You really are witless."

Tobias scowled. "Well, the only other choice to get into the room is via a window. Do you think your men outside could be relied upon not to shoot at me again?"

Leopold shook his head. "That's an unacceptable risk."

The first time he had watched Tobias scale the abbey walls, he hadn't known who he was but had been amazed by his skill. Now? He couldn't accept the risk of losing him after finally finding him again.

"No, it's not. Not when there is family involved." Tobias stripped off his coat, his footwear, and then entered the chamber next to where Edwin was being held. "Wilcox, be a good chap and wave at the servants on the grounds outside the window. I want you to stay there as long as possible so they know I'm doing this with your permission."

Tobias turned. "Brother, I'd suggest you return to the duchess. She's likely to become hysterical when the glass breaks. In my experience, most women find it a bit unsettling."

"I take it you've broken into ladies' bedchambers before."

"On occasion." Tobias shrugged. "Usually there is a bit of excitement to dampen the danger, but I don't think the mad one will be welcoming me with open arms."

"Is she mad?"

"How the devil would I know?"

"All clear," Wilcox called.

"All right then. Make way."

When Tobias threw his leg over the windowsill, Leopold's chest tightened. It was a damned dangerous thing to do, and he would be more afraid for Tobias if he had not already seen him clinging to the walls.

When he disappeared from sight, Wilcox hung out the window to watch his progress. He gave Leopold a reassuring wave to send him back to Mercy's side, and he hurried to join her. Mercy had slumped to the floor, head pressed to the wood. She was still calling to her sister to open the door.

Leopold drew Mercy to her feet and wrapped her tight in his arms. "We will have him soon, sweetheart."

"How? Oh Leopold, she won't even speak to me now. I want Edwin back in my arms. I want our son."

Leopold pressed a kiss to her hair just as breaking glass shattered the silence.

Mercy cried out, but he kept her against him as even more broke inside the chamber. Inside, Tobias swore loudly and Blythe yelped and there was a thud. There was silence for a few moments…and then Edwin started to cry.

The door handle rattled, and then was flung wide as Tobias thrust Edwin out of the room.

Mercy moaned and hugged Edwin to her, rocking him as the boy cried hysterically. After checking that the boy was unharmed physically, Leopold glanced inside the chamber.

Tobias was just settling Blythe on the narrow bed.

Leopold stalked inside. "Did you hurt her?"

"Of course not." Tobias held out his bloody hand. "She took one look me, and fainted."

"Hell's teeth, you're hurt."

"It's nothing. Just a scratch." But that scratch was leaving a tidy little patch of blood on the carpet at his feet while Tobias stood staring at Blythe. "Think she'll be all right?"

Leopold caught Tobias by the wrist and lifted his hand. There wasn't any glass that he could see in the wound so he took a chance and loosely bound his handkerchief around it. "I don't know. When she wakes up, we will have to detain and question her. Let us hope she does not faint again at the sight of you."

Tobias wiggled his fingers, and a wince crossed his face. "You should know, she put herself before the boy when I came through the window. She'd have clobbered me good and proper, too, if I'd gotten too close. Had that candlestick in hand, ready to send me to my maker. But then she wilted at the sight of my wound dripping blood. Are you sure she's the one slaughtering animals?"

"There doesn't seem to be any other possibility," Leopold murmured, while breathing a silent sigh of relief. That Blythe fainted at the sight of blood, and spirited Edwin away inside his own home, pointed to a woman who was more unhinged with grief than truly dangerous.

Tobias heaved a heavy sigh. "I hope you don't have to be too hard on her. It would be a shame for a beauty such as that to be miserable for long. She is beautiful when she smiles."

Now that was a surprise. Leopold could not remember seeing Blythe smile at all but it might take him a while to get used to his younger brother having an interest in the fairer sex. He wasn't sure how Blythe would care for Tobias' admiration, either. Watching the two of them together could have been interesting. When he'd known his brother before, he'd been young and had cared only for his hound and horses. Now, they were virtually strangers and would need to become reacquainted.

Perhaps it would be best to limit Tobias' association with proper ladies until he lost some of his rough edges.

Tobias shuffled from the room, bowing low to Mercy. "Is he well, Your Grace?"

"He is wonderful," Mercy said as she placed her hand on Tobias' arm. "Thank you for rescuing my son. Now, have that cut seen too. Wilcox will take care of you."

"Leopold was correct before in the drawing room. You do the family proud."

Mercy scowled at him. "How long were you listening, and where were you?"

"Long enough to hear my brother gush over your beauty." He glanced at the bed. "Are all the women in your family so pretty?"

Mercy shook her head. "Well, you are certainly a different kettle of fish than your brother. Honey drips from your tongue."

Tobias pressed his lips together hard, eyes alight with mischief. "If I told you what image your words evoked, I fear my brother would indeed kill me. I'd best take my leave of you. Until another time, Your Grace."

When he followed Wilcox down the hall and out of sight, Leopold's gaze moved to Mercy and Edwin where they stood clutching at each other. His heart swelled as he listened to Mercy and Edwin. His family. The two loves that would break him.

How would he bear not knowing how they fared?

Leopold took them in his arms and squeezed. They were everything to him now, his reason for living, his reason for breathing. But could he stay here with them on the outside of their lives, pretending to be happy with the arrangement and always wanting more?

Yet, the longer he stayed, the greater the chance of Mercy conceiving. She couldn't bear his child outside of marriage without facing utter ruin, and he couldn't ask her to marry him and give up her title to become his wife. So where did that leave them? His heart might break in two, but he would have to go on pretending he was happy as a cousin.

Edwin wriggled, as if to get down. When Leopold moved to give him space, Edwin jumped into his arms, clinging with a tight grip about his neck, and hung on to him as if he would never let go.

Leopold's eyes stung with unshed tears, and he closed his eyes at how much he wanted to remain with Mercy and Edwin.

"There now. Isn't that so much better?" Mercy said. "You have family now, Edwin. One big, wild family. We will likely never be lonely or bored again."

Leopold looked beyond Mercy to where Blythe lie all alone. "What do you want done about your sister, sweetheart?"

Mercy's smile dimmed. "I'm not sure what to do or think about Blythe anymore. But we should send for Dr. Heyburn. The physician can decide if Blythe's health is in any immediate danger or if she is indeed a threat to us."

Chapter Twenty-Eight

Mercy paced the hall outside the bedchamber where Blythe had been carried. Dr. Heyburn had been in there for an hour or more now, and she was long past the point of merely worrying for her sister's health. Shouldn't she have roused by now?

Mercy had no idea what to do, but she couldn't leave her spot outside the door until she heard his prognosis. She had asked Leopold to take care of their son while she waited on the doctor, and he'd been happy to put Edwin to bed. Tobias was downstairs somewhere, watched over by Wilcox and another footman, and she wanted to speak to him before nightfall.

Dr. Heyburn stepped into the hall and shut the door firmly behind him. "She is unchanged, Your Grace."

Mercy put her hand to her throat. "Surely there is some sign that she will come back to herself soon."

"Her heart beats strongly. Her skin is warm. But her gaze is unfocused, as if she sleeps."

He sat his little bag on a table and removed a bottle. "I have given a bottle of this remedy to the maid inside; I'll leave another with the housekeeper before I go. She is to drizzle a spoonful into Lady Venables' mouth on the hour, every hour, until I return tomorrow."

Mercy turned the bottle over in her hands, wondering what the concoction would do for her sister. The bottle was unremarkable in appearance and she handed it back to the doctor. "Is there anything else that can be done tonight?"

He shook his head. "From what little you've told me, she's suffered a fright of some kind. Once she's had time to rest, she may very well wake on her own with no ill effects suffered. If she does not wake on her own, I will begin more vigorous treatments to rouse her."

Mercy swallowed, afraid of what that might mean. She'd had little experience with doctors and their treatments, but if he thought such measures were required, she would have to consider them.

She hadn't told Heyburn about what Tobias Randall had done to bring Blythe to the point of collapse. Keeping quiet about the terror Tobias had caused spared his reputation. And Blythe would hate to be involved in any gossip concerning him, so Mercy held her tongue. There was nothing she wouldn't do to protect her family. "Thank you for coming on such short notice. May I see my sister now?"

He smiled kindly. "I cannot see why not. Try not to become too agitated by her state. The care of the sick can tax a woman's strength of will and cause a similar state in a perfectly happy woman."

Mercy blinked. Did the man think women were feebleminded? It was rare Mercy heard opinions of this kind voiced in her presence. Did he realize he'd just insulted a duchess with his remarks?

When he bowed, picked up his hat and hurried away, Mercy glared after him. She had thought him an open-minded fellow once upon a time.

She stepped into her sister's room. Blythe was in the center of the large bed, hair unbound; face smooth as if in sleep. Mercy moved toward the bed.

"The doctor said not to do anything out of the ordinary to disturb her, Your Grace," the young maid assigned at the doctor's request warned from the shadows.

Mercy sat on the side of the bed and picked up her sister's hand. "I have always behaved as I wish, child. Wait outside if you please."

When the maid hurried out, Mercy patted Blythe's hand. "There now. It's just us again. You can open your eyes now and talk to me. Everyone has gone."

Blythe made no response. Mercy had been hoping Blythe was merely pretending to sleep to avoid the embarrassment of her actions, as she had frequently done as a young girl.

She couldn't understand why her sister had taken Edwin and kept him from her. She was his mother. He was her responsibility.

She lifted Blythe's limp hand to her cheek and pressed a kiss to the back of it. "Wake up, Blythe. I need to talk to you very badly. What did I do to turn you away from me? Leopold fears it was you who killed those poor animals and left them about the abbey. How could you do that when little Adam had one as a pet? Wake up and tell me it cannot be? Please."

Blythe remained still.

Mercy blinked back tears. "I am so sorry that Tobias Randall frightened you by coming through the window as he did. But I had to have Edwin back in my arms. I cannot bear to be apart from him for long. You know that about me."

Mercy took a deep breath. "I hope you can hear me because I have something important to say, and I wanted you to be the first to know so there are no more secrets between us. I'm going to ask Leopold Randall to marry me. You can wake up and scold me all you like, but I love him. You were right before in the drawing room. I did meet him years ago, but I never knew his name. Edwin couldn't give me a child and the old duke demanded one. Leopold is Edwin's father. I am sure of it now. He came back to me as I'd hoped. I don't want to lose this second chance to be loved."

She searched for signs that her plans had outraged Blythe's strict sense of propriety. She would be giving up her rank, her position in society for the love of her life. But nothing changed in Blythe's bearing. Her chest rose and fell evenly. Her skin remained pale.

Mercy placed Blythe's hand beneath the covers so she wouldn't grow chilled. "I will also ask his brother, Tobias Randall, to stay here at the abbey. They have spent so much time apart, and I am willing to forgive him—slowly, mind you—for the trouble he's caused. You need to know that for when you wake. You will likely find him searching for clues about Oliver and Rosemary's location alongside Leopold and I, and I do not want you to be alarmed or feel left out. Did you get very far in deciphering those books? I wish you would wake and tell me. I want to tell Leopold about the room soon. If I have the deciphered journals to show him, maybe he will not be disappointed with me for not telling him straight away."

Mercy sat back and waited, hoping Blythe would blink and speak her mind.

When she remained silent for another hour, Mercy pressed a kiss to her brow, summoned the maid, and left her to sleep and heal.

There were worst things in life than putting your child to bed with a bedtime story and a long hug. In fact, Leopold could grow used to such events very easily. He trudged down the stairs to the library and peeked inside. Tobias sat draped over a large leather chair, drinking directly from a bottle in hand. He stepped into the room, surprised and pleased to see his brother had remained at Romsey Abbey. "Are you jug-bitten already?"

"No, only mellowing." Tobias peered at his bottle. "I must say the duke keeps a fine cellar. You have no idea the rot they serve up in some of the ports I've found myself in. Melt your boots off, but you get used to it, given enough leave."

Leopold glanced uncomfortably at Tobias' damaged hand, bound tight in fine white linen, a stark contrast to the ragged state of his clothes. He took the bottle from him, poured a generous amount of liquid in a glass, and put the bottle back on the shelf. He handed Tobias a fresh glass to help numb the pain of his injury. "Thank you, for retrieving Edwin. The duchess would say so too if she could be persuaded to leave her sister."

Tobias waved away the thanks. "After my mistake, a bit of pain will be an easy burden. Besides, once the ladies get a gander at this, they'll be swooning all over me. Women like a man with a good scar and a story to go with it."

Leopold raised a brow. "Does that happen a lot? Ladies swooning and you injured."

"It's a fluid thing. What's life if not to take a risk?" He drained the glass and held it out for more. "What did you do with the mad one?"

"Lady Venables is secured in a chamber upstairs. The doctor has come and gone and servants are assigned to watch over her.

She hasn't spoken to anyone since you broke through the window. We fear she's suffered a great shock."

"Possibly. Reminds me of the time when a young man onboard my first ship, an officer from a well-off family, froze in battle. He stood dumb like an oxen on the quarterdeck. Don't know how he wasn't killed or set upon. When the ship was taken, and we were rounded up, he didn't move. The French, being a merciful lot, dumped him over the side. He never came back up."

"Tobias," Leopold growled. "That is not very reassuring."

Tobias shrugged. "I'm out of practice. Spent most of my time staying alive, avoiding the hard jobs, rather than observing the niceties. The mad one won't have the same problems that fellow faced. Someone will clean up her drool, force food down her throat, and keep her warm. She's much better off here than not."

"What am I going to do with you now?"

Tobias lifted his empty glass and wobbled it. "I imagine you might allow your errant brother a few drinks, a decent meal, and place to sleep before kicking him out."

Leopold crossed his arms over his chest. The idea of Tobias loose on society as he was now was utterly impossible. "I won't kick you out. It will be up to the duchess to decide if you remain. It is her house."

"Then I shall await Her Grace's delicate foot connecting with my backside." He shrugged. "I'll be all right here until then."

"Do you have funds, land, friends in England?"

Tobias squirmed. "I do all right. Don't trouble yourself."

"You're my brother. I will always trouble myself for you. I have saved every penny, Tobias. Tomorrow, we will discuss what you would like to do with your life."

Tobias stood and refilled his own glass. "Are you sure you want me to stick around that long? Aren't you worried about what I might do overnight?"

Leopold snorted. "I'd be more worried if you left here. Besides, I have my spies watching you. Behave yourself, and I will see you at breakfast."

"He will see you at lunch," Mercy said from the doorway. "After this, we shall be all indulging in a quiet morning tomorrow. You don't mind if you speak with him later in the day, do you?"

Tobias waved his hand about. "Of course, Your Grace, we wild Randalls are yours to command."

An impish grin crossed Mercy's face. "Perhaps another time. Do excuse me; I need your brother as a matter of some urgency."

Tobias chuckled. "Urgent again. Perhaps this time he will slip you out of your gown before he ravishes you. Poor form, by the way, brother. Even I know a proper lady requires better treatment for a tryst than a hard wooden bench."

Leopold had forgotten what it was like to be teased by a brother. He hadn't missed this aspect of his former life and it would take a while to grow accustomed to the discomfort.

Mercy blushed. "Enjoy your brandy tonight, Tobias. Tomorrow, you and I will also have a long discussion about what a lady likes to hear in her presence. When my sister comes to her senses, you had better be prepared. You're exactly the sort of man she'll loathe. Cross her at your peril. I should hate to see you gelded at such a young age."

She beckoned Leopold to follow her and stepped out onto the terrace.

Leopold glanced at his brother. "It really isn't too late to end your life, Tobias."

"No chance of that now. Besides, life is just getting interesting. Imagine us all here at Romsey Abbey. Who'd have thought it could ever be ours?"

"The old duke. It's what he feared most." He pointed a finger at his brother. "Don't disappear while I'm gone, brother. We have a lot of catching up to do still."

"I'm not moving." Tobias wriggled to get more comfortable.

Leopold stalked to the door, eager to catch up with Mercy and find out what she wanted from him now.

Behind him, Toby called out, "I'd like another nephew when you can arrange one. Mother always said 'one' was too lonely a number."

Chapter Twenty-Nine

Evening was the time for secrets and lovers, but tonight as Mercy stepped out onto the terrace she was determined to dispense with both. She set her hands to the balustrade, listening to Leopold's footfalls come closer, and tried to steady her racing heart.

The danger to Edwin was gone, or so she hoped, but one challenge still remained.

Leopold set his hand to her shoulder. "I take it there is no change."

"None. She sees nothing. Reacts to nothing. It is unnerving to see her so still."

"You left a maid with her?"

"I left two. Wilcox was good enough to send to Walden Hall for Blythe's maid, and I have assigned mine instead of the young girl the doctor suggested. When she wakes, she will see familiar faces and they will send for me."

Leopold's sigh was loud. "I had thought you might have stayed with her tonight."

"I want to, but I had to make a choice."

"What choice was that?"

"Sit with her, or run the risk of letting you slip away during the night while I was distracted. You have no idea how relieved I was to hear you entertaining your brother just now." Mercy leaned against his shoulder. "Are we ever going to talk about that night?"

"Is there truly a need? We were both there," he said softly.

Perhaps there wasn't. They had both been pawns in the old duke's games, but in order to move ahead with her plans, Mercy needed to hear Leopold say the words. "Do you regret it then?"

Leopold set his hands to the balustrade and leaned forward. "I do not regret what we were forced to do. But he ensured we both behaved without honor. I still feel bitterness over that. My life has been manipulated by Romsey more than I care for."

Mercy sucked in a breath, startled by the heat behind his words. "Do you resent me, too?"

She couldn't bear that. She couldn't live with herself if he blamed her for the loss of his honor. Not when doing so had given her a man she could love.

Leopold's gazed fixed on hers as he smiled, showing off the dimples she loved. Her heart did little tumbles of joy. "Never. That would be impossible."

Relieved, Mercy grinned impishly and ducked under his arm. She stood between him and the balustrade. Leopold shook his head at her, and she curled her fingers into his waistcoat pocket and tugged. "I love you."

Leopold's eyes closed, yet his arms curled around her protectively and drew her against his body.

Mercy watched his face, searching for some hint as to what he was thinking. What he planned for his future. She hoped he'd be amenable to her suggestion. "I've given our situation considerable thought over the past few days, and I think it's high time you made an honorable woman out of me. You should propose. Tonight. And then we can start living respectably as man and wife. I liked waking up beside you."

Mercy bit her lip and waited.

Slowly, Leopold opened his eyes and stared at her. She smiled her most encouraging smile then looped her arms about his neck. "Really, it's the perfect solution. You get free run of Romsey to look for further clues of your siblings' whereabouts, and you get to keep Edwin and I out of trouble."

"And what are my chances of getting you to behave?"

Mercy slid her hands down his chest. "You would change me?"

"No. But almost getting caught making love to you is not how I would wish to conduct my marriage. We were lucky that Allen walked in on us and not a housemaid. The gossip will be bad enough that you're considering giving up your title to marry me."

Mercy shook her head. "Not considering. I will give it all up to be your wife as long as you promise not to keep any more secrets from me. I don't care what they are, or how scandalous, I want to be your confidant. I don't want a stuffy, proper husband who keeps me on the outside of his life. I want you to desire me and also care for my opinion. Just as I do yours."

Leopold backed her against the balustrade. The hard ridge of his erection nudged her belly. "Desire isn't a problem for us, and I'm getting used to sharing my thoughts with you. All I ask is that you be a little more patient with me."

"I can be patient about *some* things." Mercy chuckled and shifted her hips against him. "But I hope, too, that you'll be agreeable to getting me with child again as a matter of some urgency. I don't want Edwin to grow up alone. I want a large family again."

Leopold pressed his head against hers. "That's why the old duke sent me to you in the first place, you know. I overheard him complain to my father once that our side of the family reproduced like rabbits. He'd hoped I'd prove to be just as fertile when I went to your bed."

Mercy cupped his face between her hands. "No matter his motives, I am thankful he sent you and not one of his cronies, or even Allen." Mercy shuddered at the thought, and Leopold tightened his grip around her. "I think I fell in love with you that first night, you know. You were so gentle with me, so concerned that I be all right after we made love."

"You were terrified at first, as you should have been. The old man was a bastard to do that to you." Leopold's head dropped to her shoulder. "When did you discover it had been me in your bed?"

Had there really been a time that she hadn't known? She curled her fingers into his hair and held on. "Not at first, certainly. But you affected me, and I couldn't stop wanting to touch you or kiss you." Mercy looped her arms about his neck again. "But after our first night by the pond, I discovered that everything I'd loved about the night Edwin was made seemed the same, except for your withdrawal. You have quite remarkable restraint, my love. Did your mistress teach you that?"

"My circumstances taught me to never make mistakes again." Leopold's lips pressed hard against her head. "I did have a mistress in India, but she couldn't hold my interest after I had made love to you. I wanted to come back to find you, to make sure you were all right, but the threats against my family prevented my return. Do you understand? Do you forgive me for abandoning you?"

Mercy nodded as tears streamed down her cheeks. "You didn't abandon me. Family is everything to me, too. But once he was certain I had conceived, the old duke doted on my health and happiness. I believe he also discouraged his son from visiting my bed. He only shared my bed once after you came to me."

Leopold's sharp intake of breath gave her pain. "Then I may not be Edwin's father after all?"

"True, but I believe he is your son, and that is what counts. There are so many things about the two of you that are similar. Dimples for one." She smoothed her hands over his chest. "My husband never affected me the way you have, Leopold. I may be a horrid woman to speak ill of the dead, but he never was particularly affectionate toward me. You showed me what had been missing from my marriage and made me yours that night."

Leopold's hands cupped her head to hold her gaze to his. "That was never supposed to happen. We did not know one another. I should have done everything different. I should have asked your name."

"I didn't ask yours either and I should have." Mercy cupped his cheek. "We cannot change what has gone on before, but we can change our futures. I think it only fair that I claim you while I can. Marry me, so we may find Oliver and Rosemary together. I should confess that there is a hidden room inside the abbey that may contain all we need to know."

"You clever girl." His smile grew. "You found the duke's sanctuary. Father always said there were secrets within the walls."

Mercy nodded quickly. "Live here with Edwin, with our son, and love us as we love you. You belong here at Romsey. Tobias will settle down in due time, and I will show you the entrance to the room in a moment if you like. But since neither Tobias nor Edwin is in any immediate need of our attention, could we please get back to my original proposal?"

"So are you proposing now? I thought I should do it?"

When Leopold pressed his lips to her brow, she snuggled closer. "Well," Mercy sighed dramatically, "I haven't heard anything like a proposal of marriage from your lips so far. Perhaps I should be the one to get down on bended knee?"

"Were you this bossy before you became a duchess?"

He really should know the truth before he got in too deep, and he did like her for her honestly. "Oh, much, much worse. I told you my brother was glad to be rid of me. I doubt you will see any change when I give up my title and marry you."

Leopold drew away. "Your brother could have serious objections to our marriage. He will be unhappy that you're giving up your title, too. I am too. I don't want to cause further trouble with your family."

"Constantine finds little joy in life beyond his fleeting pleasures. But he will still have control over Edwin's welfare. When Blythe comes around, guilty or not of terrifying me, she will forgive us any scandal as soon as the vows are spoken. Patience will not care. She is rather broad-minded about affairs of the heart. Well?" Mercy gave Leopold a little shake.

To her surprise, Leopold threw his head back and laughed. When he finished, he wiped at his eyes, smiling so broadly that both his dimples showed. Mercy smiled up at him as tears threatened to take away her sight. How had she lived without this gorgeous man before?

"I suppose I should make a start." Leopold kissed her nose. "A kiss first, my love, and then we can begin negotiating the terms of my surrender in earnest."

Mercy pursed her lips. "It will do as a start, but don't think I won't make you work hard at the negotiations tonight."

Leopold's grin widened as he rocked his erection against her belly. "Trust me, given all you've put me through so far, I'm more than ready to engage the enemy."

The End

Wild Randalls Series

Book 1: Engaging the Enemy
Every great family has a few secrets. The wild Randalls of Hampshire excel at them.

Book 2: Forsaking the Prize
The perils of life at sea are nothing compared to the danger of attempting polite conversation with a proper woman.

Book 3: Guarding the Spoils
The adventure he never expected is closer than he ever imagined!

Book 4: Hunting the Hero
She can lose her birthright, but not her heart!

More Regency Romance...

Distinguished Rogues Series
Book 1: Chills
Book 2: Broken
Book 3: Charity
Book 4: An Accidental Affair
Book 5: Keepsake
Book 6: An Improper Proposal
Book 7: Reason to Wed
Book 8: The Trouble with Love
Book 9: Married by Moonlight
Book 10: Lord of Sin
Book 11: The Duke's Heart
Book 12: Romancing the Earl
Book 13: One Enchanted Christmas
Book 14: Desire by Design
Book 15: His Perfect Bride
Book 16: Pleasures of the Night

Saints and Sinners Series
Book 1: The Duke and I
Book 2: A Gentleman's Vow
Book 3: An Earl of Her Own

...and many more

About Heather Boyd

USA Today Bestselling Author Heather Boyd believes every character she creates deserves their own happily-ever-after—no matter how much trouble she puts them through. With that goal in mind, she writes steamy romances that skirt the boundaries of propriety to keep readers enthralled until the wee hours of the morning. Heather has published over 40 regency romance novels and shorter works full of daring seductions and distinguished rogues. She lives north of Sydney, Australia, with her trio of rogues and pair of four-legged overlords.

You can find details of her work at
www.Heather-Boyd.com

9 781925 239539